WHISPER'S
GRAVE

GIANTFUR CAVE

The Coast

THE GATHERING DARKNESS

SURVIVORS

INTO THE SHADOWS

SURVIVORS

Also by ERIN HUNTER

WARRIORS

THE PROPHECIES BEGIN

THE NEW PROPHECY

Book One: Midnight
Book Two: Moonrise
Book Three: Dawn
Book Four: Starlight
Book Five: Twilight
Book Six: Sunset

POWER OF THREE

Book One: The Sight
Book Two: Dark River
Book Three: Outcast
Book Four: Eclipse
Book Five: Long Shadows
Book Six: Sunrise

OMEN OF THE STARS

Book One: The Fourth Apprentice
Book Two: Fading Echoes
Book Three: Night Whispers
Book Four: Sign of the Moon
Book Five: The Forgotten Warrior
Book Six: The Last Hope

DAWN OF THE CLANS

Book One: The Sun Trail
Book Two: Thunder Rising
Book Three: The First Battle
Book Four: The Blazing Star
Book Five: A Forest Divided
Book Six: Path of Stars

A VISION OF SHADOWS

Book One: The Apprentice's Quest
Book Two: Thunder and Shadow

EXPLORE THE
WARRIORS
WORLD

NOVELLAS

Hollyleaf's Story
Mistystar's Omen
Cloudstar's Journey
Tigerclaw's Fury
Leafpool's Wish
Dovewing's Silence
Mapleshade's Vengeance
Goosefeather's Curse
Ravenpaw's Farewell

Book One: *The Quest Begins*
Book Two: *Great Bear Lake*
Book Three: *Smoke Mountain*
Book Four: *The Last Wilderness*
Book Five: *Fire in the Sky*
Book Six: *Spirits in the Stars*

RETURN TO THE WILD

Book One: *Island of Shadows*
Book Two: *The Melting Sea*
Book Three: *River of Lost Bears*
Book Four: *Forest of Wolves*
Book Five: *The Burning Horizon*
Book Six: *The Longest Day*

MANGA

Toklo's Story
Kallik's Adventure

THE GATHERING DARKNESS

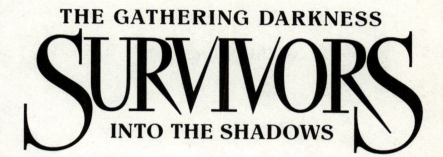

SURVIVORS

INTO THE SHADOWS

ERIN
HUNTER

HARPER

An Imprint of HarperCollinsPublishers

Special thanks to Gillian Philip

Into the Shadows
Copyright © 2017 by Working Partners Limited
Series created by Working Partners Limited
Endpaper art © 2017 by Frank Riccio

Library of Congress Control Number: 2016944446
ISBN 978-0-06-234341-3 (trade bdg.) — ISBN 978-0-06-234342-0 (lib. bdg.)

Typography based on a design by Hilary Zarycky
16 17 18 19 20 CG/RRDH 10 9 8 7 6 5 4 3 2 1
❖
First Edition

For Abby Carmichael

PACK LIST

WILD PACK (IN ORDER OF RANK)

ALPHA:

female swift-dog with short gray fur (also known as Sweet)

BETA:

gold-and-white thick-furred male (also known as Lucky)

HUNTERS:

SNAP—small female with tan-and-white fur

BRUNO—large thick-furred brown male Fight Dog with a hard face

BELLA—gold-and-white thick-furred female

MICKEY—sleek black-and-white male Farm Dog

STORM—brown-and-tan female Fierce Dog

ARROW—black-and-tan male Fierce Dog

WOODY—stocky brown male

PATROL DOGS:

MOON—black-and-white female Farm Dog

TWITCH—tan male chase-dog with black patches and three legs

DART—lean brown-and-white female chase-dog

DAISY—small white-furred female with a brown tail

RAKE—scrawny male with wiry fur and a scarred muzzle

Breeze—small brown female with large ears and short fur

Chase—small ginger-furred female

Beetle—black-and-white shaggy-furred male

Thorn—black shaggy-furred female

Ruff—small black female

OMEGA:

small female with long white fur (also known as Sunshine)

PUPS:

Fluff—shaggy brown female

Tumble—golden-furred male

Nibble—tan female

Tiny—pale-eyed golden female

PROLOGUE

The trees were impossibly tall! Their red trunks rose up forever into the blue sky, so high that it hurt Lick's eyes to stare at them. Instead, the little pup concentrated on bouncing through the high grass after her litter-brothers, whose small rumps were just visible ahead. All three of them had to work hard to keep up with Martha, the huge black water-dog who was leading them through the forest.

This is my kind of adventure! thought Lick excitedly. If she narrowed her eyes, she could imagine the grass was the whole forest, and Lick herself was a giant dog. Flanking her there were thick bushes with fleshy leaves—those could be monstrous wild forests off in the distance, far beyond the yellow-green stalks of the Grass Forest. . . .

No, she thought, blinking. *I don't need to imagine another exciting adventure. This one with Martha is good enough!* Putting on a burst of speed, Lick scampered to catch up with Grunt and Wiggle. Ahead, Martha glanced back at the three of them, her dark eyes filled with fondness.

"Not far now, pups," she growled softly.

"What kind of surprise is it?" yipped Grunt.

"Tell us, Martha, please!" squeaked Wiggle, the smallest of the pups.

"Ah, no, little one." Martha stopped to lick the top of his head. "That would spoil the surprise!"

"I want to *see!*" yelped Lick. She burst through the grass past Martha, who gave a gruff bark of warning.

Just in time, too. Lick slithered to a halt on a slope of damp, sandy earth, staring in awe. Behind her, Grunt and Wiggle shoved their way through, eager to see, and their jaws fell wide open.

"What *is* it?" gasped Grunt.

Martha sat on her haunches, her eyes twinkling. "This, little ones, is the river. It's where the River-Dog lives. Where I'm happiest of all."

Lick stared at the dark, fast-flowing expanse, which seemed to stretch to the limits of her vision. If there was a far bank, it was only a distant blur of green. She'd seen bright water gurgling in streams, of course, and tiny foaming waterfalls clattering over pebbles, and deep, still ponds among the trees. But this was so different. Out toward the middle of the river, water churned white around submerged rocks; closer to the pups, it was smoother and darker, but it was clear to Lick how fast the water ran. The great river looked powerful, magnificent, and dangerous.

And *thrilling!*

"I want to go in!" barked Grunt.

"Me too!" yelped Lick, determined not to be outdone.

Wiggle took a nervous step back. "I don't like it."

"Not so fast, pups." Martha shook her great head. "I'm going to teach you to swim, but first you must learn to respect the River-Dog. If you don't show her respect, she might eat you!"

Lick felt a shiver run along her flanks, and she nodded. For all the excitement that the river promised, she believed Martha absolutely. Martha had taken care of them after they'd lost their own Mother-Dog; she had *always* looked out for Lick and her litter-brothers, and Lick trusted every word the big dog said. Lick sat down obediently, though her tail still tapped the earth with frantic energy.

"The smells," Wiggle was saying wonderingly, as he sniffed at the sandy earth. "They're all so different! I can smell water . . . and weeds, they're like very wet grass . . . but what's this one?"

Martha nosed the ground gently. "That's river-rabbit," she told him. "We call it that because it tastes a bit like rabbit—but it's a hunter, like us! It catches fish—the river is full of fish, and some of them *bite*."

"Ooh," Wiggle breathed.

"If they bite me," declared Grunt, "I'll bite them back! Then they'll be sorry!"

Martha laughed.

"What else is in the river?" Lick asked.

"There are river-rats," said Martha, "and eels—those are long, slippery fish. And there are sometimes even snakes. And birds that can swim under the water!"

"Wow," gasped Wiggle.

"The River-Dog holds so much life in her paws," explained Martha, "and she brings life to the forest, too. It's the River-Dog who makes the trees grow so tall, and turns the grass green. She nurtures all the creatures and tends the growing things."

"She's a very special Spirit Dog," whispered Lick in awe.

"Yes," agreed Martha, a faraway look in her eyes. "She is. And swimming in the river is like playing with her. I want you to feel what that's like, pups—but be careful! When the River-Dog is in a playful mood, she can pull you this way and that, even tugging you under. And she's strong!"

Lick nodded vigorously. "Yes, I bet she is." Suddenly it didn't seem like such a good idea to plunge into the River-Dog's territory. The water did look so very dark, so cold and deep. . . . Lick backed away a little, shivering.

She felt Martha's warm tongue lash her ear. "Don't worry, Lick. Remember, the River-Dog is our friend—if you respect her. Watch me!"

The big black dog trotted confidently to the water's edge, bowing her head very slightly. Then she sprang, plunging into the water in a silver shower of glittering spray. Wiggle gave a cry of dismay, but Martha turned easily in the current and shook water from her ears, her tongue lolling. Lick could see her powerful legs working below the surface of the clear water.

Martha barked toward the shore. "See how I move, little ones? Don't fight the current; let the River-Dog support you. She can be gentle as well as wild. But don't ever swim out too far!"

Grunt was edging toward the water, nervous but eager, and Lick had no intention of letting him go first. Martha looked so happy—and even better, swimming looked like *fun!* Lick nudged Grunt firmly out of the way and waded into a shallow, eddying side current.

"It's not cold," she yelped as the water swirled around her forepaws. "It's lovely and cool!"

"Yes!" agreed Grunt, hurriedly splashing in beside her. Wiggle looked less certain, patting the water with a paw and drawing back, but Lick and Grunt waded quickly closer to Martha, the water rising up their flanks.

Lick pressed confidently forward, faster and surer—till all of a sudden, there was no sand beneath her paws. There was nothing! She gave a gasp as she sank in the water, but with an instinctive flailing motion of her paws, she found she was rising again. Her head was above the surface, she could breathe, she could move—

"I'm *swimming!*" she yelped.

"Me too!" Grunt bumped against her, swayed by the light current.

"This is *great!* Come on in, Wiggle!" In Lick's excitement, she found herself tipping sideways, one nostril submerging, but Martha's broad muzzle found her belly and righted her before she could panic too much. She sneezed and floundered, then struck out with her paws again, finding her balance in the River-Dog's gentle embrace. Martha backed off, circling farther out while keeping a watchful eye on the pups.

Wiggle looked wistful, but still anxious. He had waded out a little farther but seemed reluctant to let his paws leave the safety of the riverbed. Lick watched him, yelping encouragement.

"Look at me, Lick!" Grunt barked grandly. Lick turned her head and saw that he was halfway toward Martha in the deeper part of the river, his little body jerking in the water as he panted and paddled. "The River-Dog's not scary at all—this is easy!"

Wiggle gave a sharp squeak of alarm, and Lick turned back. Grunt was still swimming heedlessly toward Martha, but as Lick watched in horror, her bigger brother was caught in a sudden bite from the River-Dog. The great Spirit Dog surged, seized Grunt in her jaws, and swept him away downstream.

He didn't show enough respect! Lick thought, panicking. "Grunt! Grunt, come back!"

But he clearly couldn't. His head went under water for a moment, and when it reappeared, he was choking, his eyes huge with terror. Another wave washed over him. He wasn't swimming anymore; he was helpless in the River-Dog's paws as she batted him farther and farther away downstream.

Lick began to howl in fear, but she was silenced when Martha butted her sharply back toward the shore. As her small paws scrabbled on the riverbed, finding purchase, Martha was already turning in the water and swimming strongly after Grunt.

Lick scrambled ashore, her breath coming in gasps, and Wiggle pressed his shivering flank against hers. "Will Martha save him?" he whined. "Oh Martha, please get to him!"

"I can't even see him anymore!" whimpered Lick. Her legs felt terribly weak, and the river-water on her coat felt so much colder now.

"Me either . . . no! There!" Wiggle panted desperately, his ears straining toward the water.

Peering, Lick could see a dark shape growing larger as Martha surged powerfully against the current. Gripped in her jaws was a limp, bedraggled little body. It felt like an unbearably long time before the huge black dog waded ashore and laid the tiny lifeless creature on the sand.

"Grunt!" cried Wiggle in misery.

Lick couldn't even whine. Her mouth felt dry, her body cold to the core. Her litter-brother looked so much smaller now, a sodden little rag of fur and bone. "Martha, he's not moving!"

"Hush, now," said Martha firmly. Taking a deep breath, she

lifted one of her massive webbed paws and struck Grunt firmly on the softest part of his flank.

Lick gasped and whimpered. It looked painful, but Martha must know what she was doing. Surely she did?

When there was no response from Grunt, Martha hit him again, and then again.

With a sudden spasm of coughing, Grunt's body jerked and water came gushing from his mouth.

"Thank the Spirit Dogs." Martha gave a great sigh of relief.

It looked agonizing, thought Lick: the way Grunt's muscles shuddered and his legs twitched helplessly, his little chest racked with choking coughs.

But all Lick could feel was a glowing happiness. For all his painful misery and his drenched, shivering body, her litter-brother was alive! She whined aloud in gratitude to Martha—but mostly in thanks to the stern yet merciful River-Dog.

You didn't swallow Grunt—you let him go! Thank you, kind River-Dog! You didn't take my brother away after all. . . .

I swear I'll always respect you.

CHAPTER ONE

How could this have happened?

Broken shards of clear-stone, Storm realized with horror, had been concealed in the very prey the Pack dogs were about to eat. Two fat, splendid deer, the finest prey pile the Pack had seen in many turns of the Moon-Dog—and some dog had sabotaged it. *Why?*

Every dog wore a look of stunned disgust. Bella, just behind Storm, whimpered with distress, but even her loyal mate—Storm's fellow Fierce Dog, Arrow—was too horrified to comfort her. He stood at Storm's shoulder, trembling with shock. Most of the Pack was silent, staring, their hackles bristling. Breeze's howl of incredulity still echoed on the air—and Storm knew how she felt.

Storm had suspected for a while that there must be some dog in the Pack who was working against them all, but even she could hardly believe a member of the Pack had done this appalling thing. They had all been so happy tonight, sharing the spoils of a wonderful hunt—and now the Pack's Third Dog lay on the ground, choking and whimpering, while Snap eased the treacherous shards from his bloodied mouth. They glinted where she dropped them, cruelly sharp and wet with blood.

Daisy, holding Twitch's russet-furred head steady with her two small forepaws, licked his ear, whining wretchedly. "Please try to hold still. It's nearly done."

"Oh no, oh no. Oh, Twitch. You poor thing," Sunshine whimpered as she tried to help Daisy and Snap by moving the clear-stone away from their paws and into a small pile.

Since Breeze had let loose her howl of distress, since the Pack had finally realized there was a traitor in their midst, the other dogs had stood there, frozen, staring at one another in horror. But now, Storm felt a prickling down her spine as little Ruff turned and fixed her gaze on Arrow. There was accusation in Ruff's eyes. Storm glared at her, but even as she did so, she saw Bruno also turn and stare. One by one, the heads of all the Packmates were turning toward Arrow.

It's Arrow they don't trust. Just because he's a Fierce Dog!

But I'm a Fierce Dog, too, and I was the one who tried to warn them. . . .

Her heart pounded in her chest with fear and with anger at the unfairness of it all. She was certain that Arrow would no more have sabotaged the prey with clear-stone than she would herself. Yet he was the first suspect that leaped to every dog's mind.

Bruno was the first to growl his thoughts aloud. The burly dog showed his sharp teeth. "I told you. I said it all along. You can't trust a Fierce Dog."

Storm's fur prickled with resentment, but he was glaring at Arrow, his snarl menacing. "I never wanted that Fierce Dog in the Pack!"

Storm's rage boiled up, smothering her fear. She hadn't slept properly in many journeys of the Sun-Dog, afraid *she* was the Bad Dog, afraid of what she might do if she walked in her sleep again. She realized now that she wasn't responsible for the terrible things that had befallen the Pack. Knowing that she had tortured herself and worried that she was a bad dog, while all the time there had been a real traitor lurking, made her even angrier. And that Bruno should assume Arrow was the traitor, just because he, like Storm, was a Fierce Dog, was worse still.

"How dare you, Bruno? Arrow's done nothing to deserve that!" It felt good to release her fury at last, to lash out at the dog who made so many snide remarks about Fierce Dogs. "He's been a loyal Pack member from the start—even if you refuse to realize it!"

"Ha," growled Ruff softly. "We should have known."

Storm spun on the little black dog, her ears swiveling forward. "What do you mean? Say it out loud!"

"Gladly," sneered Ruff, the little black dog who had once been Omega in Twitch's Pack. "One Fierce Dog stands up for the other one. What a surprise."

Before Storm could snap back, Dart too gave a low snarl. "You don't have to stand up for Arrow, Storm. He isn't like you—it's not like he's been one of us for long. You've proven yourself to this Pack. What do we know about him? *Nothing.*"

"Nothing," added Chase, "except that he betrayed his last Pack. Didn't he?"

"Wait just a minute!" Bella sprang forward, her golden hackles raised. "Arrow betrayed the Fierce Dogs to save all of us! You've got no reason to blame him. And he couldn't have sabotaged the prey—I know it! I've been with him the whole time, ever since the hunters brought it back to camp."

"Oh yes?" Tall, scruffy Rake cocked his head, eyes narrowing. "You never took your eyes off him, then? You weren't distracted, even for a moment?"

"Every dog gets distracted," growled Woody. "Especially with Alpha's new pups around. You can't have watched Arrow *all* the time, Bella."

"Well, I did," she snapped defiantly. "I always know where Arrow is. *Always!*"

"Huh," sneered Ruff, shaking her head. "Is that so? Why's that, Bella?"

Ruff has a lot more to say than usual, thought Storm bitterly, *now that she's attacking Fierce Dogs.*

"I want to know that, too." Dart curled her thin muzzle, eyeing Bella keenly. "What makes you so aware of Arrow all of a sudden, Bella? Is there something you need to tell us?"

Bella paused for a moment, lifting her head, and Storm saw a muscle in her throat jerk. Her own heart was in her mouth, because she alone knew what was coming. Was Bella going to admit the truth now? It would be harder than ever, at this moment, to make the Pack accept it.

The golden dog's hackles were still lifted as she curled back her muzzle. "Yes," Bella told them defiantly. "Arrow and I are mates. We have been for some time."

For a long moment there was silence, except for the pained

whimpering of Twitch as Snap stepped back from him, her awful job finally done.

Then Breeze spoke for the first time since she'd howled in horror. Her voice was uncertain but clear in the quiet camp.

"But in that case . . . Alpha?" She turned to their slender leader, the swift-dog. "I'm sorry, but we *can't* take Bella's word for it, can we? If she's Arrow's mate, she's bound to defend him."

"No!" Lucky, the Pack's golden-furred Beta, barked loudly. "I know Bella better than any of you"—though Storm noticed he shot a suddenly doubtful look at Arrow, as if to say *maybe not as well as I thought*—"and she would never be with a dog who would turn on his own Pack. If Arrow was a bad dog, my litter-sister wouldn't be his mate." With a glance at Bella, he paused to catch his breath, shook himself a little, and licked his chops uncertainly. Whatever he said, Lucky couldn't hide his surprise at Bella's announcement.

Well, Storm told herself, *it was a shocking way to find out.* No doubt Bella had hoped to choose a better moment to break the news to her litter-brother, a far higher-ranking dog.

"I'm not so sure." That was Dart, who sat back on her brown-and-white haunches, tapping her tail thoughtfully. There was a spiteful gleam in her eye. "It wouldn't be the first time Bella's chosen unsavory allies."

Mickey, the kind old black-and-white Farm Dog, gave an angry growl. "That's in the past, Dart. Don't drag it up again like rotten prey."

Storm shifted uneasily. She knew what they were talking about: the time Bella had allied herself with a mob of foxes to try to force the Pack's half wolf former Alpha to share their territory. It had been a reckless strategy, one that backfired horribly, as Bella herself had told Storm.

But this was no time for Dart to bring that up! It was just another vindictive, painful dig at Bella, who was truly remorseful about her foolishness. And it was another way of getting at Arrow. Storm felt her lip curling.

All the dogs had turned to Alpha now, waiting for her answer to Breeze. The gray swift-dog looked very thoughtful, but she hadn't so much as growled.

"Well, Alpha?" Bruno nodded at Breeze, then looked directly back at his leader. "Do you agree with our Beta, or with Breeze? Are you going to rely on Bella's word, given that she's the Fierce Dog's mate now?"

Storm suppressed a gasp of shock. Such open defiance of

their Beta—she'd known Bruno wasn't fond of Arrow, but surely Alpha would slap down the burly Fight Dog now? Anger roiled in Storm's gut, but she was too confused and hot with fury to say any more. *It's up to Alpha now, to make these dogs see how ridiculous their accusations are!*

Alpha swung her narrow head, gazing around the clearing at each dog in turn. Her expression was a combination of disappointment and irritation, but her growl was cool. "It's too soon to point a paw at any dog. Every dog here needs to calm down and stop grabbing at dry bones." She nodded at Twitch, who lay exhausted with pain, his flanks heaving. "Twitch has been hurt. This is not the time for destructive quarrels!"

"But, Alpha!" barked Bruno.

"We've got to put a stop to this right now," whined Woody, "and Arrow's the most likely culprit!"

"It's obvious, isn't it?" growled Dart sulkily.

"That is enough." Alpha's snarl was deadly. She said no more, only stared into their eyes until every dog coughed and muttered, then fell into shamefaced silence. Nor did the swift-dog spare Storm; she glared into her eyes with a directness that brooked no further argument. Storm clenched her jaws and resisted the urge to howl at the injustice.

"And now," announced Alpha at last, when every Pack member looked suitably chastened, "it's time to stop chattering and squealing like a bunch of squirrels, and go to sleep. Twitch needs care and quiet; Snap, Daisy, and Sunshine, well done on your quick thinking, and for not being distracted by squabbling. It is up to me, your Alpha, to find out who did this—and make no mistake, I will. But the truth will not be discovered through arguments and gossip." She glared around at the rest of them again. "I expect every dog to be alert tomorrow. Night patrols: prepare yourselves and go on your rounds. There may be a bad dog in this Pack, but that doesn't mean other enemies aren't out there too. Back to work, all of you."

She turned elegantly and stalked toward her den, her Beta at her heels. As the two leaders walked away, Storm could see there were still raised hackles and wrinkled muzzles among the sullen dogs. Alpha had given them no answers, yet Storm couldn't help but agree with her. Now was not the time for the Pack to snap and tear at one another, not with Twitch lying there injured. He didn't seem to be badly hurt, but he was still clearly in pain—and the shocking deliberateness of the attack must have hurt him almost as much as the clear-stone shards themselves.

The Pack all seemed in a great hurry now to get to their

sleeping dens, and Chase, Thorn, Beetle, and Ruff were quick to organize themselves into patrols and set out past the border of the camp.

Storm almost wished she were going with them, despite her anger at their willful stupidity. Anything would be better than gnawing over her worries in the hunters' den. Though she turned more than enough sleep-circles, and tried to relax every muscle, it was impossible to get comfortable on her bed of leaves and moss. At last, with a heavy sigh, she stopped trying, and her ears drooped.

Why hadn't Alpha said more? She could easily have ordered the Pack to stop their ridiculous attacks on Arrow, could have forbidden any more wild speculation, any crazy accusations that only served to undermine Pack unity even more. Sure, the dogs had finally stopped quarreling, but reluctantly, and Storm didn't think for a moment that they'd give up muttering among themselves. Alpha had shut their muzzles for now, but she'd done nothing to smooth the awful undercurrents of suspicion or to quell the hostility against Arrow.

Just because he's a Fierce Dog, Storm thought, her fangs clenching. *They've got no other reason to dislike him. It's so unfair!*

All the same, as Storm twisted her head restlessly and her gaze fell on Arrow, she couldn't help feeling a small surge of happiness. Only last night, he and Bella had slept on opposite sides of the den, careful to hide their relationship from the Pack. Now the mates lay curled together, muzzles touching, Bella's tail laid over his sleek flank.

But Storm realized Arrow was as sleepless as she was; she could see the gleam of his anxious, haunted eyes as he gazed out at the den mouth. In sympathy and solidarity, she crawled to his other side, resting her flank against his rump. Gratefully, he wagged his tail. Storm heard his sad, half-suppressed sigh as he closed his eyes in another effort to sleep.

Pawsteps crunching on leaves made Storm raise her head just as Arrow did. It was only Twitch, limping toward the den mouth on his three legs, his muzzle twisted with pain. Storm sat up, concerned. Arrow just stared at Twitch, his dark eyes filled with nervousness, his pulse throbbing fast in his sleek throat.

"Twitch!" Storm exclaimed softly. "Are you feeling better?"

The Third Dog nodded, but he winced with each movement. In the faint moonlight Storm could see that his mouth was stained with drying flakes of dark blood, and his muzzle looked swollen and sensitive. He'd chomped down eagerly on that piece of deer he'd chosen; Storm couldn't imagine how painful it would be to crunch clear-stone in her teeth and feel it stab into the soft flesh of her mouth. Still, Twitch spoke firmly.

"Arrow, I don't believe you had anything to do with this," he mumbled, wincing again at a jab of pain. "I want you to—know that. I know—you'd never—"

"Thank you." Arrow rose to his paws, his sharp ears pricked forward. "Twitch, please, don't try to talk. It must hurt."

"Yes," agreed the Third Dog wryly, "very much. But I wanted you to know."

Arrow stepped forward to lick very gently at his jaw. "I appreciate that more than I can say, Twitch. Truly, thank you."

Storm felt a wave of relief that made her limbs tremble. *Twitch knows Arrow isn't guilty, that he's not a bad dog.*

But it wasn't enough, not really. The other dogs *had* to be convinced of Arrow's innocence.

But which dog did this, then? It seemed almost unimaginable. Staring at Twitch's bloodstained muzzle, Storm flinched in sympathy. "You should get some rest, Twitch," she said softly. "Don't worry about us."

"I should," he agreed, turning slowly and limping from the den. "Good night, young dogs."

They watched him go, both quivering with tension, and Storm

licked her jaws. "Poor Twitch," she murmured.

"It's hard to believe, isn't it?" Arrow gave another sigh, but he seemed comforted. This time, when he curled up on the mossy bed, he fell asleep quickly, and soon Storm heard his gentle snores. Lying down against him once more, she found the sound of his heartbeat began to lull her to sleep.

And I do still need to sleep. . . . I've spent so long trying to stay awake, afraid of the darkness inside me; terrified that I'll walk in my sleep again, that I'll hurt my Packmates without realizing it. I thought for so long that it might have been me who murdered Whisper, that I'd done it without knowing. I was too scared of my own inner Fierce Dog to let myself sleep. But now I know for sure I'm not responsible. I'm not the bad dog in this Pack. Now I know. . . .

She must have drifted into a very deep sleep, because when she woke, it was with a jolt, a tremor rippling through her muscles. Storm shook it off, reorienting herself in the starlit dimness. Her paws were twitching, and she remembered she'd been dreaming of a hunt: *an ordinary dream,* she remembered with relief, *not some frightening prophecy.* Her Packmates were asleep around her; she could hear deep breathing, faint snores, an occasional whimper or muted yelp. The air smelled of warm bodies and dry fur, grass and moss. A paw scratched an ear, jerkily, then fell back limply; its owner was asleep. Except for the small sounds of the night, all was quiet.

No. Not entirely quiet.

Storm pricked an ear, craning toward faint voices. There were definitely at least three dogs outside, maybe on the far edge of the camp, talking softly.

That sounds like Bruno.

Storm was instantly alert. Bruno was not officially on patrol, so why would he be awake and speaking in that low, insistent growl? Creeping to the den mouth, Storm glanced around, then slunk to the closest undergrowth, and followed it cautiously around till she was closer to the dogs. She heard Bruno's voice again:

"So we're agreed, then?"

Storm counted five of them: Bruno; Snap the hunter; Dart, the skinny brown-and-white dog who'd spoken against Arrow; little black Ruff, who had suddenly found her voice just to criticize the Fierce Dog; and tall, scruffy Woody. Their heads were close together but the night was still, and if Storm swiveled and strained her ears she could hear their words clearly.

"Yes, we're agreed." That was Ruff. "We'll take turns watching him."

"We'll have to be careful," pointed out Woody. "We don't want to be obvious."

"And not just around Arrow," added Dart. "There are other dogs who don't seem to see the danger he is."

"Trouble is," said Bruno, "he may not do anything while any dog is watching. He may wait till he's alone. In fact he's bound to, if he's up to mischief."

"Yes, but that's the point," said Snap. "If we take turns and keep eyes on him all the time, there's no way Arrow *can* get up to anything. We may not get any proof, but at least we'll be protecting the Pack."

"True," agreed Bruno. "Constant, quiet surveillance, that's what we need. Don't tip off Alpha or Beta, whatever you do. They wouldn't take kindly to this."

"Indeed," said Woody gruffly. "Alpha may be willing to trust a Fierce Dog, but I'm certainly not."

With nods and growls of farewell, the secret meeting broke up, and Storm realized, aghast, that they were going to walk right past her. Quickly, and as quietly as she could, she ducked down into the long grass. She held her breath as their pawsteps drew closer; then exhaled with relief as they passed her, unseeing, and headed to their separate dens to rest.

Storm lay quite still in the bushes, trying to breathe very quietly despite the thrashing of her heart. Her brain was whirling.

When all other sounds had faded to silence, she crept back to the hunters' den, where Arrow slept close to the entrance, his flanks rising and falling gently, blissfully unaware of the conspiracy against him. Bruno, Snap, and Woody must have crept in very sneakily so that they didn't disturb him.

Just beyond the den mouth, Storm could see the Moon-Dog floating above the trees. The shining Spirit Dog had turned away from the dogs down on the ground, her haunches twisted so that she was only half-visible; Storm wondered if she was angry at their suspicions, their plots, and their squabbles.

I wouldn't be a bit surprised if she was.

Storm was still tired, but sleep refused to return. The low ache of anxiety gnawing at her rib cage and belly was too intense.

I don't know what's happened to this Pack. I don't know who's caused it all, who could be so malicious. Is it one of those dogs I saw conspiring out there—or another?

She had no idea. All Storm knew, with a burning certainty in her gut, was that something terrible had come to her Pack.

CHAPTER TWO

Storm stretched her tired body, clawing the grass as she yawned widely. The Moon-Dog, angry or not, had long vanished into her den to sleep the day away; the Sun-Dog had risen instead, but he remained behind a thick layer of cloud. *Perhaps he's as angry with us as Moon-Dog is,* thought Storm. *He'll give us his light, but he doesn't want to look at us. He shows us no warmth, not today.*

The sky was a heavy gray, and for a moment it made Storm feel strangely wistful. Then she realized: it was the exact color of Whisper's fur. An ache of grief squeezed her heart when she remembered the scrawny, eager little dog, and anger tightened her throat. Whisper had been murdered brutally, without mercy, and the Pack still did not know who was responsible.

He wanted to be my friend, Storm remembered, sadness like a stone in her rib cage. *Whisper admired me even when I didn't much like myself; he tried so hard to get my attention. He should have been here right now, yapping his nonsense in my ear and following me around the way Alpha's pups follow her.*

I used to find him so annoying. But now all I want is a chance to let him annoy me again. . . .

But that would never happen. Some treacherous, murderous member of the Pack had made savagely sure of it.

Things had been so much better in the Pack before Whisper's murder.

Storm sat down on her haunches and raised a hind leg to scratch at her ear. She frowned.

Was that true? *Had* things been so much better? Thinking it over, she realized they couldn't have been. Even before that awful day when they'd found Whisper's mutilated body, one of their own had been plotting, scheming, finding ways to destroy and harm the Pack, divide its members, ruin the life they'd built for themselves here beside the Endless Lake. There had been other incidents both before and after Whisper's death, ones that Alpha and Beta seemed content to ignore: a dead rabbit in the water supply. A rat's rotten corpse hidden beneath the prey pile, poisoning their food and making many dogs sick. Worse things: a murdered fox cub, left close to the camp for the very purpose of causing war between foxes and dogs. And when Whisper was killed, Storm had known at once that no fox, no coyote had made the brutal wounds on his body.

She'd recognized dog bites when she saw them.

But it had taken a long time for the Pack to believe her. And when at last they did, they had turned on Arrow with a speed that suggested the other Fierce Dog had never been truly accepted.

No, thought Storm, *things have been very wrong in the Pack for some time. . . .*

"Storm!" A cheerful voice broke into her dark thoughts, and she twisted her head around.

Lucky was padding toward her, his golden fur gleaming even in the overcast daylight. At least he didn't look angry with her, as he so often had recently. He gave her an affectionate lick on the nose and sat on his haunches.

"Are you all right, Storm?"

She nodded, trying to put her gloomy anxiety to the back of her mind. "I'm fine."

He tilted his head and studied her; he looked unconvinced. "I know it was hard for you last night, listening to the awful things the others were saying about Fierce Dogs."

Storm felt a shiver of relief. At least Lucky understood. "It's true. It wasn't nice to listen to that."

"Well." He gave her another comforting nuzzle. "Remember, when they talk about Fierce Dogs, they don't mean *you*. They all know you're one of us."

She stiffened, feeling a small sudden chill. *Doesn't he realize that's not the point?*

"Lucky." Storm felt a strong need to change the subject. "Can you tell me more about what Dart said last night?"

He frowned. "About the Fierce Dogs? I told you, it—"

"No." Storm shook her head. "I mean, when she talked about Bella having unsavory allies. That business with the foxes. I know she teamed up with them, and it went wrong, but what happened, exactly?"

It was Lucky's turn to flinch. He licked his jaws. "That was a long time ago."

"All the same." She watched his face keenly. "What happened? *How* did it happen?"

"Bella had her own small Pack, back then." Lucky gazed at the ground. "It was . . . not long after the Big Growl, when she'd escaped with the other Leashed Dogs. They were living nearby, and I was living in the camp of the half wolf."

"Why?" Storm pricked her ears forward. Why hadn't Lucky been with his litter-sister? "I thought it was you who brought the

Leashed Dogs out of the city?"

"Yes." He sighed. "But when we came to the previous Alpha's territory, he wouldn't let us share the water and prey, though he had plenty. You remember how strong-willed and vicious the half wolf could be, Storm, and he wouldn't have us near his hunting grounds. Bella asked me to join his Pack as a spy, and I agreed."

A *spy?* Storm stared at Lucky. This was part of the story she had never heard before.

"I already knew Sweet from our time in the Trap House, and she was the half wolf's Beta, so I had a way in. But it was . . . a mistake, in many ways. And Bella had her own plans that I didn't know about. She made a deal with a bunch of foxes."

"Yes, she told me." Storm nodded sadly. "What was she thinking?"

"I suppose she thought there would be strength in sheer numbers; she didn't stop to think about what her allies were really like, what they'd want from the alliance. And—to cut a long tale short, it led to the death of one of Moon's pups."

Storm gasped.

Lucky's tail drooped. "It was never Bella's intention. She was foolish, but she didn't mean to cause such harm, and she's never really forgiven herself for what happened. It broke her heart."

"Not as much as it broke Moon's, I bet!" Shocked to her core, Storm couldn't repress an angry bark. "I understand that Bella never meant it to happen, but she didn't think it through, either!"

"No," sighed Lucky, "she didn't."

Storm felt as if her chest would burst with the unfairness. "Arrow has never done anything like that," she spat, "and neither have I! We've never done anything so terrible, but there are plenty of dogs in this Pack who'd trust Bella before either of us!"

Lucky licked his chops, wincing uncomfortably. At least he had the decency to raise his eyes to hers—but he looked so sad, Storm found she couldn't go on raging at him. Biting back her anger, she glared past his shoulder until the furious howl rising in her throat had subsided. There was no more she could say. Lucky knew exactly how she felt about this, but there was nothing he could do. Nothing any dog could do, except the ones who refused to see past their own prejudices.

"Are you taking a patrol out hunting?" she asked at last, her voice tight. "I'd like to come, if you are."

Lucky seemed relieved at the change of subject. "Actually, I came over here to ask you a favor. Alpha's tired of being cooped up; it's like a four-pup Trap House in there." He let his tongue loll to emphasize the joke. "She'd love to get out for a long run—stretch her legs, you know? Will you watch the pups for us?"

He was already getting to his paws, expectant, but Storm's brain had frozen at the words *watch the pups*. "But—but, Lucky— shouldn't you ask Moon to watch them? Or . . . or Breeze?"

Without a word, Lucky turned and padded back toward Alpha's den, and Storm was forced to hurry after him, just so she could keep protesting. "Honestly, Lucky, I don't know anything about pups. I don't have the first idea—"

"There you are, Storm." Alpha was emerging from the den, the pups tumbling around her paws, as Lucky halted and licked her muzzle affectionately. "I'm very grateful to you."

"But I can't—Moon would love to look after the pups, I know she—" Storm realized she was babbling, but panic was turning her brain to mud.

"Storm, we want *you* to watch our pups," said Alpha firmly. "Isn't that so, Beta?"

"Indeed." Lucky was watching Storm with some amusement, but he looked implacable.

Storm opened her mouth, then closed it again. Doubtfully she glanced down at the four pups. *Alpha and Beta are showing how much faith they have in me,* she realized. *Isn't that what I said I wanted? This proves to the whole Pack that they trust me with these tiny pups. . . .*

And the pups *were* kind of cute.

"All right." Storm hunched her shoulders. "I'll take care of them, Alpha, don't worry. They're so little; how hard can it be?"

She must have been hearing things, she thought as Alpha and Beta loped quickly away to find the other hunters. Surely the two Pack leaders couldn't be *laughing?*

How hard can it be? Storm didn't think she'd ever regretted any hasty words so much. Her head buzzed and she was dizzy with the effort of keeping her eyes on four pups at once. *I didn't think anything so small could move so fast,* she wailed inwardly. For the umpteenth time she twisted and grabbed Fluff before the shaggy little brown creature could dart out of the den mouth. Storm had visions of her running straight into the open jaws of a coyote.

"No, Fluff! It's dangerous!"

"Storm!" she wailed. "Mamama!"

"I am *not* your Mamama—hey, stop that!" Tumble, the golden-furred male pup, had thrown himself onto his distracted sister and now they were rolling over and over in the dirt, growling and play-biting and giggling. Exasperated, Storm pried them apart. She was terrified that Tumble's leg injury from the fox bite would open up again, although it did seem to be healing nicely. She held him firmly in place with one paw to check, but as she peered closer, Fluff took her new chance and bounded clumsily out of the den, yapping with wicked delight. Storm scrambled after her, but the pup hadn't gone looking for coyotes; she was spinning in a circle, biting and snapping at her own tail. The other pups were tumbling from the den now, joining in the game, and with a sigh Storm went after them.

It's like trying to round up sharpclaws, she thought as she dashed to grab Nibble. Before she could reach the tan-colored pup, Storm felt a sharp pain in her own leg, and she yelped in surprise. Whipping around, she found herself staring at Tiny; the pale-eyed golden pup was crouched, ready to play, panting happily. *She's supposed to be the runt!* Storm thought irritably. "No, Tiny, that hurt!"

Tiny ignored that, bouncing up and down at the paws of her huge Fierce Dog minder and darting in for more attempted nips. Storm backed off, confused and thoroughly nervous. *By the Sky-Dogs, this is more exhausting than the fox battle!*

"For Lightning's sake!" The irritated bark came from the patrol den, and Thorn's black-and-white face appeared, half-asleep and grumpy. "Aren't you supposed to be watching those pups, Storm? I was patrolling all night and I only just got to sleep."

"Sorry," yelped Storm. "I'll—ow, Tiny, stop that!"

"Storm! Play, play, play!" There was another volley of yips as the other three pups joined their littlest sister in harrying Storm.

Why the other Pack members couldn't help out, Storm had no idea. They seemed content to bask in the hazy daylight, watching indulgently as the pups ran rings around her. Moon huffed with amusement as Tumble evaded Storm's paws yet again and bounded toward the edge of the camp.

As Storm seized him by the scruff, with as much gentleness as she could manage, a movement in the trees caught her eye. A dark shape and a golden one walked side by side through the dappled shadows: Arrow and Bella, their flanks pressed close as they left the camp together. For a moment Storm felt a little twinge of pleasure at their happiness; then she saw a third shadow, slinking a rabbit-chase behind them. Between the trunks, the light caught a tan-and-white hide. . . .

Snap. So the conspirators had put their plan into action already. They were watching every move Arrow made.

Storm shook herself. She had no time to be angry when the pups needed so much focus. Determinedly she turned and carried Tumble back to the den, where she dropped him on the soft moss. He bounced back up straightaway.

"Tumble," she growled. "Stay with me."

He blinked at her, seeming to know he'd pushed her quite far enough for the moment. Glancing around, he found mischief available inside the den: "Fluff!" He launched himself at his sister again, knocking her over.

Sagging onto her belly, Storm panted in exhaustion. She felt a squirming, warm body cuddle up against her and looked around to see Nibble taking a moment's rest. *Aw. Nibble's sweet. Quieter than the others . . .*

No sooner had the thought gone through her head than Nibble jumped up again, tearing toward Tumble and Fluff. With a muted groan, Storm laid her head down and watched them wrestle.

Where do they get the energy? I'm sure Wiggle and Grunt and I never behaved this badly!

A screeching yelp brought her back to her aching paws. "Nibble! Don't bite so hard, you're hurting Tumble." Storm padded grimly over and began to sort out the heap of pups. *Golden, shaggy—Tumble, check. Dark brown—that's Fluff, check. Tan—Nibble, there she is. Gold again, pale eyes, the littlest—*

Storm started back, eyes widening. Where *was* the second golden pup? "Why are there only three of you?" she growled, uneasiness lifting the fur along her spine.

"Storm! Play!" The three pups gazed up at her, bright-eyed and panting, but Storm could only gape at them, throat tightening with panic. Apart from the cluster of pups before her, the den was empty. It didn't matter how hard she looked.

Where's Tiny? Turning, Storm bolted out of the den, her blood thrumming in her ears and her heart thundering like an angry Sky-Dog.

She slithered to a helpless halt, twisting her head this way and that, peering into every corner of the camp, swiveling her ears in desperation. There was no sign of the little golden pup. *And I have no idea where to start looking!*

"Looks like you could use some help." At the amused voice behind her, Storm spun around.

"Breeze." Storm hoped she didn't look too pathetically pleading. "Oh, please. I can't find—"

With a wry look, Breeze nodded down at her front paws. Following her gaze, Storm saw the bundle of golden fur, the big shining eyes and the lolling little pink tongue that was . . .

"Tiny!" Storm thought she might fall over in gratitude.

"I found her trying to chase a squirrel," laughed Breeze. "It was almost as big as she is, so I don't know what she planned to do when she caught it."

"Oh, Tiny, you had me chasing my own tail with worry," Storm scolded her, but she licked the little golden head till Tiny wriggled and made a face.

"So would you like some assistance?" Breeze's eyes twinkled.

"Oh, yes. Yes, *please*."

"Come on, then." Breeze yelped softly at the other three pups, who had come out of the den to stare at their litter-sister among the bigger dogs. "Gather round, pups, and I'll tell you a story. Would you like that?"

A chorus of high-pitched yaps greeted her suggestion, and the pups fell over one another as they rushed to her. Breeze settled them, nudging and licking, then shepherded them gently toward the pond that lay just beyond the camp. She sat down on the edge. "This is a story about four pups who went on a great adventure to the Endless Lake," she told them.

Storm could only follow, staring in admiration. How did Breeze *do* that? The pups were all behaving perfectly, and Tumble didn't so much as swipe a paw at his sister Fluff. They looked entranced by Breeze's voice.

"The four pups were called—let me see—Tuggle, Fuzz, Nimble, and Titchy, and they were great friends. 'Let's go to the Endless

Lake!' said Titchy one day. 'Oh yes,' said Tuggle. 'The Endless Lake is where the world ends. It's where dogs find everything they could possibly need.' So the pups walked and they walked and they were *very* tired, and they thought they would never find the Endless Lake. But do you know what? They did!"

"More, Beeze!" barked Fluff, her eyes glowing. "Tell more!"

"All the pups could see was water, and they were a *bit* disappointed." Breeze swished the pond's surface with a paw, making it ripple, and Tumble looked on, mesmerized. "But a big friendly dog came to meet them. And they realized this was the River-Dog!"

"Ooh!" the pups chorused. Storm tilted her head in amusement, remembering her own puphood. *Maybe it's Martha in the story,* she thought, *not the River-Dog at all. That's who I'd have pictured. . . .*

"The River-Dog said they had to go down a *secret tunnel* under the waves!" went on Breeze. "And they did, and the pups found a secret special land there. There were swimming ponds and sticks and soft, green grass. And the sky was blue all the time. And there was everything the pups could want to eat or drink or play with. And they lived there very happily for ever and ever!"

Storm smiled to herself. It wasn't exactly a Spirit Dog tale, but the pups were obviously bewitched; Tumble's mouth hung open in awe. Nibble and Tiny snuggled closer to Breeze as she lay down, and soon Tumble and Fluff were yawning too.

"Another story," mumbled Fluff as her eyes drooped and she nestled against Breeze's belly.

"Very well. I'll tell you about an adventure the pups had once they got to the Secret Land of Underlake. One day, Tuggle saw a rainbow. . . ."

Two of the pups were already asleep, making squeaky snores. Storm, amused and beyond grateful, backed carefully away, leaving them in peace with Breeze, who gave her a nod of reassurance.

They're much better—and safer—with Breeze, decided Storm. Besides, she was eager to see how Twitch was doing, so she took her chance to pad across the clearing. The Third Dog lay resting outside his den, shaded by branches that dipped in the light breeze.

"Twitch." She licked his ear gently. "How are you feeling?"

"Better, Storm, thank you." He lifted his head to blink affectionately at her. His mouth still looked raw and swollen, but he could speak a little more clearly. Storm still flinched at the sight of the ugly cuts.

"They do look like they have healed a little today," she managed to say, quite truthfully. "They don't seem poisoned. There's no bad blood in them."

He nodded slightly. "Thank the Sky-Dogs. I was lucky."

"I still can't believe some dog did this to you," said Storm angrily.

Twitch sighed. "I know. I really do believe Arrow is innocent—but I can't imagine who else could be responsible. You know, Storm, it could well have been some intruder. Some strange dog could have slipped into the camp, unseen. It's possible."

Storm clenched her jaw. Twitch seemed to be hanging on to that hope, and his faith in the Pack, but she herself didn't believe it for a moment. There had been no scent of an intruder, after all. *There's a traitor. Deep down, Twitch must know it.*

As if reading her mind, he gave another, sadder sigh. "Ah, Storm. Things were so hard after the Big Growl. When Blade died, it seemed everything was suddenly going to be better. I suppose we hoped for too much, didn't we?"

"There's nothing wrong with hoping for the best," Storm insisted, "and we should be able to trust each other! We—"

An angry growl behind her made her stop what she was saying.

"Storm! Why aren't you watching the pups?"

"Lucky!" Storm stared at her Beta, and at Alpha behind him. She hadn't expected them back quite so soon. "The pups are fine. They're with Breeze! She—"

"I didn't ask Breeze to look after our pups," said Lucky coldly. "I asked *you*."

"But I . . ." Storm licked her chops. He had a point, but she had left the pups in safety, with a dog who cared for them and understood how to keep them happy and *quiet*. "I'm sorry, Beta. I just thought—"

He shook out his shaggy coat, as if shaking off her explanation. "I'm disappointed in you, Storm."

It was all he said. He turned briskly away, and he and Alpha stalked toward the pup den without another word.

Storm gaped after them. *That's not fair! I did what was best for the pups. Yes, it suited me too, but still!*

Lucky used to spend time with me, she thought sulkily. *He used to teach me important things. And now all he thinks about is those pups.*

Annoyance made her throat feel so tight, she couldn't even bark an angry answer at her Beta—and that was probably just as well, she realized grimly. She did not need to get in even *more* trouble right now. . . .

Some dog was barking, though. Storm jerked her head up and pricked her ears, searching for the source of the sudden, frantic sound. It was coming from High Watch, she realized, and she stiffened.

It was Daisy, sounding the alarm.

CHAPTER THREE

"Breeze!" barked Lucky. "Stay with the pups!" He and Alpha ran for the edge of the clearing, Alpha already outpacing him on her long, slender legs. At Storm's side, Twitch was trying to rise to his three paws, but she nudged him with her nose and he subsided easily.

"You wait here, Twitch. We'll be back soon!"

Storm bounded toward the cliffs, aware that other dogs were racing to join her. Mickey appeared at her side, tongue lolling as he ran, and Moon, Thorn, and Beetle were right behind him. The cliff path was steep and their claws scrabbled, sending pebbles skittering down the steep slope, but they kept close behind Beta and, some yards ahead of him, the swift-dog Alpha. Daisy's barks were loud on the clear, cool air; they sounded urgent but not desperate. Storm was thankful for that. *We don't need another crisis right now!*

As they crested the ridge of High Watch, Daisy ran toward

them, her little white ears pricked and her tail quivering.

"What is it, Daisy?" called Alpha, slowing to a trot. "What's happening?"

Daisy turned toward the Endless Lake and nodded. "Out there. Another longpaw floatcage, see?"

All the dogs turned to look at the huge expanse of water, regaining their breath as they gazed out. Just as Daisy said, there was a floatcage on the gray surface of the lake, bobbing like a piece of driftwood on the river. Its head, sharp-pointed and blue, nosed through the waves, and tall, thin spines bristled from its back; its body tapered toward where its tail should be, and on its low-slung flank stood—

"Longpaws!" growled Lucky.

"Not again!" Moon's hackles sprang erect, and her lips pulled back from her fangs.

"What are they doing?" Daisy sniffed the salty air, her tail wagging hesitantly.

Storm stared in fascination. The longpaws didn't look like the ones she'd seen before, blank-faced and yellow-furred; these had visible faces, and their forelegs were also bared to their hairless hides. Daisy was right to be curious. They were dragging trap-meshes out of the Endless Lake. Why? The trap-meshes were sagging, almost bursting with glittering silver fish.

The longpaws were barking to one another and hauling hard on their weighty trap-meshes till their loads of fish collapsed and slithered into the belly of their tame beast. *Too preoccupied to take any notice of us,* Storm realized, *thank the Sky-Dogs.*

"They're hunting, I'd guess," mused Alpha. "What else would they do with all those fish? But they're taking so *many.* How much does a longpaw need to eat?"

"Oh, they don't eat much all at once," said Lucky knowledgeably, and Storm remembered that in his Lone Dog days he'd lived very close to the longpaws, on the streets of the city. "But they like to hoard their prey. It's like our prey pile, I suppose, but they keep theirs for much longer. In cold-boxes, sometimes. And other huge boxes, just filled with food."

"I must say," Daisy growled softly, "these look more like *proper* longpaws. They're not like the horrible yellow-fur longpaws at all."

"What do you mean?" barked Moon. "Longpaws are longpaws, and they're all evil."

"Well," said the little white-and-brown dog diffidently, "when I lived in the city, my longpaws were nice. And these ones aren't trying to hurt us, are they? They're just hunting. And we can see their faces. I think the yellow-fur, faceless ones were only around after the Big Growl."

"Daisy might have a point," growled Lucky softly. "There are lots of different kinds of dogs, aren't there? Well, maybe there are different kinds of longpaws, too. I knew some kind ones in the city. There was one in a Food House who used to give me the most amazing scraps."

Moon gave him a slightly contemptuous, disbelieving look, but Mickey nodded. "My longpaws were kind to me, too," he agreed. "And what about that one last Ice Wind, the one we saw on the edge of the lake? We saved him from the great wave, and he was grateful. He was friendly! He wanted to take me with him."

"Take you with him?" muttered Thorn darkly. "He probably just wanted to capture you and torture you."

Daisy ignored the young dog. "Mickey's right! These ones"—she twitched her ears toward the floatcage—"they're normal longpaws, like friendly, good dogs. And the yellow-fur ones, they're more like—"

The little dog's voice seemed to catch in her throat just as her excited eyes met Storm's, and she snapped her jaws shut before she could say more. But Storm felt a twist of unhappiness in her belly, and her heart sank.

I know what you were going to say, Daisy, she thought grimly. *If these longpaws are like Good Dogs, then those awful yellow-furs are more like Fierce Dogs.*

Moon took a pace forward, lowering her ears and growling. "I don't care what kind of longpaws they are," she said. "They're bad, like all longpaws."

"I agree," snarled Beetle, coming to his Mother-Dog's side. He and Thorn looked as furious and scared as Moon, Storm realized, and no wonder—their Father-Dog, Fiery, had been killed by those vicious yellow-furs. "We'll have revenge on the longpaws one day. Right, Thorn? For our Father-Dog."

"Oh yes, we will," growled his sister. "We'll hunt them down, and they'll get what they deserve for killing my Father-Dog. And I don't care what you Leashed Dogs think!"

"Foolish pups!" Moon's bark made them start back from her in surprise. "Longpaws are dangerous, and don't you ever forget it!"

"But Mother-Dog," protested Thorn, her tail submissively low but her eyes stubborn. "They need to be taught a lesson."

"You can't teach longpaws anything! The only thing to do is to *stay away from them!* Remember what they did to your Father-Dog, and keep your distance, both of you!"

Beetle and Thorn could only meet her angry blue gaze for a few moments before dropping their eyes and nodding. But as soon as Moon turned away, Storm noticed, the two young dogs were exchanging rebellious looks.

"They're leaving, anyway," Moon pointed out in satisfaction, her tail quivering as she stared out at the Endless Lake. "See? And good riddance."

Sure enough, the floatcage was moving slowly across the bay, the thrum of its growl just audible on the clear air. The dogs watched as it rounded the point of the headland, then vanished. Storm licked her chops, glad to know it was gone along with its longpaws. She didn't know what to think. Were the former Leashed Dogs right, that not all longpaws were hostile and savage? Could some of them be trusted?

Storm shook herself from head to tail, releasing the tension. No: she was inclined to agree with Moon and her pups. After all, longpaws had kept Fierce Dogs like her as their obedient Fangs, and trained them with callous, cruel methods designed to make the dogs callous and cruel in turn. Longpaws were dangerous, and better avoided.

Alpha touched her slender muzzle to Daisy's. "Well done, Daisy. You were right to warn us, and sharp-eyed to see the float-cage out there. Let me know if any more appear—especially if they come closer to the shore."

"I will," yapped Daisy proudly, returning to her post.

"Storm," Lucky called as the dogs made their way down the cliff path once more. "I think it's time to take out a hunting patrol. Take Bruno, Arrow, and Mickey, will you? Dart can be your scout dog."

Storm nodded, panting happily. "Of course, Beta!" Finally, a proper job, and one she was good at. *I might be terrible at looking after pups, but I can hunt as well as any dog!*

Storm had been so thrilled to be asked by Beta, and so energized by getting out into the forest to stretch her muscles, she hadn't paused to consider the makeup of the hunting party Lucky had chosen. But now, as they threaded their way cautiously through the forest, nostrils alert and ears pricked for prey, she glanced nervously back at her companions.

It's not the team I would've chosen, she thought ruefully. *It's barely a team at all.*

As they made their way through the undergrowth and over grassy tussocks, the only dog who seemed happy in the company of two Fierce Dogs was Mickey, who was busying himself with scenting and tracking. But Bruno's muzzle had taken on a slight curl; he looked both distracted and sullen. And Dart, who was supposed to be scouting ahead, was hanging back at Bruno's flanks, muttering to him, or casting suspicious looks at Arrow.

Lucky probably meant to force us all to get along, Storm realized. *But if that was his plan, it's failing.*

"Dart!" growled Storm as her patience ran out. "Get up ahead and look for prey or threats! You're supposed to be scouting, not gossiping with Bruno."

Dart shot her a killing look, but she obeyed, trotting forward with her tail at a sulky angle. Arrow wrinkled his muzzle sympathetically at Storm, and Storm felt a twitch of amusement. Arrow had known exactly what Dart was up to. *Snooping on his every movement! But it doesn't bother him; he shakes it off like river-water.*

Arrow was so tolerant of the Pack's hostility, thought Storm; and that made it even more unfair that he should have such a bad reputation.

Don't worry about that right now, she told herself. *You want to make a good impression on Lucky with this hunt—especially after you made such a rat's-ear of pup-sitting. . . .*

No sooner had Storm made up her mind to forget Arrow's troubles and focus on hunting, than Mickey suddenly bolted into a patch of sagebrush, quick and silent. There was a violent rustle of scrub and a squeak of distress, cut abruptly short. Then Mickey emerged triumphant, a limp squirrel clamped in his jaws.

Storm panted happily, nodding to Mickey. *A good start! O Forest-Dog, I hope that's an omen!*

It seemed indeed to be a good sign, because not much later, she scented something at the same moment as Arrow: the warm, sweet smell of rabbit. The creature had wandered too far from its burrow, and Storm and Arrow together found it simple to harry it toward Bruno. The big dog crouched in wait, springing up just as the panicked rabbit spotted him and tried to dodge. Bruno's jaws snapped on its spine, and he shook it with pride.

"The Forest-Dog's kind today," he mumbled through his mouthful of fur and flesh, and Storm panted happily in agreement. Bruno was so pleased with himself that, though he didn't exactly thank Arrow for his help, he did at least stop glaring at him for a few moments.

After stashing their two fine pieces of prey between the roots of an ancient pine, the hunting patrol moved on with increased confidence through the trees. Storm's heart had lightened so much, she even stopped checking on Dart and Bruno.

Which was a mistake, she realized with a spurt of anger as the hunters headed down a slope into a grassy glade. The patches of tall bracken at its far side looked like a promising hunting ground, but when Storm gave a sideways glance to check that Bruno was in position, she spotted a familiar brown-and-white shadow at his side. Dart was muttering to the big dog again, and Bruno was nodding, his face set once more in a glare.

"Dart!" barked Storm, too enraged to keep her voice low. "You're our scout dog. So scout!"

Dart gave an angry whine. "I only came back to report to Bruno!"

Storm could hardly believe her ears, and she wrinkled her muzzle in a snarl. "Bruno's not the hunt leader today! *I—*"

She was interrupted by a horrible, guttural, grunting roar. Instantly she fell silent, her ears pricking straight up as the undergrowth crashed and snapped, and her fellow hunters stiffened, nostrils flaring. The sound was awful, and it was growing louder and angrier.

"The bracken," gasped Mickey. "It's moving!"

They all spun to face the shifting, rustling brown fronds; just as they did, a massive head broke through, glaring at them with bright, vicious eyes. It was covered in dense bristly hair, and savage yellow tusks curled upward from a thrusting jaw.

They were almost on top of it, Storm realized with a surge of panic.

A tusknose!

CHAPTER FOUR

It had to be a tusknose, didn't it? Storm had never seen one, she thought as she stared at it in horror, but there could be no other animal as ugly and ferocious as this. She'd heard stories from the older dogs, who were tough and experienced hunters—and even they wouldn't willingly get into a fight with a tusknose. *Best left alone,* they'd told her. *You don't want to mess with a tusknose, young Lick!*

She could believe that. The creature looked lethal—and intimidatingly huge. *It's bigger than me!* Its tusks gleamed dully in the overcast light of the Sun-Dog, its eyes were lit with red rage, and slivers of drool escaped from the corners of its jaws as it glared menacingly at the dogs. The hunters could only stare at it, frozen with horror, each dog seeming to wait for the others to do something, to move, to run.

They were still lost in panicked indecision when the tusknose charged. It hurtled forward, crashing through the bracken, and lunged straight for the nearest hunter—Storm.

She gave a yelp of horror, aware that the others were scattering for the edges of the glade, their tails tucked low. At the last moment, just before the vicious tusks could rake her flank, she flinched and shot away to the side, scrambling for the thickest, thorniest scrub.

This might have been a mistake! As thorns tugged and tore at her hide, she struggled on through, only to hear the tusknose plunge after her. It must be completely indifferent to the spiky undergrowth, she realized in panic, with its tough skin sheathed in coarse hairs. *It's faster in this cursed tangle than I am. And it's getting closer!*

Desperately Storm shoved and scrabbled, claws raking the dry earth. She felt a momentary surge of relief as her head and shoulders burst clear of the bushes and into open air, but it was short-lived. The tusknose was so close she could feel its hot snorting breath on her rump. Then, as she broke free of the thorns altogether, she skidded to a halt, almost plowing nose-first into a vast pine trunk.

Twisting swiftly to face the tusknose, she drew back her lips from her fangs. *It might kill me, but I'll hurt it first!*

There was a volley of barking behind the creature as it paused to paw at the ground and grunt that hideous roar, but Storm couldn't even see her Packmates beyond its bulk—and anyway, she knew they were too far away. *And how could they hope to drag it off? It's too big, too angry, too brutal . . .* if she tried to turn and run, it would be on her before she could even begin.

I need to surprise it, that's my only hope!

She lunged for its throat, snarling viciously. With a burst of triumph, she snapped her teeth down on its burly neck, but her eyes widened as she felt how tough its hide was beneath that wiry hair. Her fangs did little more than scrape across its skin, leaving a deep graze that only enraged it more. Its shoulders heaved, its neck muscles flexed, and Storm's grip failed as she was flung aside.

The breath was knocked out of her as she hit the tree with her full weight. Stars exploded behind her eyes. Stunned, she struggled to roll over and get back to her feet, but the huge shadow was already on top of her, that deafening roar hammering her sensitive ears. The creature jerked and swung its head, and Storm felt a sickening rip of agony in her shoulder. She opened her jaws in a screaming yelp.

I'm dead, was all she could think through the pain.

Then even her own thoughts were drowned out by the furious barking of her Packmates. They must be right at the tusknose's rump, and it couldn't afford to ignore them any longer. With a squealing snarl, it twisted with astonishing speed to face the hunting patrol. Gasping and panting, Storm sank her claws into the earth and dragged herself out from beneath the beast. That was all she could manage before the pain in her shoulder made her collapse onto her side, the wound leaking a scary amount of blood.

As it turned on them, the dogs harrying the tusknose had to back off, and it began to lumber around to attack Storm once more. But with a truly Fierce Dog snarl, Arrow darted in from its side and sank his fangs into its muzzle. The beast screamed and shook him off, and Arrow retreated swiftly, but he'd gotten its attention. It swung away from Storm, eyes blazing with red fury, and charged after him.

The sound of its hard paws on the dry earth was a terrifying thunder; it was amazing, thought Storm through a haze of pain, how fast that massive thing could move. Blinking, she could make out the dark shadow of Arrow's lithe form as he led the tusknose away from her, twisting and turning between the pine trunks, diving through scrub. It pounded after him, still roaring. Arrow was barely able to stay out of reach.

The other dogs were barking furiously, but holding back, and Storm realized that all they could do was try to distract and disorient the beast. If another dog tried to intervene in the chase, or cut off the tusknose's charge, it would only get itself trampled. But the hunting patrol howled and yelped, maddening the creature as it lunged for Arrow. It swung its head as he dodged and darted, its tusks only just missing his hind leg.

Arrow paused for a moment in his crazy chase, his tongue hanging from his jaws, his breath coming in rapid pants. He looked exhausted. The tusknose didn't hesitate. Lowering its massive head, it screamed and charged.

Storm was sure her fellow Fierce Dog was doomed. The monster was unstoppable, and its tusks were aimed straight at Arrow's chest. But at the last possible instant, Arrow bunched his haunches and leaped out of its path. The tusknose slammed into the broad pine trunk behind him, and it felt to Storm like the impact made the Earth-Dog quiver.

The sound of the collision echoed through the glade as the tusknose staggered, then sagged, then lurched forward onto its knees. One flinty paw struck the ground, as if it was trying to recover and rise, but it didn't get the chance. Bruno, Mickey, and Arrow launched themselves at its thick neck, Dart flew in for its throat, and for long moments there was the sound of frantic snapping and biting and tearing as the dogs raced to di.. creature.

Through her haze of exhaustion, Storm saw blood spatter the golden pine trunk with dark red. The beast made one last attempt to stand, swinging its head wildly, but its roar was feebler now, and it staggered. Arrow attacked again, and Bruno's jaws closed on its squealing snout. As Storm managed to drag herself upright at last, the creature finally toppled with a crash into the leaf litter and lay still. One hind leg twitched, then sank back.

One by one, the dogs backed away from the enormous carcass. They were all panting, their flanks heaving; Dart's leg was bleeding from a shallow gash, and a clump of Bruno's shoulder fur had been torn away. But the fight could have gone a great deal worse for all of them.

No thanks to the fool who let this happen! thought Storm furiously.

Limping forward, she bared her fangs and snarled in Dart's face. "This was your fault!"

"My fault?" Dart's eyes widened, and her own teeth showed. "I helped kill it!"

"You nearly got all of us killed!" Storm glared around the circle of dogs, blinking. The pain in her shoulder was intensifying into a burning agony, but she refused to sit down.

"Now just wait a minute," began Bruno gruffly, but Storm barked sharply to interrupt him.

"If Dart had done her job, we wouldn't have been in this position. But she was busy gossiping with *you*, Bruno! We barely escaped with our lives." Rage mingled with pain, making Storm's vision redden and blur. "You were our scout, Dart; you should have scented this beast and warned us in time. But you didn't. And you almost killed me. You *almost killed us all!*"

CHAPTER FIVE

Storm was the last to release her aching jaw-hold, and the carcass of the tusknose thudded and rolled down the shallow slope into the clearing, bumping to a stop against a white stump. The hunters could only stand there for a long moment, heads hanging low with exhaustion, their breath coming in panting gasps, as every dog in camp got to its paws and stared at them.

Storm opened her jaws as if in a yawn, stretching the muscles. Around her, her fellow hunters were doing the same, shaking their fur and extending their tired forelegs to claw at the ground. None of them had the breath to speak after dragging the gigantic tusknose all the way through the forest. Even Storm's fangs hurt— but not nearly as much as the slash of agony that went through her shoulder every time she moved. Twisting her head, she tried feebly to lick the wound, as Alpha and Beta walked slowly forward from their den. The other Pack members in the camp simply gaped at the lifeless tusknose.

Storm sat on her haunches, then lay down on her belly, exhausted and aching. "We found some prey," she told Alpha dully.

Lucky barked a hoarse laugh. "You can say that again!"

Alpha's ears pricked high, and her eyes were shining. "Well done, hunters!"

The other dogs were gathering around the tusknose now, yelping in delight and admiration. "Oh my goodness!" Sunshine kept yapping in high excitement. "Oh my goodness!"

I should be proud, thought Storm as she watched them all. *I should be as excited as Sunshine.*

Instead anger still roiled in her belly. *I almost died, thanks to Dart. It may not look like it, but this hunt was a disaster.*

But more than anger, she felt only a longing to curl up in her den and sleep, forgetting them all. She could still feel the warm trickle of leaking blood on her shoulder, and it was beginning to make her light-headed. Dragging the tusknose back to camp had taken all the energy she had left; she hadn't even snarled at Dart, not since she'd scolded her back in the woods.

But I'm still angry. That stupid, mean-minded, vindictive dog: she's so obsessed with Arrow, she couldn't even do her job and protect us. And Bruno's no better.

"Storm, you've done a wonderful job." Alpha was standing beside her, she realized, and Storm staggered to her paws. "All of you have. This is a very fine catch indeed!"

"The Pack will eat well tonight—and tomorrow!" Lucky licked Storm's muzzle. "But you're hurt, Storm! Are you all right?"

"Not really," she admitted, sagging where she stood. "It's—"

"Storm found the beast!" barked Mickey. "And Arrow tired it out."

"Every dog helped," put in Arrow modestly. "It took all of us to bring it down."

"Fantastic teamwork," agreed Lucky, his tongue lolling with happiness.

Storm wanted to swipe that pleased look off her Beta's face. Suddenly, her rage boiled over, and her hackles sprang erect as she snarled in fury.

"It was anything but teamwork! It was the opposite of teamwork!"

Lucky's ears pulled back in surprise. "What?"

"We ran into the tusknose by accident," she barked. "I only

'found' it because I nearly fell over it. And it came within a claw's-width of killing me!" She nodded at her shoulder wound; even that small movement sent shards of pain through her whole body. "It was pure luck and the mercy of the Forest-Dog that brought us this prey, Alpha. Not skill and not teamwork either!" Turning on Dart, she growled fiercely. "Dart *didn't do her job*. She let us walk straight into a death trap!"

For a moment there was stunned silence in the glade. Alpha stared at Storm, then at Dart. Then Bruno gave a sharp bark of objection.

"Dart *was* doing her job," he insisted gruffly. "She'd just come back to report to me, remember?"

Alpha stared coolly into his eyes. "And why," she asked softly, "was Dart reporting to you, Bruno? Storm was your hunt leader."

"Because she wasn't reporting to him at all!" barked Storm. She hated being the one to whine tales to Alpha, but she was frustrated beyond endurance, and now that she'd opened her mouth, the words wouldn't stop coming. "She was sneaking and gossiping instead! Until we came upon the tusknose, Dart and Bruno spent the entire hunt whining to each other about Arrow. It was all they could think about, all they could talk about. I watched them."

Arrow sat back on his haunches, looking startled and hurt.

Dart curled her muzzle, and Bruno's face grew surly and resentful. Lucky tilted his head and looked sharply at Storm. "Why would they do that, Storm? Maybe you were imagining it. If they were whispering, you couldn't have—"

"No!" She'd had enough of the Pack and their secret conspiracies. *In for a rabbit, in for the whole warren,* she decided. "They're all plotting against Arrow all the time. I heard them talking about it during no-sun in the trees on the edge of camp. Not just Bruno and Dart. Snap and Ruff and Woody, too. They've been following Arrow around, spying on him, because they don't trust him—and all because he's a Fierce Dog! How is that good for the Pack?"

Alpha and Beta looked stunned, their ears back and their eyes wide. Arrow got slowly to his paws.

"I . . ." The Fierce Dog swallowed, glancing around at the dogs Storm had named. "I know some of the Pack suspected me of being the bad dog, but—I never thought—I didn't imagine they would *spy* on me. . . ."

Storm gave him an understanding *ruff.* Despite her anger, despite the tormenting pain in her shoulder, she felt a massive sense of relief. *It's out in the open,* she realized. *I've been carrying this around like a stone in my paw, and I'm glad I told the Pack.*

There was movement behind Alpha and Beta, a flash of

sunlight on golden fur, and Bella walked forward silently. Every dog turned to watch her as she paced to Arrow's side, turned, and stood there, shoulder to shoulder with her mate, giving her Pack-mates a cold and defiant glare.

The rest of the Pack was stirring now, shocked out of their silence, and they were beginning to mutter and yelp among one another. Beetle stepped forward, his brow creased with anxiety. "Storm's right. This is bad for the Pack!"

"Agreed," yapped his sister Thorn. She glared at Dart. "What you're doing is wrong."

Other dogs were nodding, or growling in agreement—Mickey and Rake, and little Daisy, who yelped her disapproval.

"Packmates need to trust each other," growled Rake, "or what's the point?"

"I agree," added Chase, blinking. "Pack is the most important thing, whatever you might think of individual dogs."

Storm, though, kept watching the others. Moon and Twitch looked uneasy, but not very shocked, and Dart's expression was defiant.

"Yes, we've been watching Arrow," the scout dog barked, her eyes steady on Storm's. "And *that* is for the good of the Pack." She glowered at Thorn and Beetle. "If we think there's a danger to our

Packmates, we have to guard against it. Am I right?"

Bruno and Ruff growled in agreement.

"You should be grateful, Storm," Dart added with a sneer and a disdainful flick of her ear. "We're trying to prove the *bad* Fierce Dog did it—we're not accusing *you!*"

Storm's stomach plummeted, and for a moment she couldn't speak. *Whatever that sneak Dart says, they don't trust me any more than they trust Arrow. Just because we were born Fierce Dogs!*

In the awful silence, Dart grunted. "I bet Alpha agrees with me. This is how we protect the Pack, and that's the most important thing of all. Right, Alpha?"

Storm turned desperately to the graceful swift-dog. Alpha was perfectly still, only her tail twitching, and her dark eyes were flinty.

"Indeed," she said at last, crisply. "You are quite right, Dart. Protecting the Pack *is* every dog's priority."

"Exactly." Dart's smug smile made Storm want to bite off her nose. Bitterness filled her mouth till she felt she would choke.

"However," Alpha went on, lifting her head to glare around the Pack. "Protecting the Pack means that we all do our jobs. When a dog is given a task, he"—she fixed her steely eyes on Dart—"or *she* must do it to the best of their ability. And you, Dart, did not. You failed to do your job, the job I gave you in the best interest of your Packmates. You should have been scouting ahead of the hunting party as Storm asked you to do. If even that simple assignment is beyond you, I can relieve you of your duties as scout dog."

Dart's jaw dropped open, and her throat muscles worked. But Alpha glared into her eyes until she fell silent, licking her chops.

"You, Dart, will eat last today," Alpha announced. "As for the rest of you: you will return quietly to your duties. I want to hear no whining, and no arguments." She shot a sidelong glance at Storm. "*Every* dog is to calm down."

Dart looked as if Alpha had scraped the earth out from under her paws. Sullen, she hung her head. "Yes, Alpha."

Turning with a dismissive flick of her tail, Alpha stalked off to join Twitch, Lucky at her heels. As the other dogs began to disperse, silently, in ones and twos and subdued groups, Arrow and Bella huddled together, murmuring to each other. They sounded distressed as they padded out beyond the camp boundary, and their quiet misery only made Storm more angry.

That solved nothing at all! she thought, her muscles quivering as she stood in disbelief. Yes, Alpha had punished Dart—but what did that really matter? It would be humiliating for the chase-dog to eat last, but not especially hurtful, not when there was an entire tusknose to go around. *And Alpha said absolutely nothing about those dogs stalking Arrow!*

Storm couldn't bear to submit calmly like the others. She limped as determinedly as she could toward Alpha, Lucky, and Twitch. Lucky glanced around, one ear flicking back in alarm as he spotted her, but even his warning look couldn't stop her.

"You know Arrow's not the problem," Storm barked as she shouldered her way into their group. "Arrow didn't sabotage the prey. He didn't kill that fox cub. And he *certainly* didn't murder Whisper!"

"Lower your voice," snapped Alpha.

Storm's hackles rose. Was that all Alpha cared about—what the other dogs thought? "Why aren't you doing something about those dogs who are persecuting Arrow? They accuse him of everything, and you don't say a word, Alpha!"

"That's enough, Storm," growled Lucky.

"No, it's not! Why don't you tell those dogs it's unacceptable? You need to stop their gossip right now!"

"Storm, be quiet," said Lucky. "You're right; we know Arrow's not the bad dog."

"And we know it was the foxes who killed Whisper, and we've gotten rid of those beasts," added Twitch reassuringly.

Storm stared at him, and then at Lucky. "Beta, you know I don't believe that the foxes were responsible!" she growled. "And you know why!"

"That's not the issue here," Lucky admonished her. "I know you think it's unfair that the Pack is blaming Arrow, but it's just the way things are right now."

Alpha sighed. "Storm, you think this is hard on Arrow, and you're right. But for the moment, it's good that there's only one suspect, that the Pack is focusing all their hostility on a single dog. Arrow is strong. He can deal with this. And Beta, Twitch, and I can make sure that suspicion is as far as they go, that things don't get out of control. Until we can set a paw on the real culprit, this is all we can do. It's hard, but it's necessary. If every dog had doubts about every other dog, the Pack would fall apart. Can't you see that?"

No, thought Storm furiously, *I don't see why Arrow has to take all the weight of this by himself.* But she kept her jaws firmly shut; she'd spoken her mind, and it was clear Alpha didn't want to listen.

"We'll keep our eyes and ears alert," Lucky reassured her. "Someday soon, under the Sun-Dog or the Moon-Dog, this traitor will make a mistake, and we'll catch them. The bad dog will be punished, Storm; it's just a matter of watching, and waiting. Be patient."

But I'm not sure patience is the answer, Lucky. Hunching her wounded shoulder, Storm turned and walked away sadly. *Patience doesn't give Arrow any comfort. Or Whisper any justice . . .*

Storm licked the last juicy traces of tusknose from her jaws. The Moon-Dog above her remained half turned away, her eye averted from the Pack, and Storm was sure she was still angry. *I know that happens with every journey the Moon-Dog makes, but no-sun feels different these days. It feels wrong. It feels dangerous.*

The meat of the tusknose had been delicious, rich and dark with a strong tang, and the Pack had wolfed down its flesh and crunched its bones with joy. But the taste in Storm's mouth was one of bitterness. Her accusations had been brushed aside by the Pack, and the three leaders had dismissed her like some yapping pup; it hurt, and it rankled in her belly. No tusknose could dispel the sourness of that.

Her shoulder hurt, too, with a stabbing pain that only occasionally faded to a dull ache. Every time it did, just when she could almost believe she might fall asleep at last, the sharp agony would bite again and jolt her back to miserable wakefulness.

Why are they so happy to let every dog think badly of Arrow? Lucky says it's only for now—but what if the true culprit is never found? And it's not fair that

Arrow has to go through this at all. He's a good dog, and Lucky knows it.

There was a soft voice nearby, and Storm tilted an ear toward it. Breeze was telling stories to the pups again, she realized. The sound was soothing.

"The battle was glorious," Breeze murmured. "The monster was the fiercest the brave hunting dogs had ever met, with its fiery red eyes and savage tusks, but they fought on, for the good of the Pack. Bruno flew at it, and might have been gored, but Mickey caught it by the throat and held on. . . ."

Storm strained her cocked ear. Breeze hadn't mentioned her yet, or Arrow. She hadn't mentioned Dart's name either, but still . . . was Breeze leaving out the Fierce Dogs deliberately? Did she think even a mention of them would frighten the pups? Was Breeze against the Fierce Dogs, too? She'd spoken out against Arrow, that night the broken clear-stone had been hidden in the deer . . . but on the other paw, Breeze had always been kind and friendly toward Storm herself. . . .

"And as the Sun-Dog sank down over the Endless Lake, the tusked monster began to tire. The sky turned bloodred, and so did the sand. Bruno and Mickey were finally beginning to overcome it. . . ."

So the setting of the story had changed, too: Breeze had moved it to the Endless Lake. Storm sighed, her ears drooping. *Maybe the story works better with just two dogs in it. Maybe any more would confuse the pups.* Storm's eyelids grew heavy; Breeze was good at this. Her gentle voice could lull an angry tusknose to sleep. . . .

It wasn't no-sun after all; it was still twilight, with a soft gray glow blurring the edges of the glade and turning the tree branches into a shadowy spiderweb above the Pack. The dogs lay content, bellies full, murmuring to one another. Every dog was happy, and no dog whined or snapped. It's so peaceful, thought Storm. This is better. This is how it should be, always. . . .

She made her way across the glade, setting her paws down lightly between her resting Packmates. Her shoulder didn't hurt anymore, and she was comfortably well-fed; this was a very good evening. She spotted Twitch relaxing at the foot of a gnarled oak, his single forepaw stretched lazily before him. She would go and sit with him.

No, something's wrong.

Storm glanced over her shoulder, and her brow furrowed. Something bad. It's following me.

It's right behind me!

Worried, Storm twisted around and stared. No, there was nothing there. It was her imagination, that was all. Creating monsters when there weren't any.

When the Pack was happy and at peace. A few eyes glanced her way, but they were only curious, not alarmed. The others had seen nothing behind her. She'd imagined it.

Storm walked on, more slowly this time. She seemed no nearer to Twitch, so she picked up her pace. And felt it again: that crawling in her hide, the prickle in her fur.

She spun around. Still there was nothing behind her. Still her Packmates saw nothing.

But the shadows at the edge of the glade: were they a little darker now? Were they spreading, drawing closer? Surely that was her imagination too, and yet . . . the shadows slid as she watched, seeping into the glade, obscuring the last light of the Sun-Dog. Darkness crept between the groups of dogs, crawled up over their haunches, obscured their faces. Her Pack was being swallowed by the shadows, yet they didn't move, didn't bark; they simply sank into the darkness.

And there were other dogs there too, she knew it, she could see them now. They were dogs made of shadow and night, dogs that took form as she watched. The shadow dogs moved among her Pack, filling up the glade. They whispered things Storm couldn't hear, muttered in the ears of her shadow-faced Packmates. And one by one, at the urging of those dogs made of night, her Packmates lifted their heads and stared at Storm. Their eyes were sparks of light in the darkness, and they were all Storm could see of her Packmates' faces now. Bruno's eyes, suspicious and sullen. Rake's, bright and afraid. Alpha's eyes, shocked . . . Shadow *dogs were whispering into the ears of Ruff, and Breeze, and Daisy. . . .*

And then there was a voice in her own ear. A soft, warning voice. One she knew.

The darkness, Storm . . . the evil is coming . . .

Whisper? *she thought.* Is that you? Whisper!

The darkness, *he told her silently.* Oh, Storm. The darkness. It's spreading through the Pack. . . .

Pain shot through Storm's shoulder, jarring her awake. Panting, her heart thundering in her rib cage, she realized she'd tried to stand up in her sleep; she was propped up on her forepaws, wobbling. The eerie twilight was no longer around her, the camp no longer haunted by black shadows; it was night again, a soft unthreatening darkness lit by the glow of the Moon-Dog. Around her there were no ghostly voices, only the peaceful breathing and the gentle snores of her Packmates.

And the furious, thudding echo of her own terrified heartbeat.

CHAPTER SIX

"Absolutely not," Alpha scolded firmly. "You are not hunting, Storm. Not today."

The sleek swift-dog stood over her, shaking her elegant head as she stared down at Storm's shoulder. Storm knew that the wound from the tusknose looked as red and raw as it felt.

"That wound was much worse than you let on," Alpha added. "It's all very well being tough, Storm, but you also need to be sensible. This Pack relies on you a great deal, so take the time to get better."

"But there's hunting to be done. That tusknose won't feed us forever. . . ."

"No more arguments, Storm. That's my decision. Stay in camp, relax, and rest that shoulder."

Storm opened her mouth to argue more, but one look at

Alpha's steely expression told her it would be useless. With a sigh, she slumped back onto her bedding. "All right."

"That's better." Alpha nodded approvingly, then turned to watch the hunting parties as they organized themselves and headed out of the clearing. Storm watched them too, a growl of resentment rumbling in her throat. *It's just a cut,* she thought grumpily. *I could manage a couple of rabbits, for the Sky-Dogs' sake. And I'm going to be so bored here. . . .*

Her prediction was very quickly proved right. *Is this really all that goes on in the camp all day?* Alpha and Beta did nothing more than lay in the weak sunshine, gazing approvingly at their pups as they tumbled and rolled around a grassy knoll, playing some game called Alpha-of-the-Pack. When Tumble and Fluff grew bored of that (and no wonder, thought Storm: they'd spent the whole game taking turns at being Alpha, without giving Nibble and Tiny a chance), they started hopping around at Omega's heels, jumping up to lick her chin and chasing her tail as if it were a fluffy white butterfly. Storm was amazed that Sunshine wasn't irritated, but the little Omega actually seemed to enjoy the pups' antics. She flicked her tail to the side as Tumble batted a paw at it, then sat down to let him catch it after all. The pups seemed to adore her as much as she loved them, Storm realized sulkily. *Why does every dog but me know exactly how to make pups happy?*

Tired of watching the youngsters, Storm rolled over to see what the adult dogs were up to. Twitch was talking to Moon, and the white-and-black dog laughed at something he said. A few of the dogs from Twitch's old Pack were still in the clearing, too; Ruff, Woody, and Breeze were deep in conversation, but they were too far away for Storm to hear any of it, and besides, their voices were drowned out by the squealing of the overexcited pups. With a disgruntled growl, Storm laid her head on the ground and put her paws over her ears.

The nudge of a small wet nose against her flank made her start. "Storm!"

Storm sighed, but she stretched out her muzzle to give Nibble a friendly lick. Nibble was the quietest and most sensible of the pups; Storm reckoned she could just about manage her—so long as her littermates didn't come over too. . . .

"You a hunt-dog, Storm?" The little dog's ears were pricked with enthusiasm.

"That's right, Nibble," Storm told her patiently. "I catch prey for the Pack."

"Yes!" The little pup's tail wagged. "Strong and fast like my Mother-Dog and my Father-Dog. I be a hunt-dog, too, when I *big*."

"That's good, Nibble," Storm murmured. "You'll grow up big and strong." Nibble really was quite cute, she decided, as the delighted pup covered her muzzle in licks from her small tongue. When Storm's face was thoroughly wet, Nibble drew back in satisfaction, then turned and toddled off to rejoin her littermates.

The conversation between Twitch's former Packmates seemed to have come to an end, because Ruff and Woody got to their paws, stretched, and padded over to Twitch. The three-legged dog raised his head, pricking his ears at their questions, and nodded.

As Storm watched, the two dogs left Twitch and strolled across to the prey pile, where torn pieces of the tusknose still lay—a haunch and half a shoulder, as well as quite a lot of the flank. Pawing a chunk of meat from the carcass, Ruff settled down. Woody joined him, and they began to gnaw contentedly.

There was a bark of angry surprise from Alpha, and she rose and loped toward them. "What do you think you're doing?" she demanded.

Woody looked up, blinking in surprise. He licked some tusknose juice from his nose.

"You're eating without my permission!" barked Alpha, looking from Woody to Ruff. "What are you two thinking?"

The two dogs exchanged an uneasy glance. "But, Alpha," said

Ruff indignantly, "Twitch said it was fine."

Twitch scrambled to his paws and limped over to where Alpha stood glaring at the two dogs. "Alpha, I'm sorry. I didn't think there'd be a problem. There's so much tusknose left, I didn't see the harm in it."

Alpha's hackles bristled on the nape of her neck. "That's not the point, Twitch, as you well know. And we—"

"Alpha." Lucky was at Alpha's shoulder by now, and he nuzzled it gently. Lowering his voice, he murmured to her, so quietly that Storm couldn't hear the words. At last Alpha took an impatient breath, then walked away and sat down, looking irritated.

This was crazy, thought Storm. Every dog was bored: that was why they were eating food they shouldn't, and getting into quarrels. *I don't want to spend all day in the camp doing nothing, like this lot!*

Rising to her paws, she winced slightly, but the pain was bearable. Perhaps she would wander out into the woods for a walk, see if she could sniff out a mouse or two. . . . Alpha surely couldn't object to *that* much exertion? Trying to look innocent, she padded languidly toward the border of the clearing, but when she was within a sniff of freedom, she heard a gruff yap from Lucky.

"Storm! That doesn't look like resting." He trotted to her side. "You're supposed to be healing that shoulder, remember?"

Rolling her eyes, she sighed and turned reluctantly toward him. "But, Beta, I'm so *bored*."

"That's not important," he scolded as he shepherded her back into the clearing. "What matters is you getting well enough to hunt at your full ability. Now, why don't you sit down with Sunshine?" He led a dejected Storm over to where the little Omega was pawing through a pile of soft leaves and sagebrush. "If you're really that bored, you can help Omega with her chores."

It's not the escape I was hoping for, sighed Storm to herself, *but it's better than nothing.* Her head drooped as she plodded over, but Sunshine turned with such a happy, welcoming expression that Storm's mood lifted despite herself.

"Storm!" yapped the little Omega, her bedraggled plume of a tail waving. "Oh, this is wonderful—I haven't had a chance to talk to you recently!"

"Just make sure she helps you as well as chatting," warned Lucky with a twinkle in his eye. "Thank you, Sunshine. Have fun, Storm."

I doubt there's much chance of fun here, thought Storm darkly, but Sunshine was all bounce and enthusiasm, and Storm couldn't help but be glad to see her.

"Tell me the whole story about the tusknose again," yipped

Sunshine, her tiny pink tongue lolling. "I haven't heard it from you, and I know it must have been frightening and Dart was silly to get you into such a mess, but oh my goodness, it sounds like an incredible adventure. Let me know if your shoulder wants licking, and I'll help. Oh! Lucky wanted me to show you how to do this. Well, see these leaves?" She nosed a couple of brown aspen leaves from the pile. "These ones are too dry and old, they wouldn't be comfy to lie on. So we take these ones out, here, like this. Look for the ones that are still green and soft, and then we can mix them with some nice moss, and if we put sagebrush underneath them, there's a good base for the softer bedding. . . ."

So much for telling Sunshine about the tusknose, thought Storm affectionately—she'd be lucky to get a word in. But just listening to the eager little dog made her heart much lighter. The Omega was so happy with her place in the Pack, so keen to make herself useful. Storm almost envied her. *Sunshine doesn't waste her days worrying about what other dogs think of her,* she realized. *She doesn't fret and fume and plan status fights with the other dogs so she can rise higher in the Pack. She's content to be helpful. I don't think I've ever seen such a happy dog.*

And really, I don't know what the Pack would do without her. Storm gave Sunshine an impulsive lick on the crown of her head, and the little dog started, then wagged her tail.

"What was that for?" she asked happily.

"I just—well, thanks, Sunshine. For all you do. And for letting me help today. I was going out of my mind with boredom. Here, show me again which leaves go on top?"

Sunshine was more than happy to give Storm a further lesson on leaves, in detail that would usually have driven Storm crazy. But maybe just for once it *was* nice to stay behind in camp, to have time to talk and relax and simply enjoy another dog's company.

And at least, thought Storm, she hadn't been asked to pup-sit again. . . .

She glanced toward them. Tumble, Fluff, Nibble, and Tiny were romping in the middle of the glade, devotedly watched by their parent-dogs. Storm was surprised by a pang of envy. *The pups don't have any worries either,* she thought. *For now all they have to do is play, and be safe and looked-after.*

Following her gaze, Sunshine paused with one paw on the leaf pile. "I always knew Lucky—I mean, Beta—would make a good Father-Dog," she murmured. "Didn't you, Storm? After all, look how well he cared for you when you were little."

Storm nodded wistfully. "I couldn't have asked for a better Father-Dog," she agreed. Sighing, she added, "Sometimes I miss those days. Sometimes I wish I could just let Lucky take care of everything for me, the way he used to. Silly, isn't it?"

"Every dog misses their pup-days sometimes," Sunshine reassured her. "It was simpler then. A bit like being a Leashed Dog! My longpaws were like my parent-dogs, I suppose. And yes, I sometimes remember how easy life was in those days, being petted and brushed and walked and cared for. But I wouldn't go back now!"

"I guess you're right," said Storm with amusement.

"There's nothing odd about missing those days," Sunshine went on. "You can still look back and remember, and miss it just a little bit. It's nothing to be ashamed of, so long as we know we're grown-up Pack Dogs now!"

Storm couldn't help laughing at Sunshine's bright and breezy attitude. *Things must have been so much easier for Sunshine then. But she's all Pack Dog now.*

As Storm settled into the routine of leaf sorting, she was surprised to find how relaxing it was. As the piles of separated bedding grew around her, and Sunshine's happy voice bubbled on in her ear, she let her mind drift, and her eyes wandered back to the pups. She cocked one ear in interest. Breeze was approaching Lucky and Alpha, dipping her head in respect.

"Breeze! Breeze!" The pups gamboled to her, hopping up and down as they tried to lick her nose. Breeze crouched to meet them, nuzzling Tiny fondly and letting adventurous Tumble climb almost on top of her head.

"Alpha," Storm heard her say as the pups finally lolloped away and returned to their game, "can I talk to you for a moment?"

Alpha's eyes were warm as she nodded. "Of course, Breeze. What's on your mind?"

"I'm sorry . . . I'm not sure I should even be saying anything. It may be nothing important. It's just—" Breeze hesitated.

"Go on," Lucky urged her. "You can tell us, Breeze."

Storm cocked her ear, the better to hear. Breeze sighed, and sat down. "I'm just a little worried," she said. "The way the dogs of Twitch's old Pack . . . the way they still tend to treat him as their leader. Don't get me wrong, Alpha! I think it was a great idea to make him Third Dog. But he isn't Alpha—you are. And Twitch is a wonderful dog, and it's not as if he encourages them, but . . . I worry, that's all. About Pack unity." She lowered her voice, as if ashamed even to bring it up, and Storm had to strain to hear her next words. "You're our Alpha. And we should all be one Pack, that's all."

Alpha nodded slowly, thinking. "I understand why you're worried, Breeze. I really do. But try not to let it prey on your thoughts."

Lucky nodded. "The three of us have worked well together

so far," he reassured Breeze. "And you can be sure that Alpha and I are aware of any . . . tensions. We keep our ears pricked. Don't worry, Breeze."

Breeze nodded and backed away, still a little shamefaced. As she turned, Storm looked quickly away, not wanting to be seen eavesdropping. But even Sunshine's chatter couldn't shift her renewed sense of unease. She didn't like the way Alpha was now gazing at Twitch, so very thoughtfully. *Oh, Breeze. I know you meant well, but did you have to draw Alpha's attention to this?*

Oblivious to Alpha's stare, Twitch was busy organizing the evening patrol. He was talking in his usual measured, cheerful way as he assigned duties and sorted the dogs into groups, and they stood around him, nodding attentively.

Storm felt her heart skip a little as Alpha rose to her feet and stalked over to Twitch. She stood at the edge of the group, watching, until all the dogs fell silent. Finally Twitch became aware of her and he stopped speaking, too, turning with a quizzical tilt of his head.

"Twitch," came Alpha's clear voice, "you should let Moon do that. She's the head Patrol Dog, after all. It's her job."

Twitch's ears pricked in surprise, and, nonplussed, he glanced around the circle of dogs. At last he nodded, cleared his throat, and sat down. "Of course, Alpha. Moon?"

Moon stepped forward, looking almost as surprised as Twitch. With one questioning glance at him, she took over and began to assign the remaining duties. Twitch watched her quietly, but Storm thought he looked a little confused.

Storm's heart was heavy again. *Oh, Alpha. How does making Twitch unhappy help the unity of the Pack?*

It wasn't a big deal, she told herself. It was such a minor incident, after all. No dog had protested, no dog had quarreled.

But the atmosphere was just a little darker than before; Storm could feel it in the prickling of her hide. To conceal her deep sigh, she shoved her nose into the leaf pile in front of her, scattering it into the air.

"Oh, Lightning strike me," she cursed as the leaves fluttered around her head.

"Don't worry," Sunshine told her kindly. "That's happened to me a lot! We'll straighten it out again in no time."

I wish I could say the same for the Pack, thought Storm morosely. Even Sunshine's sweet, cheerful face couldn't reassure her about that. She could foresee nothing for her Packmates but gloom and conflict and darkness.

I can't help it. It's too clear to me. Everything in this Pack is going wrong.

CHAPTER SEVEN

The next morning, before she had even woken completely, Storm became aware of a biting ache in her shoulder, as if a weasel were hanging on to her muscle by its teeth. And when she stood up and stretched out her forepaws, its fangs suddenly became very sharp indeed. Storm winced, swaying where she stood.

Morning light filtered into the den; the Sun-Dog was already climbing up the sky. Storm limped out into the clearing as fast as she could. *I don't want to be left behind again, like yesterday. Sunshine is sweet, but I don't think I can stand another day of leaf sorting. . . .*

"Hunt-dogs, to me!" Lucky was barking. He stood at the old stump, which was still stained with dry tusknose blood. But the colossal carcass was almost all gone now, and they'd need more prey to add to the pile. Eagerly Storm hurried to join the other hunters.

Lucky's ears swiveled toward her, and he blinked as she nosed her way to the center of the circle.

"Storm, I didn't expect you to be here. Are you sure you're up to a hunt?"

Storm nodded. "I'm fine, Lucky. Truly I am. It barely hurts at all," she lied emphatically, hoping the desperation in her voice wasn't too obvious.

"Well . . ." Lucky cocked his head doubtfully, then swished his tail in agreement. "All right, then. You can join the hunt, but I want you to be careful." He sniffed cautiously at her wound. "That cut is still quite fresh, and it's only just healed. If you overexert yourself, it might open up again. I'm warning you, take it easy."

"I promise, Lucky!" Delighted and relieved, Storm let her tongue loll in a grin. "I'll be very careful. But I *can* help."

"Very well." Lucky raised his head to study the dogs who had gathered at the stump.

I'm not at my best, Storm thought. *So he's bound to pick Arrow, just to make up for me being below my usual ability.* She blinked expectantly at Arrow, who was waiting with his usual stoic patience.

"All right: Breeze, you'll be the scout dog for this party," said Lucky. "Bruno and Bella, you'll join me and Storm. We will leave right away. There's a lot to do today."

Bella tilted her head, frowning, as if she expected Lucky to say more. When he didn't, she cleared her throat.

"Beta, shouldn't we have more hunters? This is a small patrol, and Storm's not even fully fit. We have four pups to feed as well as the grown-up dogs. If we want the best chance of finding prey, surely there should be more of us?"

Lucky shot her an irritated look, his tail twitching. "This is the hunting party, Bella. That's my decision, so all of you, follow me." He jerked his head to signal that the discussion was over, then turned away to lead them out of the camp.

Storm shared a surprised glance with Bella, then frowned after Lucky. *We'd be much more efficient if Arrow came too.* Surely Lucky knew that—and if Lucky had made a point to stick up for Arrow, wouldn't that have *forced* the others to start accepting him?

Bella, though, had clearly decided not to argue. She wore a stubborn, proud look as she paced with the others out of the camp, and Storm fell in at her side.

Should I stand up for Arrow? If Lucky won't listen to Bella, would he listen to me? Storm's heart began to pound faster with anxiety. *Would every dog think I was speaking up just because I'm a Fierce Dog, too? This isn't like Lucky at all.*

Still, Storm had always trusted Lucky; yesterday's conversation with Sunshine had reminded her of that. She badly wanted to trust him now—*needed* to trust him—so for today, she would keep her niggling concern to herself.

After all, there's hunting to be done for the Pack. And the Pack is all that should really matter.

Small gusts of wind stirred the overhead branches and ruffled the dry grass of the forest as the hunting patrol made its way silently through the trees. They kept to their well-practiced formation, and as experienced hunt-dogs they knew just where and how to place their paws to create the least disturbance. Storm felt a ripple of satisfaction at their instinctive teamwork. *Despite all the problems, we are still a Pack. We fit together as naturally as a flock of birds. Whatever's wrong, it can surely be fixed. . . .*

A dark-brown shape appeared through the trees ahead, and Lucky halted as Breeze trotted up to him. There was urgency in her stride; clearly she'd caught some kind of scent. Unlike Dart, she'd done her job as scout. And just as well, thought Storm as all the dogs clustered around Lucky and Breeze to hear her report; they were headed toward less familiar hunting territory today, closer to the cliffs than usual, and they'd need to keep their wits sharp and their senses alert.

"I've scented prey up to the left there, but it's faint," Breeze told them softly. "We'll have to be cautious. It might hear or smell us coming from some distance."

Lucky pricked his ears and sniffed the wind. "Let's spread out in pairs," he instructed them. "Move forward slowly. If we make a wide enough sweep, we can cut off any escape route. Don't forget the cliffs are ahead."

They all nodded, attentive.

"Storm, you take the right flank with Breeze," Lucky went on. "Bella and Bruno, you two take the left. I'll advance in the middle. That should give the prey less of a chance to escape."

Bruno gave a low coughing bark. His tail flicked. "Maybe I should go with Breeze?" he suggested. "She's not a natural hunter. If we're attacked by foxes or coyotes, I'd be the best choice to protect her."

Lucky gave the big Fight Dog a cool look. "I trust Storm to do that job," he said firmly. "Besides, you and Bella are good, experienced hunters, and you're not injured." He glanced apologetically at Storm. "When the prey is sighted, the two of you together should be unstoppable. We'll have a better chance of running down this prey if you're working as a team."

Storm eyed Bruno out of the corner of her eye. The shaggy

Fight Dog didn't look very happy with Lucky's orders, but he shut his jaw and gave a throaty growl of assent. He padded off in his assigned direction, Bella following. The two dogs seemed content enough to work as a hunting team, but they kept their flanks a good distance from each other.

Storm couldn't help feeling that disturbing tremble in her fur again. She nudged her Beta. "Did you see that, Lucky?"

"What?" He glanced at her.

"Bruno. He looked so uneasy about being paired with Bella."

Lucky hunched his shoulders. "I know what you're going to say, Storm, but it's nothing to worry about. Bruno and Bella will work perfectly well together."

"Are you sure about that?" She could hear that her own bark was sharper and more challenging than it should be, but she couldn't hold the question back.

Lucky huffed. "I agree Bruno's in a strange mood, but he's probably having trouble understanding how one of his Packmates could grow so close to a Fierce Dog. I know he has his prejudices, Storm, but try to make allowances for him. He'll get over it."

"Arrow's a Pack Dog as much as he is," said Storm in a low voice.

"Yes, but don't forget, Bruno used to be very close to Bella.

They were good friends before the Packs ever joined—before either of them were even *in* a Pack. It's bound to take him some time to get used to the new choices Bella's making."

Storm closed her jaws. She didn't dare ask the next logical question.

What if Bruno never gets used to those choices? What then, Lucky?

Suppressing a sigh, Storm turned away and padded off to the right as she'd been instructed, gesturing for Breeze to follow her. The short-furred dog came close to her flank, and after a moment she spoke in an uncertain whine.

"Storm, I don't like all this tension. You feel it too, don't you?"

"Quiet," Storm warned her in a low voice. "You'll scare the prey." *And I really don't want to discuss this with any dog but Lucky.* "We can talk about it later—when we have full bellies and we're all feeling better."

Storm sensed Breeze come to a sudden halt behind her, and she glanced back questioningly, hoping she wasn't going to argue. But Breeze was casting about, sniffing the air, an expression of concentration on her face.

"The prey scent, Storm. I just caught it again."

Storm flared her own nostrils, searching, but the scent eluded her. She shook her head. "I can't smell anything," she told Breeze, lowering her voice even further, "but you smelled it earlier, so you'd recognize it before I would. It must be some distance away—let's keep going."

They pushed through the long grass, Storm focusing on filtering out its dry, sun-warmed smell to find whatever was beyond. At last she detected something else, not too far away now: a musky, slightly sweet odor that made her mouth water.

"Rabbit," she whispered. "And only just over this ridge. Well found, Breeze!"

Breeze halted. "What now?"

"You don't know what to do?"

Breeze licked her chops and panted uncertainly. "I don't—not really. This part isn't what I'm good at."

Of course Breeze didn't know what to do next; it wasn't her fault. She was a scout dog, not a hunter.

Cautiously Storm took a couple of paces forward, trying not to stir the grass more than necessary. Some way off to her left flank she saw movement, a flash of sun on a golden shape: Lucky was stalking forward, positioned right between the two pairs of dogs as he'd promised.

If I do this right ... Lucky should understand. We've hunted together before.

Storm twisted her head to nod at Breeze. Her voice was barely more than a breath. "Stay behind me, and don't make any sudden moves. And try to keep quiet, all right?"

Breeze inclined her head obediently, and Storm began to creep through the grass to her right, stalking in a wide circle away from the others. The rabbit was clearly visible now, the tips of its ears twitching above the grass. It lolloped a few paces, paused with its head erect, then began to nibble again.

Storm was in position now. Bunching her haunches, she sprang forward, tearing toward the startled rabbit.

As she expected, it spun with a flash of its white bobtail and bolted, far faster than she could run—but it was fleeing straight toward Lucky. Storm gave a yap of warning, and Lucky jerked round in surprise. He dashed to intercept the rabbit.

But he was just a claw's-width too slow. The rabbit saw him coming and veered with a sharp twist toward the cliff; Lucky's jaws snapped on empty air.

Storm was at his side now, as the two dogs turned together to pursue the rabbit. Not far behind them, Storm heard Bella and Bruno join the chase, paws pounding. But no dog could hope to catch a rabbit that had a head start, not without setting up an ambush. The rabbit was a blur of brown fur and white bobtail, streaking away through the grass, and when it vanished into a cleft in the rocks on the edge of the cliff, Lucky barked, "Stop!"

Both dogs skidded to a halt, sending up flurries of sandy soil. Disappointed, Storm sat back on her haunches, panting. Bruno and Bella trotted up behind them.

"Bad luck, Storm," said Bella. "That was a fat one, too."

"I know," said Storm dejectedly, and they all fell quiet.

Into their morose silence came the sound of the Endless Lake butting against the rocks; it was fairly calm today, but it never stopped flinging itself landward, and the sound was a ceaseless rhythmic rush. Peering over the cliffs, Storm could see the foaming waves breaking against the shore before withdrawing with a sucking roar over sand and pebbles.

Where are we going to find prey now? We'll have to backtrack quite some distance.

A few paces away, Breeze was craning to look over the cliff too. The short-furred dog tilted her head and cocked an ear.

"Why don't we try the cliffs?" she said.

"What?" Lucky frowned.

"We should at least have a look, don't you think?" Breeze panted. "We don't pay the cliffs much attention unless we're on High Watch. There could be prey down there. There are certainly plenty of those white birds swooping in and out all day long. They can't be on the wing *all* the time."

"I don't know," said Lucky hesitantly. "The rocks are pretty steep."

"The rabbit went that way," Breeze pointed out. "We know there are paths, and once you get over the edge, there's a bit of a slope. It doesn't fall straight down to the lake."

"And neither will we, I hope," grunted Bella.

"It might be worth a try, you know," put in Storm. "It's not as if there'll be much prey left up here, not after the noise we made chasing that rabbit."

"All right." Lucky tapped his tail thoughtfully. "As you say, Storm, it's worth a try. But be careful, everybody."

He eased himself down onto the narrow and rocky trail that wound down the cliff face, his forelegs stiff, and with only a moment's hesitation, Bella followed him. Bruno was next, his burly body trembling nervously. When the big Fight Dog was safely on the path, Storm took a deep breath. *My turn now—well, I did say I thought this was a good idea.*

The worst part was the first step. Storm felt her stomach lurch as she placed a paw carefully over the edge of the cliff. A breeze seemed to rise the moment she had all four paws on the steep, sandy path, and she hesitated for a moment, feeling her ears lift in the updraft. But she got used to it quickly enough, and followed the other three dogs as they trod cautiously down. It was a thin, winding path, like a long tail with many kinks and breaks, and it constantly doubled back on itself. *Rabbits probably made it in the first place,* thought Storm, and the Sky-Dogs knew that rabbits never took a straight trail anywhere. Behind her she heard the crunch and skitter of tiny stones as Breeze at last joined the line of nervous dogs.

Storm's heart lurched again at the first sharp turn, but she twisted and followed close behind Bruno's quivering tail. The Endless Lake seemed somehow even farther away than it had from the top of the cliff; far below, the churning waves flung up white spume, as if the lake itself were trying to reach up and drag them from their precarious position. Swallowing, Storm decided she would try not to look down again. Instead she glanced up at the blue sky; those birds were still there, wheeling in distant circles, close to the Sun-Dog. They seemed to pay the dogs little attention, and why would they? There was no way Storm could reach up and grab one. She sighed.

Even the track itself was distracting; tiny sharp stones bit into her paw pads, and the dusty coating of sand was treacherous. It was more painful even than running hard on flat, rough ground, and Storm found that her hesitant, wincing efforts to protect her paws were making her shoulder wound ache painfully. She clenched her jaws against a whine of pain.

We're not even a proper hunting patrol anymore, she realized as she risked a glance forward at the others. The dogs were strung out in single file, nose to tail, and they were too busy keeping their footing to worry about finding traces of prey. They had no plan, no formation—and worst of all, the path seemed to be growing *narrower* as they went on.

If they had to run, Storm realized—if they spotted prey, or if some danger suddenly threatened them—there would be chaos. *We'll collide with one another, block one another's escape. This could be very bad.*

One of us might shove another, by accident. One of us could easily fall. . . .

Ahead, Bruno came to a halt as Bella and Lucky in front of him did the same. That was another worry, thought Storm—their stop-and-start pace. And as she stared in frustration at Bruno's shaggy rump, she realized she *hated* not being able to see what was ahead.

Bruno twisted awkwardly and spoke out of the side of his muzzle. "Lucky says there's prey ahead."

Now, that was better news—though Storm was beginning to wonder what they could possibly do about it. She flared her nostrils, seeking the scent. It was a salty, faintly acrid smell, mixed with the thick odor of droppings. *Some kind of bird,* she decided.

Very hesitantly, Storm leaned to the side and peered around the line of dogs. Her eye was caught by a cluster of grayish-white, a little way down the precipitous slope. In a clutter of sticks and moss and seaweed there was a litter of bird-pups, fluffy and help-less, their wings barely more than stubs of down. They were small, and they'd hardly fill a couple of dog bellies. But it was a start.

If we can reach them, she thought dolefully.

Bruno muttered again, "Lucky's going to try to slide down the slope a bit. We're supposed to wait here, and he'll try to grab them one at a time and pass them up."

Storm licked her chops as a pang of anticipation went through her stomach. But no sooner had Lucky placed his forepaws on the stiff, short grass by the path than a screech sounded above them.

Storm jerked her head up. Against the brilliant blue of the sky she could see shadows swooping down, broad-winged and aggres-sive. A wingtip brushed her ear and she flinched as the first huge bird dived. And suddenly the sky seemed full of them, soaring and plunging and shrieking in anger.

"There's a whole Pack of them!" barked Bruno.

Lucky yelped in alarm and backed swiftly onto the path as a

white bird dived at his head. Behind Storm, Breeze whined in fear, and her frantic paws sent stones skittering over the edge. Bella was snarling angrily at the birds, but that was pointless; they took no notice of her, simply forming up again to renew their attack.

"They're defending their pups," barked Lucky, ducking from another assault. "This is no use!"

Storm tried to leap up and snap at one bird, but as she landed, her paws skidded dangerously. Her heart thrashing, she tried to back away from the edge. It was impossible to attack the brutes. *This is their territory,* she realized. *Dogs don't belong here!*

Bruno backed up suddenly, bumping into her face. Storm felt Breeze's shoulder bash into her flank as the scout dog spun in panic. Bella yelped in alarm, crouching to avoid Lucky as he, too, slithered backward to avoid the ferocious beaks.

"We'll fall off the cliff!" barked Storm. "We have to retreat!"

"Retreat!" echoed Breeze's terrified yelp as she turned and slipped on the path. More pebbles and grit scattered over the edge, bouncing down into the void, and Breeze froze in terror.

"Get moving, Breeze," Bruno snapped.

For one horrible moment Storm was forced closer to the drop as the big dog squeezed past her, but then he scuttled through and began to shepherd Breeze back toward the cliff top, while the birds continued their furious assault. Storm wheeled around to look for Bella and Lucky.

"Come on!" she yelped.

The two golden dogs were still cowering from the birds, but they began to shuffle back toward Storm, half-crouched. As white wings sliced through the air toward Bella, Storm barked in anger and sprang forward, driving the bird back into the sky. Ducking her head, Bella crept ever closer to Storm, with Lucky at her heels.

Her barking seemed to have kept the birds at a distance, so Storm carried on, sending a volley of furious growls and yaps in their direction. Bella and Lucky were hurrying now, ears and tails flat, but as he picked up his pace, Lucky's paws suddenly went out from under him. Loose rocks bounced into the empty air, and with a yelp of terror Lucky stumbled, his hindquarters slipping over the edge.

"Lucky!" Bella darted to grab him by his scruff.

Storm joined her, sinking her teeth into his thick neck fur. Lucky's eyes were wide with panic, showing the whites, and his claws scrabbled desperately at the pebbles and rocks of the path. Storm and Bella dug their hindpaws into the ground and hauled with all their strength, and Lucky finally tumbled back onto the path.

"Quick!" barked Storm. "Back to the top, *hurry!*"

Then she was the last dog left on the path, yelping in fury at the birds as they swooped in wider circles. They seemed to be holding back now, keeping in close view of their pups. The creatures soared higher, contemptuous, as the dogs scrabbled back up the cliff. With one last frightened glance back, Storm hauled herself up onto level ground and flopped onto her belly.

The others lay close by, panting frantically. Level ground, Storm thought, had never felt so beautiful. Her claws were dug deep into the soft earth, and she found she didn't want to loosen them, not yet.

Lucky was the first of them to get to his paws, but he was still trembling, and his hackles were erect and quivering.

"Back to the forest," he growled. "If we find prey on the way, so much the better. But let's get away from here right now!"

As her muscles sagged in relief, the pain shot back into Storm's shoulder with a vengeance. But she didn't even have the energy to wince. She rose to her shaking paws, desperate to put as much distance as possible between herself and the terrifying cliff top.

CHAPTER EIGHT

Even before the dejected hunting party pushed through the last of the trees to enter the camp, Storm could hear a clamor of barks. Glancing anxiously at Bella, she picked up her pace and trotted into the clearing after Lucky. But when she saw what was going on, Storm came to an abrupt halt. Just behind her, she heard Bella take a shocked breath.

Arrow stood stiffly in the center of the clearing, his ears pricked and quivering. Around him, Snap, Dart, Ruff, and Woody stood in a circle, their shoulders lowered, their tails stiff. They were facing him down, giving harsh, sharp barks of accusation.

"You don't belong with this Pack, Fierce Dog!"

"How are we supposed to trust you?"

"There's hardly a dog in this Pack who would risk turning their back on you!"

Lucky bounded forward, his fur bristling. "What's happening here? Calm down!"

But the dogs around Arrow were too worked up to listen; Storm doubted they'd even heard their Beta. Woody scraped at the earth with his claws, agitated. Ruff's fur was standing on end, and Dart's voice was hoarse with fury.

"Go and find some other savages to run with!" she yelped.

Storm felt hot anger shoot through her when she heard that word. The memory of the old half wolf Alpha trying to name her "Savage" still stung.

"That is enough!" Lucky's bark was like the thundering voice of the Sky-Dogs, echoing from the trees as the sound faded. Storm bolted past him to shove her way into the circle of dogs, snapping her jaws.

"What's this about?" She shouldered her way to Arrow's side and stared around at the others.

"Don't look at us," snarled Dart. "This is all the Fierce Dog's fault."

"I've done nothing," Arrow began to protest, but he was drowned out once more by furious yaps.

"How can there be any peace in the Pack with him around?"

"Exactly, Ruff! He was one of Blade's dogs!"

"Why can't he go find a Pack of his own?"

Storm shook herself in frustration. "Whatever started this, it's pointless! You all talk about 'protecting the Pack'—well, how does this help? You're not promoting teamwork and harmony, are you?"

"Keep your snout out of it, Storm," growled Woody. "This is none of your business!"

"It's every dog's business!" barked Bella, pushing her way through at last to stand on Arrow's other side. She was panting and her flanks were heaving—more from anger, Storm thought, than from the effort of shoving the hostile dogs aside. "What does Arrow have to do to prove himself to all of you? He's never done anything wrong! He's been a good Pack Dog, but none of you will give him a chance!"

"You can stay out of it too, Bella," snarled Dart. "Why should we trust anything you have to say? You're blinded by your misguided feelings for this brute. I'd say you weren't even right in the head to begin with, if you chose *him*."

"*What did you say?*" Arrow lunged forward so suddenly, Storm had no chance to stop him. He shouldered Woody aside, making the big dog stumble and slip, and was on Dart in an instant. Rearing up, he slammed his paws into her, knocking her flat. She was too stunned to resist; holding her there with his strong forepaws, Arrow lowered his jaws to her ear, his fangs clenched.

"Keep your insults to yourself," he snarled. "How dare you? You're not fit to lick Bella's paws."

Arrow's teeth had not even grazed Dart's neck, but she trembled under his paws, her eyes full of terror—and Storm couldn't really blame her this time. The sight of an angry Arrow would make any dog regret insulting his mate. She didn't blame Arrow either; he'd been pushed beyond endurance, and it was high time some dog stood up to Dart.

But Arrow had made a mistake, Storm realized with a sinking heart. As he loomed over Dart—fangs bared, eyes glittering, drool dripping onto her terrified face—every dog in the Pack emerged from their dens, drawn by the commotion. Approaching hesitantly, they gaped at the scene before them. Alpha walked through them to the front of the Pack, eyes locked anxiously on the Fierce Dog.

"Arrow!" she began in horror.

Arrow turned his head to give her a glare that silenced her. Alpha looked shocked, and suddenly nervous, but she said no more.

Storm swallowed. Arrow was much bigger and stronger than Dart, and the small patrol dog shivered as she cowered beneath his paws. He wasn't hurting her, but Storm knew exactly how this must appear—especially to any dog who hadn't heard him being baited and provoked. Arrow simply looked like a huge dog bullying a smaller, weaker one. He certainly seemed like a dog to be feared now.

He looks truly . . . Fierce. A small shiver ran down Storm's spine. It wasn't fear *of* Arrow: right now she was very afraid *for* him.

In the sudden ominous silence, a dog made a coughing sound. Storm looked up to see Breeze step forward from the hunting party, her ears flicking nervously.

"This is just a misunderstanding," the brown dog yapped. "It really doesn't help any dog. The Pack doesn't need this kind of tension."

"Exactly," growled Ruff, and Storm turned to glare at the black dog. "This *tension*, as you put it—all this mayhem and trouble and *violence*—it follows Fierce Dogs around. It sticks to them like fleas and ticks."

"That's not fair!" barked Storm. "Arrow didn't start this!"

"And how would you know?" Woody's eyes were narrowed to

aggressive slits as he ground his forepaws into the grass. "You only came in at the end of the fight. You and all the hunters. You didn't see anything."

Storm gaped, silenced by shock. *That's an outright lie, and he knows it! The real fight didn't start until Dart insulted Bella!* Did Woody want Arrow out of the Pack so badly, he was willing to deceive his Pack-mates?

How can we live and work together when dogs hate one another so much they're willing to tell outright lies? A Pack like that doesn't have a future at all.... She stole a glance at Alpha, longing for their leader to take swift and decisive action. But the swift-dog seemed utterly flummoxed, and she was doing nothing to stop the awful fight. *She doesn't know what to do,* Storm realized. *She's afraid to say anything!*

A creeping sense of horror crawled in Storm's spine. *She's let it get to this point, and now she can't control the Pack! By the Sky-Dogs, we don't even have an effective leader!*

The clamor of barks was rising again, as the dogs argued and threw accusations—but a sudden, sharp howl from Arrow cut through the racket. Every dog turned to look at him, their ears flicking forward in surprise.

"I've had enough," he snarled, staring around at them all with contempt. "The best thing I can do is leave this Pack."

"No!" barked Storm, shocked. All around her she could hear murmurs of agreement, growls of confirmation, a mutter of "Too right!" that came from Bruno. "Arrow," she barked louder, trying to drown them out. "You mustn't!"

"No dog wants me here—or not enough of you." Stepping contemptuously away from the cringing Dart, the Fierce Dog curled his muzzle as he glared around the Pack.

"Arrow, don't be hasty!" barked Lucky.

"No, please don't." Little Omega trotted forward, her dirty plume of a tail waving. "I'd miss you so much, Arrow. And I know we can fix this, all of us. As a Pack!"

Her little pink tongue lolled as she gazed pleadingly up at him, and Arrow dipped his head to lick her floppy ear. "You're such a good dog, Sunshine. But I don't have a choice." He gazed steadily at Lucky. "I'm certainly not being *hasty*. I've been putting up with this nonsense for too long."

Storm shot a glare at Lucky. *You were wrong. Even Arrow couldn't stand that pressure forever.* And as she looked around at the other dogs, she realized that not one of them was opening their muzzles to stand up for Arrow. She felt her lip drawing back in a snarl, but she made herself push away her rage. Anger wouldn't help now.

"Please don't go, Arrow," Storm said. "You belong here, with your Pack." She glared at the others, daring them to disagree. But even the dogs who were usually sympathetic toward Arrow looked awkward and shifty. *Are they hoping for an easier life? Hoping that if Arrow leaves, all the trouble will go with him? They don't know how wrong they are. Just for some peace and quiet, they're willing to let a good dog take all the* blame. Storm's muzzle twisted in disgust. *Lucky isn't even really trying to stop him—and Alpha...?*

Craning her head, Storm stared over the assembled Pack at their swift-dog leader. Alpha stood well back, her pups now clustered around her paws. The little dogs were wide-eyed, their ears straining forward, but they stayed as close as they could to their Mother-Dog. Obviously, Storm thought, they did not understand the reason for the crackle of hostility in the air. Nibble was actually trembling as she stared at Woody's snarling features, and her litter-brother Tumble edged closer to her, as if reassuring her.

Right now, those pups have more dog-spirit than any other member of this Pack, thought Storm angrily. *If they don't understand this nonsense, it's because they have the right instincts—not the so-called grown dogs!*

But while her pups looked both astonished and anxious, there was no expression on Alpha's face at all. She simply watched, impassive, as the dogs of her Pack faced Arrow down.

I can't believe it, thought Storm. *She's not going to say anything. She's not going to intervene to protect him. . . .*

Another dog did, though. Bella barged forward to stand firmly alongside her Fierce Dog mate. Her eyes were narrowed with anger as she glared at the Pack dogs.

"If Arrow goes," she growled, "I go with him."

"Bella!" Lucky's shocked whine was hoarse. "No!"

"Yes!" Bella was almost snarling as she turned on her litter-brother. "It's not as if you've fought to keep us, *Beta*. No dog wants us here, that's obvious. And we don't have to put up with this, day after day. The whispers, the accusations, the *spying*. No dog should!"

Storm could barely believe this was happening. Desperately she licked her jaws, searching the faces of the Pack for any sign of shame, for any trace of sympathy for Arrow. The dogs who met her gaze looked aggressively defiant, and the others looked away, avoiding Storm's eyes.

Even Mickey? she thought in disbelief. The Farm Dog was always reliably kind and good-natured, but now his eyes were downcast. When he finally looked up to meet Storm's pleading stare, he only twitched an ear and shook his head very slightly. *Yes, even Mickey,* she realized in despair. *Even Mickey won't speak up for them.*

"How can you all just stand there while a good dog is driven out?" Storm barked, glaring around at the Pack.

"Be quiet, Storm," Woody snapped. "You're just as biased as Bella."

Storm glared at him. *You're the one who's biased.*

Twitch gave an awkward cough. "Arrow can look after himself. He's tough, and so strong. He doesn't need us to defend him."

"Just as well," snapped Bella, "since no dog here ever does. He hasn't got many allies, so what's the point of either of us being in a Pack at all?"

"But, Bella!" cried Sunshine. She darted up to the golden dog and placed her small white paws against her shoulder. "You can't leave the Pack. Neither of you! This is all so *silly!* We've all been through so much together. And the Pack needs every dog. We *need* you and Arrow!"

Bella nuzzled her gently. "I'm afraid it doesn't look that way, Sunshine. Not for most of the Pack."

"Omega's right," murmured Lucky miserably. "The Pack needs you, Bella, and it needs Arrow. We can't do without clever, strong hunters like you."

Watching him, Storm realized that despite his last-ditch plea, he looked resigned. Like he wanted to beg Bella to stay but knew that there was nothing he could say to keep her.

Bella gave a growl that was bitterly amused. "That's not how it seems to me, Lucky. The way these dogs are talking?" She nodded disdainfully at the group around Arrow. "It's more like they can't wait to be rid of us."

"It's not *you* we want to be rid of," barked Ruff.

In the horrible silence that followed, every dog's eyes turned to Arrow—some filled with shame, some with vicious glee. Arrow himself looked confused, but defiant. Then, gradually, the muscles of his face relaxed, his ears drooped, and he looked only sad. He gave a heavy sigh.

"I just don't understand why all of you—"

"Don't, Arrow!" Bella barked sharply, pressing closer to him. "Don't give them the satisfaction." Glaring around at the other silent dogs, she wrinkled her muzzle in contempt. "Tomorrow, when the Sun-Dog begins to run, we'll leave this camp. Let this so-called 'Pack' hunt their own prey, Arrow. If they don't want us, then we certainly don't want them."

As she watched the Sun-Dog slink down toward the horizon, his light dimming and the shadows growing around the clearing, Storm felt a sense of dread that had nothing to do with the oncoming night. *When he stretches and rises again,* she thought sadly,

Bella and Arrow will leave. And there's nothing I can do to make them stay.

Her heart heavy, Storm padded toward the biggest den in the clearing, the one where Alpha and Beta lay huddled protectively around their sleepy pups. As he saw her approach, Lucky rose to his paws, extracting himself from the tangle of tiny pups, pushing Tumble gently off his foreleg. Tumble yawned, showing baby teeth, and squirmed into a new position between Fluff and their Mother-Dog.

Storm saw Lucky nod in acknowledgment, so she halted and waited for him to pace quietly over to meet her. Then he beckoned with a jerk of his head, and she followed him out into the pines that surrounded the clearing. The air was still and cool, tinged with the salty tang of the Endless Lake, and Storm flared her nostrils to inhale more of it. A faint, familiar dog-scent came to her too, and she turned slightly to peer into the gathering dark. She could make out the forms of Bella and Arrow, nestled together in their new sleeping place on the very edge of the camp. They'd settled down as far as they could get from the rest of the Pack without leaving altogether. It was the most basic of dens, a shallow scrape in the earth that Arrow and Bella had lined with dry grass. After all, Storm realized sadly, they wouldn't be using it again after tonight. . . .

"Lucky, are you going to let this happen?" she asked softly. "Are you really going to let them go?"

Lucky gave a sigh, his head and tail drooping. "I don't think there's anything I can do to stop them, Storm. I've never been able to make Bella change her mind before—and I don't think she will now."

Storm bit back a whine of despair. "But can Arrow and Bella even survive by themselves? Without a Pack to rely on? Without Packmates to watch their backs and care for them?" She shook herself miserably. "Doesn't *every* dog need a Pack?"

For a long moment, Lucky said nothing; he just stared at his litter-sister and her mate. Bella stirred slightly in her sleep, and Arrow shifted and licked her ear.

"Some dogs are better off without a pack. I lived without a Pack for a long time," Lucky said at last. "They're both strong dogs, and good fighters. Perhaps they really don't need any other dog, Storm." He half turned away, glancing back once more. "They'll be all right. But—" He licked his chops and met her eyes, seeming a little unsure of himself. "You aren't thinking of leaving, right?"

She pricked her ears in surprise. "I hadn't imagined—"

"Good." He nodded, his ears flopping with relief. "Don't ever think that the Pack doesn't want you, Storm. We need you. We love you. All right?"

With that he turned and padded back toward his den and his pups. Storm watched him go, unable for a moment to move. *Why couldn't he have said the same to Bella and Arrow, before it was too late? Everything's falling apart. The Pack is collapsing. And I don't want to lose Bella and Arrow. . . .*

Storm glanced back toward them, and her heart skipped a beat when she realized Arrow's eyes were open. She could see their sad gleam in the starlight, and he blinked once at her. She gave him a small nod, wishing there was something she could say to him.

But what? She couldn't think of a single thing that would comfort him. After all, she knew all too well how it felt to be a Fierce Dog—to know that your Packmates were afraid of you, even when they didn't show it. *To know that they'll never trust you . . .*

But however nervous her Packmates had been around her, she'd never been threatened with exile. She'd never made her friends so afraid of her that they drove her out of the Pack.

I can't even imagine how Arrow must feel right now.

Or how angry Bella must be . . .

* * *

This was the saddest walk she had ever taken, thought Storm the next morning as she paced at Arrow's side through the trees. On his other side walked Bella, her golden head held high and proud. Next to Bella was Lucky, far more subdued than usual. Their only other company was faithful Sunshine, trotting fast to keep up with the much bigger dogs. Perhaps it was just as well the little Omega was out of breath, thought Storm: she looked as if she might howl with misery if she had energy to spare.

They had already left the camp far behind. Storm had been glad when the trees closed in behind them and the clearing was no longer visible. All the same, it felt as if the stares of the other dogs were still burning into their rumps. She was so impotently angry, she almost wished she was leaving with Arrow and Bella, despite what she'd said to Lucky last night. Her heart ached for the two dogs who were walking away from their lives as her Packmates.

Storm was so distracted by her thoughts, she was taken by surprise when Arrow came to a halt beside her. She realized they had reached the edge of the forest; open ground sloped away toward a valley in front of them, a brisk breeze stirring the lush green grass.

"Arrow and I will go on alone from here," murmured Bella.

Arrow nodded, nuzzling her ear.

"Where will you go?" Lucky sounded desolate.

"To be honest, I'm not sure." Bella looked at him more kindly than she had for days. "Lucky, don't be so sad." Affectionately, she nudged his shoulder. "These last few seasons, since the Big Growl—let's see them as fortunate. We were separated when we were just pups, and if our lives had gone on as they were planned, we would never have found each other again. Maybe we're not really meant to be together."

"That's hard to believe, Bella," sighed Lucky. "We were litter-mates. We were always together, till the longpaws came for us. . . ."

"Well, I got you back for a short time, litter-brother." She touched her nose to his. "I'm almost grateful to the Big Growl for that."

"Oh, Bella." Closing his eyes, Lucky pressed his head against hers.

"And I'll miss you both too. So much." Sunshine padded up to Arrow, creeping right underneath his belly as if seeking his protection. Peeking her head out, she blinked up at him. "There's nowhere safer than right here. I wish the rest of the Pack could have seen that."

Arrow swallowed, looking touched. He bent his head to lick the top of the little Omega's. "I'll miss you, Sunshine. But don't worry. You'll be safe with the Pack; they'll look after you."

Storm stepped forward, trying to think of a pleasant way to say good-bye, but she still felt too angry for that. Instead, she spoke bluntly, stumbling over her words. "I wish this hadn't happened. It's wrong, and I'm sorry."

Arrow licked her ear. "We'll miss you too. Just remember that you are a good dog, Storm. No matter what any other dog says."

Storm felt a strange lump in her throat. She glanced away from Arrow and Sunshine, only for her gaze to light on the two golden littermates, Bella and Lucky. They stood close together, their heads still touching. The painful twinge in Storm's belly was somehow familiar. *I felt something like this when Martha died. . . .*

Perhaps she shouldn't be surprised. She was losing Bella, a dog she'd known since she was a tiny pup, and Arrow—her last connection to her Fierce Dog heritage and possibly the only dog who could ever truly understand her.

It's not like they're dying, she told herself with a brisk shake. *I might see them again. . . .*

But I don't know that I will. This could be the last time I see either of them. And what if it's worse than that . . . what if I see them again, and we're fighting them over territory or prey?

Storm tried to swallow her sudden, terrible misgivings. *What if* we have to battle them, like we once battled Blade, and Terror?

What in the name of the Sky-Dogs would happen then?

Storm's paws were in the sand, and a stiff, salty breeze lifted her ears and chilled her hide as it gusted off the Endless Lake. Behind her, waves pounded the shoreline, rushing in and foaming up over her paws. For a moment Storm was perplexed. How did I get here? Then she heard a familiar sound and looked up.

There was the cliff above her, and the great white birds soaring and swooping in angry circles.

Bella, Bruno, Lucky, and Breeze were strung out along the narrow cliff path just like they had been before, but she was standing on the beach below and she could do nothing as they crouched, backing away and trying to dodge the birds. They were becoming hopelessly tangled, getting in one another's way as they shoved and slipped, and she couldn't help! Heart in her throat, barely able to breathe, Storm watched her Packmates try to struggle to safety.

And then one of them slipped. A golden dog fell over the edge, twisting and turning in the air. Lucky!

Storm gave a shrill bark of terror. Somehow even from this distance she could make out the horror in his eyes and hear his petrified howl as he plummeted toward the pounding waves at the foot of the cliff. Storm tried to bound forward to reach him, but her paws felt heavy, as if something was dragging on them; then, as Lucky disappeared beneath the waves, she felt herself sinking too.

Please, River-Dog, don't drag me under!

Lucky was gone, vanished forever beneath the surface. And now a huge wave cascaded over Storm, forcing her under, filling her nostrils and jaws as she sank into darkness. She couldn't help Lucky, not when she couldn't think, or even breathe. . . .

When she startled into wakefulness, Storm almost expected to find herself standing in water, as if she could have walked in her sleep all the way to the Endless Lake.

But no: the ground beneath her was warm and dry, and the sound of crashing waves had been replaced by the breathing and snoring of her sleeping Packmates. Some dogs' paws scuffled against the earth, as they ran in their own dreams. Storm lifted her head and panted softly till she felt calm again.

If she hadn't sleepwalked, even in the midst of that awful, vivid dream, maybe she'd finally gotten over it. Maybe it would never happen again. Storm felt a small surge of hope, despite the images in her mind that lingered from the nightmare.

I can still see Lucky plunging into that water. I can still hear him. . . . Storm shook herself violently. No. She wouldn't give in to despair. It was just a dream.

Those horrible moments on the cliff hunt must have affected

her more badly than she'd realized. It was haunting her dreams because it had been a close escape, that was all. Lucky was asleep in his den, right now, at Alpha's side. He was safe.

It was a hideous vision of what could have happened.

That was all it was.

CHAPTER NINE

"Packmates, to me!"

Alpha's clear bark brought every dog loping to the center of the clearing, where she stood with her ears pricked and her eyes bright. As her Pack huddled in close to listen to her, Storm had the feeling that the swift-dog was putting on the bravest face possible. *And she needs to,* thought Storm grimly. *If she'd acted more like a leader last night, she could have stopped Bella and Arrow from leaving.*

Storm looked around at the rest of the Pack. Didn't any other dog care that Arrow and Bella were gone? To Storm, their loss left glaring, empty spaces at the middle of the Pack where the two hunters belonged. Lucky seemed a little sad, she thought, but most of the dogs looked just like their usual selves. Bruno's head was high and his eyes were bright. *He thinks he's saved the Pack by driving them out,* Storm realized. *But he's wrong. Arrow wasn't the threat, and nothing's going to get better with him gone.*

"We need to appoint two more dogs as hunters," Alpha announced. "Now that Bella and Arrow have left the Pack, we must reassign all dogs to the roles where they are most needed."

"But, Alpha." Moon sounded weary as she stepped forward. "There are barely enough Patrol Dogs as it is. We can't jeopardize our safety!"

"Moon," growled Alpha, "we can't protect ourselves if we're starving. Hunting is the priority right now. Every dog will have to put in just a bit more effort."

"This is all Bella and Arrow's fault," muttered Ruff. "We'll go hungrier now, *and* our borders will be less secure."

"Typical," growled Woody in agreement. "They never thought of any dog but themselves."

Storm stared at them both in sheer disbelief. She wanted to howl at them. *You drove them out of the Pack! You and your cronies!*

But what would be the point? These dogs would never accept that they were at fault. Pointing it out would only create yet more division, more strife. Snapping her jaws shut, Storm swallowed her fury as Woody crept forward, Ruff behind him.

"We should be the two new hunters," mumbled the bigger dog. "We're senior Patrol Dogs, and we hunted for our old Pack, when Twitch was our Alpha."

Though it was Woody who made the case, Storm could tell from Ruff's anxious eyes and twitching tail how desperate she was for the promotion. And it would be a big promotion, for a dog who had once been an Omega. Dart paced forward too, though.

"We've always been more skilled hunters than Twitch's old Pack," she growled. "We had to think for ourselves, rather than being ordered around by a maniac."

"Well," coughed Twitch, "I heard that Breeze did well on the last hunt." He nodded at the dark-brown dog. "I believe she even had the idea to hunt up on the cliffs."

"And look how well that turned out," growled Snap.

"Anyway," said Thorn, glaring at Twitch, "you're just trying to get the job for one of your old Pack."

"That's enough, Thorn!" barked Moon. "Be quiet."

Thorn gave a sulky whine and backed down, but Storm noticed she didn't apologize to the Third Dog.

"Snap does have a point, Third Dog," said Alpha calmly. "Breeze's idea almost got my Beta killed."

Her pups whimpered and huddled tighter against her. Nibble, looking terrified, had begun to shiver. It was surely the tension in the air that was scaring them, Storm thought, not the idea of their Father-Dog dying. They were far too young to understand death—*thank the Sky-Dogs. They* shouldn't *have any concept of what death is, not yet.*

"So how are we going to decide?" Rake's voice drew Storm's attention away from the pups. "Perhaps we should have trials to choose the new hunters." He drew himself up, and Storm realized he was confident of performing well in any hunting trials that might take place.

But Alpha shook her elegant head. "We don't have time for that. All trials will do is set dog against dog—and I don't think we need more fighting, do you?" Her gaze on Rake was steely. "I will make this decision myself."

Rake shifted his eyes away, Storm was satisfied to see. *So much for trying to promote yourself.* She turned back to watch Alpha—who was studying Thorn and Beetle, her face thoughtful.

No, thought Storm with a frisson of disbelief. *I'm not crazy about Rake and Ruff, but you can't seriously be considering Beetle and Thorn as hunters . . . they have no experience!*

"Thorn and Beetle," the swift-dog said at last. "You two will be our new hunt-dogs."

Storm felt her whole body tense. Thorn and Beetle gave delighted barks. "Thank you, Alpha!" exclaimed Beetle.

"We'll make our Father-Dog proud," added Thorn. "We promise you!"

Storm could hear a low, dissatisfied growling from some of the dogs of Twitch's old Pack. Rake and Woody were muttering to each other, and Storm found she couldn't blame them. But the Third Dog himself limped forward and bowed his head to Alpha.

"If that is your wish, Alpha," he said, "I will support your decision."

Storm sat back and scratched at her ear. Twitch was almost too gracious about this, she thought. *Thorn might be all right, but Beetle's not suited to hunting. He's not exactly the fastest or the strongest dog. . . .*

Storm risked a glance at Lucky. The Beta wouldn't meet her eyes, but she thought she detected an unease in his expression. His eyes were slightly narrowed, and he licked his chops briefly. But he said nothing.

Even if he disagrees with Alpha, he's not going to say anything, Storm realized. *That's probably as it should be.*

But I hope this does work out. Because we need good hunters like never before.

The long grass of the meadow stirred as Storm stared intently through it. Crouched low, she resisted the urge to sneeze at the tickling of the blades—and hoped that the inexperienced Beetle would do the same. Scaring off prey-creatures was never a good thing, but now it would be disastrous.

Storm cocked an ear. Without looking to either side, she was aware of Thorn and Beetle at her flanks; she could smell Beetle's nervousness—it made her delicate nostrils tingle even more than the grass did—but he managed to remain still.

Just a small hunt to start with, Storm, Lucky had told her. *Take our new hunt-dogs and see how they get on. Let them practice their skills in the meadow, where they won't alarm any sizable prey.*

"The grass, Storm," whined Beetle softly. "It's tickling my nose."

"Quiet," snapped Thorn. "You'll disturb the prey!"

No more than you will, squabbling with him, thought Storm with an inward sigh.

"Stop bossing me around," snarled Beetle.

"We have to be stealthy," announced Thorn in a scolding voice. "So we can sneak up on anything we see!"

This is ridiculous! "Both of you," growled Storm in a low murmur. "Stop arguing—that makes more noise than anything! Be focused and be *patient,* for the Forest-Dog's sake!"

They both glanced at her, ears drooping and tails flattening against the ground. "Sorry, Storm," muttered Thorn.

"I don't want to hear another word from you," added Storm, narrowing her eyes. "Unless it's 'There's the prey.'"

As the two young dogs settled down quietly once more, with only an occasional fidget, Storm tried not to roll her eyes. Thorn and Beetle were full-grown dogs, the same age as Storm herself, but right now she felt like she was back in the den trying to keep an eye on Alpha's pups. *I think I'd rather be out here with Ruff and Rake. . . .*

She cocked one ear in surprise at her unexpected thought, but it was true. Ruff and Rake and Woody were too quick to distrust Fierce Dogs, and she didn't like that mean streak they sometimes showed—but they were more experienced than Moon's pups, and much more disciplined.

But I'd rather have Arrow and Bella than any other dog, she sighed to herself. *They knew how to hunt, but they also knew how to behave on a hunt. I'm wasting valuable time teaching new hunters the basics—while the rest of the Pack wasted their time driving away the best hunters we had.*

A dark shape appeared at the edge of the trees, sheltering beneath them as long as possible to stay concealed. It was Breeze, returning from her scouting venture into the meadow. Storm huffed a soft greeting, pleased to have a distraction.

"There's a gopher up ahead," Breeze murmured as she approached.

Small prey. But it's a start. "That's good news, Breeze. Thank you." Storm nudged her two apprentices. "Thorn, Beetle—we're going to move forward in the formation we practiced. Thorn, take the left; Beetle, on my right flank. Carefully, now. Don't rush into it, Beetle, however excited you get."

The dogs crept forward, low to the ground, picking up and placing their paws with delicate care. Beetle seemed to be focusing very hard on doing as he'd been told, and moving as silently as possible. Gradually Storm began to feel reassured. *He listened to me—and that's just as well, because a gopher is tricky. If we scare it too early, it'll go underground.*

Perhaps she should have warned Beetle about that particular trait of gophers, she realized. As soon as a flash of fur was visible through the grass, Beetle bounded forward, yapping in uncontainable excitement, tearing after the creature. The gopher raised its head, momentarily startled; then it bolted swiftly backward and vanished into a tunnel.

Beetle's eyes widened and he careered toward the hole, crashing into it in a shower of earth, and tumbling head over tail. The tunnel had collapsed on impact and his head disappeared into it;

for a moment his legs flailed as if he were still running. Then he twisted awkwardly around and scrabbled backward, yanking his head out and sneezing dirt.

There were still clumps of earth clinging to his muzzle and whiskers when Thorn bounded up and clouted him with a paw. "Idiot litter-brother! You scared off the gopher!"

"Don't call me an idiot!" Beetle spat out soil.

Storm growled in frustration. *He hasn't just scared off that one gopher—between them, he and his sister must have cleared the meadow! Anything within earshot will be long gone now.*

The pair of them were still snapping and snarling at each other, so Storm paced up and forced herself between them, laying back her ears and baring her fangs. Thorn lunged once more at her brother, trying to dodge Storm to snap at him, and Storm lunged back, shoving Thorn away with her shoulder. As she did so a sharp, searing pain went through the muscle and Storm gasped.

There was warm wetness on her fur, and she twisted her head to stare. The wound she'd gotten from the tusknose had opened up again and was bleeding freely. *That's the last thing I needed! The last thing the* Pack *needed!*

Storm curled her muzzle in fury and snapped her jaws at Thorn, then rounded on Beetle.

"Stop your nonsense, both of you! You're acting like pups. Tumble and Fluff would be more use than you two, with your stupid squabbling!"

They both cowered, crouching low, their eyes full of guilt and shame. "Sorry, Storm," whispered Thorn. "I didn't mean to—"

"You didn't mean to, it just happened because you were foolish!" A stab of pain pierced Storm's shoulder, stirring her anger to new heights. "You're making unnecessary mistakes, and those are what cause the Pack to go hungry. If you don't start to behave, I'll recommend to Alpha that you eat after Omega tonight!"

They were shuffling away from her now, their tails tucked firmly against their rumps, their ears pressed low. Small whimpers came from both dogs' throats.

"Sorry, Storm. We're so sorry!"

"Sorry doesn't catch any rabbits," snapped Storm. "Do better for the rest of this hunt, both of you. Or you won't like the report I'll be taking back to Alpha. . . ."

Curled in her den later that day, Storm licked and nosed at her shoulder wound. The bleeding had stopped, and in truth it wasn't as bad as it had first seemed, but the reopened wound stung viciously, and her irritation at the two new hunters didn't help.

"Storm, how's your shoulder?"

She turned to Twitch, who was hobbling anxiously toward her. "It's all right," she said, a little grumpily.

The Third Dog tilted his head and blinked. "And how was the hunt?"

Storm hesitated for a moment. Alpha had overruled Twitch's suggestions about the hunt dogs, and he might resent that—should she be stirring up his discontent by telling him just how badly this hunt had turned out?

But she could hardly keep it from him. Storm sighed. "It didn't go very well, to be honest. Thorn and Beetle are—well, a little inexperienced. And rash."

Twitch turned to gaze thoughtfully at the two young dogs, who were on the other side of the clearing, practicing their hunting moves. One at a time they stalked forward, before crouching to let the other make their move. If they could focus as well as that on a real hunt, thought Storm grouchily, they wouldn't be half bad.

"They're young," Twitch said at last. "It was their first time, Storm, and look how keenly they're practicing now. If they made mistakes today, at least it looks as if they've learned from them." He let his tongue loll as he turned back to Storm. "A dog can achieve anything, with enough determination. Look at me! I've learned how to manage with only three legs, haven't I?"

Storm inclined her head. "That's true. You haven't let anything get in your way. And Thorn and Beetle are determined, too. You're right, I'm sure they can learn to be good hunters." She lowered her head onto her forepaws with a huge sigh. "But, Twitch, the Pack isn't worried about tomorrow, not right now. We're not thinking about the future. We're worried about *today*. About what dogs will eat each night."

"Another hunt will be going out later." Twitch licked her ear consolingly. "A proper hunt, not a practice one. It'll be all right."

"Yes, but every day now we'll have to send Beetle and Thorn out to hunt. And if this goes on happening, we'll all be eating like Omegas. And how will that do the pups any good?" She glanced worriedly across at Alpha and Beta's den. "Tumble and Fluff and the others won't grow big and strong on a diet of spiders, will they? And then—" She clamped her jaws shut, afraid she was saying too much.

Twitch sat down at her side and placed a paw gently on her flank. "You've gotten quite attached to those pups, haven't you?"

She grunted. *That isn't what I was saying . . . but I've got to admit it's true.* "I just worry, Twitch. That they won't grow properly, that they won't be strong. The Pack *needs* them to be strong. And I worry even more about . . . well." She cleared her throat, licking her jaws unhappily, and went on in a quieter voice. "Twitch, you know as well as I do, Arrow and Bella weren't responsible for the clear-stone, or Whisper's death. Their leaving doesn't fix anything! And what will Alpha do if she thinks her pups are in danger? If she thinks they'll grow up underfed and weak? Any Mother-Dog might make rash decisions in those circumstances."

Twitch shook his head and growled soothingly. "Try not to worry, Storm. Alpha knows what she's doing. Has she ever let us down? No dog has ever lost by trusting her."

That's not true. Bella and Arrow certainly lost when they were driven from the Pack. But it would do no good to argue anymore with Twitch. "All right," she said at last, gruffly. "Maybe you're right."

He licked her neck fur. "Get some rest, Storm. Try not to worry so much." He rose to his three paws, stretching awkwardly. "Things have a way of working out—especially with a good dog like Alpha in charge."

Storm said nothing as she watched him limp back to his den. She couldn't quell the gnawing sensation of anxiety in her gut, but at least some of what he'd said was true. *Look at how well he gets around, despite losing an entire leg. Twitch has adapted and thrived. So will the pups.*

Even as she watched, she saw Breeze step respectfully out of the Third Dog's path, and he nodded in acknowledgment. The brown dog dipped her head, then turned away to join Ruff and Woody.

Twitch has more authority than most four-legged dogs, and it's all about his attitude, his confidence, the way he holds himself. If he can do it, we all can.

And if we all work together, as a Pack, to look after the pups, then they'll be fine too.

CHAPTER TEN

Storm raised her head high, scenting the wind by the Endless Lake, looking for prey. She wasn't on the sand; she was making her way along the lowest part of the cliff, through rocks and crevices and around outgrowths of coarse shrubs. She paused to take another deep breath of the salty air, then glanced up at her four Packmates. There they were above her; faint silhouetted outlines of dogs, making their way down the winding, precipitous pathway. This time they would be safe. This time.

Storm narrowed her eyes, her heart skipping a beat. Something else had joined her friends on the narrow track: dogs made of dark mist, oozing out of the rock face to walk at their sides. It was as if each hunter had an extra, ominous shadow. And those shadows were edging closer to the real dogs now, shouldering them nearer to the cliff edge. And the worst of it was, the dogs didn't realize. Unconsciously they obeyed the prompting of their sinister shadows, their paws moving closer and closer to the terrible drop.

Lucky nearly fell when we hunted here. . . . No, wait! Last time I saw this, he *did* fall. I couldn't save him.

I can't let it happen again!

Above her, white birds wheeled beneath the blazing Sun-Dog. Storm blinked against the dazzle and saw a flash of yellow-gold.

No!

The golden dog slipped once more, losing his footing, tumbling over the edge. This time Storm began to run immediately, desperate to reach him. She might not get to him before he hit the water, but she could swim out to him, drag him to safety—

The splash of his impact echoed in her ears, and the Endless Lake glittered as he vanished beneath the waves. But she was sprinting into the water now, racing to reach Lucky before he could sink, her legs kicking frantically—

And then the currents were pulling her down, down. . . . How could she save Lucky when she couldn't even save herself?

The water closed over her head, and Storm sank into darkness.

She woke kicking and thrashing, still fighting the water. Almost at once she became aware of Alpha standing over her. Startled, Storm growled and the swift-dog stepped away, alarmed. Storm, coming to her senses, rolled over and jumped to her paws. She blinked and shook herself violently, trying to scatter the clinging remnants of the dream.

"Alpha," she mumbled. Her heart was still thrashing as she saw the Sun-Dog beyond Alpha; his light wasn't glaring and hot, but soft and hazy as he began his climb up the sky. *It was a dream: calm down, Storm, calm down.*

"We need to talk," said Alpha.

Storm stared at her leader, but the swift-dog's face was unreadable. She turned without another word and walked off toward the forest, and Storm had no choice but to follow at her slender heels.

It was cool under the trees, the light misty and blue-green, and at least Storm had time as she padded after Alpha to reorient herself, and to come to terms with her dream. *Lucky falling to his death—again. It's as if I go on and on, reliving that day on the cliff, with a worse outcome every time.*

"Storm? What are you thinking about?"

She realized that Alpha had turned and was watching her curiously. Storm shook herself again. "Nothing, Alpha."

"Are you sure you're all right? You looked very preoccupied just now."

"I'm fine. Really, Alpha." She couldn't tell the swift-dog about her dream; how would Alpha react to a member of her own Pack dreaming repeatedly of her beloved Beta's death?

She might even see it as a sign of my Fierce Dog savagery. . . .

"Very well." Alpha tilted her head. "How did the hunt go?"

Storm took a breath, hesitating. She could answer Alpha honestly, tell her the hunt had been an unmitigated disaster; but she found she did not want to be the dog who told tales and spoke out of turn. *I'm not the troublemaker in this Pack, after all.*

She hunched her shoulders noncommittally. "You saw the prey we brought back, Alpha. It wasn't the best hunt I've ever been on, but I'm sure it'll get better as the new hunters gain experience."

Alpha gave her a long, steady look. "That's not what you told Twitch."

Storm swallowed, taken aback. *How does she know that? Twitch didn't tell her, I'm sure of it.* "But I—"

"Don't ask me how I know." Alpha tossed her graceful head. "But, Storm, dogs whispering among themselves is not good for Pack unity. If dogs from Twitch's former Pack think that I value Thorn and Beetle more, simply because I have known the two of them longer, they will grow dangerously discontented. So it wasn't good to complain to other dogs about how that last hunt went!" Sternly she eyed Storm. "If the dogs don't respect me, the order of the Pack will crumble, like an anthill when a giantfur crushes it."

Storm could only stare at the swift-dog. *She sounds like the old*

Alpha—the tyrannical half wolf! He always believed his way was the only way. He thought he should be obeyed without question, without argument.

"Alpha," she said, alarm creeping into her voice, "I'm sorry if I acted out of turn. I didn't mean to—"

Alpha grunted. "That's not what I meant, Storm. I just wanted to give you some advice: be careful who you trust. Be careful what you say. Arrow has left the Pack now, and do you know what that means?"

Slowly, Storm shook her head.

"It means that the first place the Pack's suspicion will fall is on you. Give them an opportunity to accuse you of some crime, or to pick a fight with the last Fierce Dog, they will. So be very cautious with your words."

Speechless, Storm gaped at her, her heart sinking. Didn't Alpha see how unfair this was? Wouldn't she defend Storm if the other dogs turned on her? It was *Alpha's* Pack. Would she really stand back and let the other dogs turn on Storm, the way she had with Arrow? But Alpha only nodded, turned, and padded unhurriedly back to the clearing.

Storm sat down on her haunches and scratched an ear with a hind leg. Her mind was racing.

Is Alpha even really concerned about me? Or is this just a strange, contorted way of stamping her authority? Storm found herself clenching her teeth in anger. *Did she just use Thorn and Beetle to get at me?* Licking her chops, Storm growled deep in her throat. *Maybe Alpha's trying to manipulate me. Maybe this is all about control within the Pack.*

But who had told Alpha about Storm's discussion with Twitch? She was sure it couldn't have been the Third Dog. *Twitch is too discreet. He wouldn't do that.*

But if it wasn't Twitch, which dog had done it?

After prey-sharing, her muscles pleasantly aching and the pain in her shoulder dulled at last, Storm lay with her head on her paws and watched Alpha and Beta's four pups as they tumbled and play-fought around an old white stump. The Sun-Dog was low behind the trees, and the light was fading, but Storm kept a keen eye on the pups. It wasn't her assigned job today, thank the Sky-Dogs, but their play was very energetic and she didn't want it to get out of hand—especially with Tiny right in the middle of it all.

But as she watched, she began to realize she was worrying unnecessarily. The battle game was good-humored, and the littermate bond between the four pups was clearly strong. As Tiny disappeared under the others, squeaking in protest, Tumble grabbed her by the scruff and dragged her clear. She gave him a grateful yip and a lick before launching herself at him in a renewed attack, and Tumble toppled backward, squirming in delight. His wound from the attack by the foxes had almost completely healed. It looked like it wouldn't even leave a scar.

These four will always look after one another, thought Storm suddenly. *They won't turn on one another the way Fang and I did. Or rather, the way he turned on me.* She felt a twinge of sadness and regret, deep in her rib cage. *I did try to make things good between us again . . . but it wasn't meant to be. He was too loyal to Blade. And she made him pay the ultimate price for that.* Storm shuddered. *She killed him in the end.*

Storm was glad to be distracted from her unhappy memories by Daisy's voice coming from the edge of camp. The little dog was talking to Woody, and Storm heard her own name. Curious, she cocked an ear to listen more closely.

"I still worry about what Storm said," Daisy was telling the scruffy dog. "She doesn't think a fox killed Whisper at *all*. Do you think it could have been coyotes, Woody? Should we keep a lookout in case any of those come near?"

"I suppose we should be alert for any strange animal," Woody conceded. "But—"

"Storm thought it might have been a *dog* who did it," Daisy went on, her voice becoming tense. "But I don't know. I can't believe a dog would be so vicious!"

Storm breathed very quietly, waiting for Woody's reply. She wished the whole subject of Whisper's murder could be buried, like Whisper himself. She hated to think about the little gray dog; it gave her a sharp pain below her ribs, and an ache in her gut. Was that guilt?

Woody was speaking again, she realized, lifting her head to focus.

"Some dogs are that vicious," he growled. "A Fierce Dog could do it."

"Oh, Woody," protested Daisy. "I don't believe that!"

He hunched his shaggy shoulders. "Well, why did Arrow decide to leave like that? Surely that means *something*. He left the Pack and our territory, all that security, and he did it voluntarily. It doesn't make sense. Unless he was hiding something. . . ."

"Oh, I don't think so," whined Daisy. "And I feel so sorry for Bella. She's out there in the cold without us, without the Pack to protect her. I hope they're finding enough prey."

Woody gave a snort. "Bella never struck me as a stupid dog. She's latched onto one of the best hunters we had. I'm sure she's being very well fed."

From the corner of her eye, Storm noticed a golden dog

crossing the camp, passing quite close to the two gossiping dogs. Lucky gave them a glance, but even though they must have seen him, Woody and Daisy simply went on chattering.

Woody's sniping about Beta's own litter-sister, thought Storm angrily. *And he doesn't even care that Beta could hear!*

Grumpily, she put her paws over her ears, unwilling to listen to Woody's nonsense any longer. But tiredness and irritation defeated her; she couldn't get comfortable again. The Sun-Dog had curled up in the west and sunk below the horizon; only his lingering amber glow showed between the tree trunks. The pups had disappeared now, sent into their den to sleep by an affectionately stern Alpha. There was nothing more to see anyway.

Storm rose to her paws, stretched, and padded to her own den. The breeze was rising into a gusty, quarrelsome wind, stirring the waving branches and making the leaves shake above the clearing with a hissing rustle. A few dead twigs and leaves left over from Ice Wind bowled and bounced across the camp. A withered leaf caught in Chase's fur, and she shook it loose.

Maybe it was the wind that was making her unsettled, thought Storm. Or maybe it was the fact that the prey had been so meager tonight, and that no dog's belly had been properly filled. The thought of having to wait till the next day to eat again filled her with a dull, niggling irritation. She was sure hunger pangs would wake her in the night.

Well, it'll make a pleasant change from nightmares about Lucky dying. . . .

Turning her sleep-circle, she felt a sharp jab in her paw pad. Glancing down, Storm pawed in annoyance at the leaves and dry grass. A loose stone, maybe, or even a big twig: something must have blown in with this aggravating wind. Huffing impatiently, she raked her claws deeper into her bedding in search of it. This time she felt an even sharper stab, right in the sensitive spot between two claws.

"Ouch!" she yelped, and stopped clawing at it, leaning down instead to sniff suspiciously. More carefully, she batted away a clump of grass and pulled aside a green leaf with her teeth. When she saw what was beneath it, Storm gasped and took an abrupt step backward.

That's no pebble! It glittered very slightly in the dim twilight, and its edges were savagely sharp. *Clear-stone!*

There was broken clear-stone in her bedding! Storm gave a stifled whine of shock and licked at the shallow cut between her claws. It wasn't too painful—but the implications were.

Did some dog put this here? Storm could hardly bring herself to believe it. Yet when she dragged the grass and leaves cautiously apart, Storm could see more shards and chunks of the horrible stuff, buried in among her bedding.

Her whine rose to a violent snarl of outrage. She wished she could have suppressed it, but she was too angry—and now the other dogs came running over, slowing their pace as they saw she was in no danger, but sniffing and pricking their ears in curiosity.

"Storm?" asked Snap. "What happened?"

Daisy bent over the bedding. "Clear-stone," she gasped.

"No!" Sunshine's whimper was disbelieving. "I prepared Storm's den myself! There wasn't any clear-stone in the leaves, I swear it, Storm! I swear to the—to the Forest-Dog! I wouldn't be so careless!"

"Of course you wouldn't," gritted Storm, managing to give the little Omega a lick of reassurance. But now other dogs were joining the fascinated group, crowding closer to examine the sabotaged bedding.

Ruff cocked his head, confused. "But who would have done this? Arrow and Bella aren't here anymore. And even if they were, Arrow wouldn't attack another Fierce Dog."

Beetle wriggled through the press of bodies, followed closely by his litter-sister. He stared at the gleaming clear-stone. "This had to be one of Twitch's Pack," he barked. "None of *us* would do it!"

"What did you say?" Woody turned on the young dog, his muzzle wrinkling in fury. "It's more like a trick the half wolf would have taught. That brute probably had lots of nasty strategies that you all picked up. Twitch's Pack never played these vicious pranks!"

"Never mind the half wolf, what about Terror?" Beetle snarled, refusing to back down. "Who knows what you learned from that crazy dog? I don't think I could trust *you* on a hunt, Woody!" he yapped.

Storm tried to get between them and butt Beetle's shoulder aside. *Oh Beetle,* she thought angrily, *don't make this worse.*

But the two dogs ignored her, still barking furiously at each other. "I don't know how you've got the nerve to say that, Beetle," snarled Woody.

"It's my old Pack that always had *nerve,*" snapped Beetle back. "*Your* Pack didn't even dare challenge the mad dog who led you!" His litter-sister Thorn was at his flank now, growling in support.

I should never have made a sound! thought Storm. *I should just have gotten rid of the clear-stone and hidden it. Now they're fighting again!*

Breeze gave a sudden sharp bark that made both Beetle and Woody turn in surprise, their ears pricked. "Stop it! Stop squabbling. This is horrible—Storm could have hurt herself badly on that clear-stone. It'd be mad to think she'd put it there herself!"

Alarmed, Storm looked around the gathered dogs. Several of them eyed her back, blinking warily. *Oh no. Are some of them really thinking that?* Which dog had suggested she'd sabotaged her own bed? Storm's eye twitched with anxiety. She appreciated Breeze speaking up for her, but it hadn't altogether helped. "I think it was an accident," piped up Rake. "Look how windy it's been, and it's almost blowing a gale now."

"Rake's right," agreed Mickey. "Anything could have blown in here since Sunshine prepared the beds. It's no dog's fault."

Bruno nodded vigorously. "It was an accident, no question."

"Exactly," said Breeze firmly. "There's no need for every dog to get worked up and worried. Storm didn't do this and neither did any other dog."

I wish she'd stop saying that! thought Storm in exasperation. But she still wagged her tail gratefully at the brown dog. "Yes, and I didn't mean to bark," she told them gruffly. "I was surprised, that's all. You'd better all go back to the dens."

With many exchanged glances, and surreptitious sniffs at the den floor, the dogs began to turn and make their way back to their own sleeping spots. Storm watched them go, a sense of unease creeping through her fur. Dart's eyes seemed to hold hers a little too long, while Daisy was gazing at Storm anxiously out of the corner of her eye.

I don't like the looks they're giving me. She licked her jaws. *They can't be wondering if Breeze is wrong, can they? Are they starting to think I did this myself?*

No, that was crazy. Storm felt her ears drooping unhappily. It wouldn't make sense to any dog. Didn't they all think that Fierce Dogs were vicious? Surely, if that was true, Storm would attack another dog before she'd do it to herself!

Still, that chill would not leave her hide. Some of the Pack had twisted every action of Arrow's so that they could believe he was a threat. He'd only tried to be a good Packmate, but they'd driven him out. Could the same thing happen to Storm?

Did some of the Pack now hate Fierce Dogs so much, they'd believe anything?

CHAPTER ELEVEN

Beetle and Thorn are finally starting to work as a team. Storm eyed the two apprentice hunters with satisfaction as the party made their way back to camp the next day. The litter-siblings had gotten their act together today and had cooperated well with the other hunters. Perhaps there was hope for the Pack after all—this patrol was bringing back a good haul of prey, including two rabbits, a couple of lazy pigeons, and a fat gopher. *Beetle certainly learned his lesson with that first gopher; he kept the noise down this time till the very last moment.*

It wasn't like hunting with Arrow and Bella, though. Arrow, Storm knew, would never have let that squirrel reach the safety of a pine tree, as Thorn had; and Bella always managed to sniff out the most potential prey.

It was funny how much Storm missed having another Fierce Dog in the Pack. So many of the dogs saw her as something different, something Other—and it had felt good to have an ally. When Arrow had been here, she had known that there was at least one dog who understood.

Now she was on her own.

The weight of the realization hit her just as she reached the edge of the clearing, and she came to a halt. She felt a sudden reluctance to walk into camp, where so many dogs of her own Pack distrusted her.

Lucky glanced back at her, then nodded to the other hunters. "Go ahead and take the food to the prey pile. We'll eat soon."

When they had trotted on, to be greeted by a chorus of grateful yips from the dogs still in camp, Lucky turned and padded back to Storm. Sitting back on his haunches, he eyed her keenly.

"What's wrong, Storm? You've been unsettled for the last few days. Is there something troubling you?"

Storm licked her chops and sighed, averting her eyes. "It's— well, ever since my den was sabotaged . . ."

"We can't be sure that was deliberate, Storm," he said. "Maybe it was just—I don't know—bad luck. You don't think a dog is targeting you, do you?"

I doubt any luck is quite that bad, she thought drily, but she said nothing. "It's not that," she told him instead, quite truthfully. *After all, I can handle myself.* "It's just that since then, they've all looked at me strangely. Beta, I'm not blind. I can see the suspicion in their eyes. I'm sure they think I did it myself."

"Why would they think such a thing?" Lucky huffed a laugh. "Don't let it bother you, Storm."

"I can't help it." She heaved a sigh. "It's not quite the way they looked at Arrow, but their expressions . . . it's like they think I'm . . . strange, somehow."

Lucky leaned in to lick her jaw. "Please, Storm, don't let it worry you. It's words and gossip, that's all. And words can't even rumple a dog's fur."

"They're rumpling mine," she growled.

"Ignore it, Storm," he told her, a little impatience creeping into his voice. "There are much more important things for the Pack to be anxious about. Let it go; I'm sure there's nothing to worry about at all."

Lucky got up to walk away, and Storm's chest ached with sadness. Lucky had practically raised Storm, but even he didn't understand. No dog could, perhaps. No dog but Arrow.

Prey-sharing that evening was satisfying, and the Sun-Dog was beginning to lope toward the horizon once more when Storm got to her feet and glanced around. For once, no dog was watching her. Her belly felt pleasantly full, but she wasn't happy. She slipped out of camp, keeping low so she wouldn't attract attention. Arrow and Bella hadn't gone too far, she knew—she'd caught their scent several times while out hunting. If she could find their camp, maybe Storm could talk to them about what had been happening to her—how her Packmates seemed to be turning on her. They would understand.

A few paces out of camp, Storm halted, surprised. Lucky must have quietly left camp before she did. She could make out the Beta's shape as he padded through the tree trunks, barely more than a golden ghost. The wind had subsided now, but the light rustle of the breeze in the branches was enough to conceal any noise his paws made.

It wasn't like him—Lucky might have been a wanderer once, but since the birth of the pups, he had tended not to go off on his own. Curious, Storm crept stealthily after him.

The trees were great black shadows around her in the deepening dusk, and mist was beginning to form in the hollows. Storm reckoned Sun-Dog must be close to turning his sleep-circle, though she couldn't see the horizon; the light was fading to blue-gray and when she glanced up, she could see the first of the stars winking. Twilight at this time of the year was always prolonged, but no-sun was on its way.

Still Lucky didn't turn back; he plodded remorselessly on, and Storm kept her distance as she tracked him. It felt like stalking prey, and the thought made her feel uneasy.

Lucky's ears must have been sharper than she realized, though. As she paused, one paw in the air, he turned to look over his shoulder, and his eyes met hers. He said nothing but waited until she had caught up to him.

"What are you doing here, Storm?"

She felt a little sheepish. "I wanted to go see Arrow and Bella. And when I saw you, I suppose I started wondering what *you* were doing."

His eyes slanted to the side. "I'm going to see Bella and Arrow."

Storm's ears pricked up in surprise. "Oh!"

"And now that you're here"—he tilted his head—"I suppose you'd like to go together?"

"Very much!" Storm gave him a quick lick, but Lucky seemed preoccupied and didn't return it. He sniffed the air, frowned, then turned to head in another direction.

He was heading now for the horizon where the Sun-Dog rose, Storm realized as she padded dutifully after him. *He seems to know where he's going, so there's no point in me trying to help.* "Lucky, have you visited them already? After they left the Pack, I mean?"

He licked his jaws noncommittally. "I suppose I've . . . seen them. Yes."

"How are they?" asked Storm. She couldn't be cross with him for hiding this; she was too excited at the prospect of seeing Arrow and Bella.

He hunched his shoulders, staring straight ahead. "I haven't asked."

"What do you mean?" She frowned, but Lucky seemed not to hear her, concentrating too intently on the path ahead. He bounded across a ditch, then crossed a narrow strip of open grassland before entering another copse of trees.

Storm sighed inwardly. The Beta dog was being *very* evasive. . . .

I recognize this place, she thought suddenly. *We're near the old Fierce Dog cave, where Blade and her cronies had their camp.* Letting her tongue loll, she gazed with interest at the familiar surroundings. The memory of Blade still sent a small chill through her fur. *But there's no need to fear her now—I made sure of that when I killed her. And I avenged my brother Fang. . . .*

It didn't look like much of a camp now, she realized. The

undergrowth had reclaimed the areas Blade and her Pack had cleared, and there was no sign of neatly organized bedding. Lucky gave a soft growl of greeting, and Storm saw the two dogs emerge from beneath an overhanging tree.

Bella walked forward and nuzzled her, and Storm licked her friend's jaw with delight. "It's good to see you, Bella—and you, Arrow! We've missed you."

"Yes," agreed Lucky, gently butting his litter-sister's neck. As the two siblings and Arrow murmured to one another, exchanging fragments of news, Storm studied the camp again. *There's not much for Bella and Arrow here.* Storm couldn't help thinking the two dogs didn't look great. Arrow's formerly glossy coat was dull, and he was visibly thinner; Bella's fur was bedraggled, and the bones of her face more stark.

"You've had so much to do," Storm told them brightly. "Would you like me to go on a quick hunt for you?"

Bella gave her a warm bark of gratitude. "That's good of you, Storm, but you mustn't."

"No," agreed Arrow. "You mustn't, though we do appreciate the offer." He gave her neck a swift nuzzle.

"They're right," Lucky told Storm as she began to protest. "What if one of our Pack saw you out hunting—and then no prey made it back to our camp? They'd think you were hunting self-ishly for yourself—or that you were a traitor."

Storm had to admit that made sense, though she felt a nig-gling sense of resentment that she couldn't hunt on behalf of old and dear friends. Why was every dog so ready to brand Storm a traitor? "All right, Beta. I wish I could help, that's all."

"Don't worry about us," said Arrow cheerfully. "Come see our new den, if you like. We're making our sleeping quarters in the old Fierce Dog cave."

Storm nodded. "I recognize it. It's a good, secure place. And sheltered." She decided she wouldn't mention the sense of unease that clung to her fur. Blade's Fierce Dog Pack might be long gone, but there was something about that cavern: a throbbing darkness in the atmosphere, as if the hearts of the Fierce Dogs were still beating here. *It's a feeling of evil,* she realized. *As if there are ghosts . . .* She almost imagined she could hear the echoes of savage snarls in the depths behind the shadow.

Fang breathed his last here. This is where Blade ripped out his throat. She couldn't repress a shudder.

I loved Fang, but please, Sky-Dogs: I don't want to see his ghost. . . .

* * *

Despite her fears, Storm had sensed nothing frightening in the cave. It had been good to talk to Bella and Arrow again, to exchange news and tell stories about the pups. Storm hadn't felt comfortable confiding in Arrow about the way the Pack was treating her, not in front of Lucky, but she was reassured to see him and Bella still healthy—if thin—and still happy. Indeed, they seemed far happier away from the nasty atmosphere in Alpha's camp, though it still gave Storm a sharp pang of regret that Bella and Arrow had been forced to exile themselves.

Storm felt tired but peaceful as she and Lucky made their way back to their own camp. Lucky seemed quiet, but perhaps that was only because of the late hour. *And of course, he must be thinking about his litter-sister. The things they talked about together, and the things they couldn't say . . .*

"Are you all right, Lucky?" she asked him after a few long, silent rabbit-chases.

"I'm fine," he growled. "Just weary." He plodded on through the darkening evening.

She hesitated, but this was as good an opportunity as she would get, while they were alone in the peace of the late evening. "It's just—you've seemed a bit troubled lately, Lucky. Are you worried about the pups, now that we're short of hunters?"

He grunted, still not turning to look at her. "I'm not happy that prey is so hard to come by. But in a way that's a good thing. The pups will grow up tough and strong if they know a little hardship in their early lives. It didn't do me any harm."

"All the same, it must be an anxious time. . . ."

He shook himself irritably. "Really, Storm, that's not what's bothering me."

Quietly she said, "So what is?"

He gave a sigh, and halted at last. "All right. It's the idea there's a traitor in the Pack, Storm. That's a horrible thought."

"I know," said Storm sadly.

"And it's the worst thing in the world for the Pack right now. It doesn't really matter which Pack the traitor is originally from— whether it's one of Twitch's dogs or one of the old Wild Pack. The dogs still identify themselves in that way, they still cling to those old loyalties. Whoever is responsible, it'll set one half of the Pack against the other. Our Pack will be torn in two, Storm."

There was nothing she could say; all his fears were hers, too. Storm felt a tightness in her throat and chest, a sense of dread and sadness. As Lucky turned and walked on, she followed dejectedly at his heels.

"I'll tell you what, though, Lucky," she said after a while, pricking her ears forward. "Whichever Pack they originally belonged to, all the dogs love your pups. Tumble, Fluff, Nibble, and Tiny— they might keep the Pack together."

Lucky huffed a laugh. As he thought it over, his tongue lolled and he looked happier. "Maybe you're right about that, Storm. If anything can keep us together, I suppose it's the pups."

Storm gave him an affectionate nudge with her nose. "They're our hope for the future, in more ways than one. Even if I'm not very good at looking after them!"

Lucky chuckled again. "It's true you aren't the best pup-sitter in the world, Storm, but still—I hope they'll grow up to be like you. You're kind, you're brave, and you see the good in others. What better example could they have?"

Storm felt a hot tide of embarrassment. "That's nice of you, Lucky."

"I mean it. I know how hard you had to fight your own Fierce Dog instincts as you were growing up. You were bred to be a fighter, by longpaws who wanted vicious dogs, and you struggled against that. But you won!" He pressed his head to hers. "You've made yourself into a good, kind, strong dog, Storm. That's something to be proud of."

Storm found her throat was a little too choked to speak.

Lucky shook himself and began to pad on again toward the camp. "It's not easy to fight your nature, is it?"

His words made the fur rise abruptly along Storm's spine. *Is he saying that it's my nature to be vicious?* she thought, startled. Did even *Lucky* believe all Fierce Dogs were naturally cruel and violent? But she was too taken aback to respond.

"Yes," he went on, sighing. "I've got to admit that the Lone Dog inside me barks very loudly sometimes. It tells me not to trust any dog; it tells me to suspect every dog's motives."

"Well," suggested Storm, recovering herself, "that can be useful. Sometimes it's sensible not to trust too much."

"True. It means I'm always vigilant for trouble. But I do wish sometimes that I could trust in other dogs more easily."

The camp was close now; Storm could smell the scents of her Packmates, including the warm milky softness of Lucky's pups. The Beta's eyes brightened as he too caught the scent.

"Do you miss it sometimes, Lucky?" Storm ventured. "Being a Lone Dog?"

He hesitated for a long moment. At last he said, "I was happy as a Lone Dog, I really was. I loved being on my own, taking care of myself, having no responsibilities. If it hadn't been for the Big

Growl, that's how I'd still be. It was the best life I could imagine for a dog."

Storm remained silent as they walked on, her paw pads cool in the evening dew. Lucky still seemed to be thinking.

"But," he said at last, "I was wrong, Storm. So wrong. It was just that I couldn't imagine a life with responsibilities, with duties, with . . . friends. Companions. Pups." His dark eyes softened. "And now? I would never go back, Storm."

His eyes lit up with contentment as they walked through the camp border. "Not ever."

CHAPTER TWELVE

At the edge of the clearing, Lucky halted to lick Storm's ear. "We should go back to camp separately. Best not to have any dogs think we're in some kind of conspiracy," Lucky murmured. "Good night, Storm."

It was sad, thought Storm as they went their separate ways, that they had to consider such things, but it had felt good to talk to Lucky alone for a while. It had been like old times, having him to herself and confiding in him, and hearing some of his secret thoughts in return. Determined, she pushed away the uneasy feeling in her stomach at the memory of Lucky's unsettling words about Fierce Dogs as she padded over the cool grass toward her den. *I'm not going to think about that.* A little white shape was busy with Storm's bedding, clearing it out and replacing it from a heap of fresh leaves and grass.

"Hello, Sunshine," said Storm, nuzzling her furry neck. "You didn't have to do this at this late hour!"

"I wanted to." Sunshine gave her a friendly lick. "It gives me something to do. I thought I'd check your fresh bedding again, after what happened last night. And I thought it would take my mind off things, but . . ." The little Omega breathed out a sad sigh. "But as soon as I started, I remembered the clear-stone wasn't an accident." She glanced up a little nervously, as if any dog might be listening. "Some dog in our Pack did this," she whispered.

It felt wrong to see the little Omega, usually so spirited and cheerful, look so glum. Storm turned to look around the camp, at the Pack and their usual evening activities. There was an edge in the air, she realized, that hadn't been there before: an unpleasant tension. Beetle and Thorn were dutifully practicing their hunting moves, but Rake rose to snap at them.

"Do you two have to make so much noise? It's late! You're running wild."

Moon, in turn, barked at Rake. "They're keeping their hunting skills sharp! That's more important than you getting even *more* sleep. At least they'll be able to bring back more food for the Pack!"

Rake growled angrily, and Woody came to his side. "Hunting's an instinct," Woody declared, glaring at Moon. "And obviously these two don't have it."

"How dare you?" Thorn turned from Beetle to snarl at him. "Just because we're not natural hunters doesn't mean we shouldn't practice and get better!"

"Exactly," growled Beetle. "Maybe *you'd* be better if you practiced more."

Storm cast a weary look up at the sky, almost dark now. *Is it going to be like this every day? Bickering and squabbling, never working together . . . that isn't Pack life!*

She blinked, realizing that the pale glow behind the trees was the Moon-Dog rising. She was full again, facing the dogs, casting all her silver light on them. *She's not showing us her rump anymore. I know her turns happen all the time, but I was worried she'd never look at us again!*

She's giving us a chance.

But the Pack should have anticipated this night, thought Storm with a flush of guilt. *Have we been so wrapped up in our own disagreements, we forgot to keep track? We've made no plans for a Great Howl tonight!*

Storm gave a sharp, echoing bark. "The Moon-Dog is full tonight. This should be the pups' first Howl!"

Silence fell as the dogs turned toward her, even the quarreling hunters staring in surprise. They really hadn't noticed, she thought. "Look!"

Raising their heads, every dog stared at the Moon-Dog as she bounded gracefully above the tree branches. Alpha came out of her den, pacing to the center of the clearing.

"Storm, you're right." Alpha turned her dark eyes toward her. "A Great Howl is what we need right now—the Moon-Dog is telling us so. It's time for Tumble, Fluff, Nibble, and Tiny to howl properly with us for the first time." She leaned down to nuzzle Fluff's head. "Sleep-time will be later than I realized, my pups—tonight you'll find out what 'Pack' truly means!"

The four pups yipped in delight—more at the deferred bedtime, Storm thought fondly, than at Alpha's promise of an important ritual. *But they'll soon find out just what the Great Howl is about. They'll understand how it feels to be a member of a strong, loving, united Pack.* Her heart surged with renewed hope.

Then her eyes caught Lucky's, and she saw the sadness in them. Of course—he must be thinking of Bella, his litter-sister, and how she and her mate would not be howling with them. The pups were Bella's blood too, yet she was going to miss their first real Howl.

It's times like these a dog really misses its kin, thought Storm sadly. *I always remember Wiggle during our Howls—poor Wiggle, who never survived his puphood. And Grunt, who became Fang—I miss him so much too, despite what happened between us. I know exactly how Lucky feels.*

All the same, as the four pups scampered and tumbled in excitement around the glade, Storm saw Lucky's tail begin to wag and his jaw drop open with amusement. His grief must be balanced with happiness—and hers was too, Storm realized as her own tail began to wag with joy at the pups' antics. *They don't really understand yet,* she thought, *but they'll bring the Pack new hope when they Howl. That's part of being Pack, too.*

Enthusiastically the dogs began to form their usual cluster for the Great Howl. As the pups scrambled and bumped into one another, Alpha nosed them into position, her face gently stern.

"Calm down now, my pups. This is a solemn occasion. You must respect the Howl."

One by one the pups quieted and became still, their excitement showing only in their quivering tailtips. They blinked up obediently at their Mother-Dog, and she licked each pup lovingly before raising her head to the Moon-Dog and releasing the first musical howl.

One by one, the dogs in the circle joined her, harmonizing

with their Alpha's voice. Storm tilted back her head and let out her own cry to the Moon-Dog.

Something disquieted her, though, and from the corner of her eye she spotted some of the other dogs. Breeze was part of the circle, but she wasn't howling. Of course, some of Twitch's old Pack had always kept silent during the Howls, terrified of attracting the Fear-Dog's attention, but hadn't they gotten over that superstition yet?

Twitch himself either hadn't noticed Breeze's silence, or if he had, did not seem to mind; he simply went on howling blissfully. Storm shut her eyes tight and let the howl rise louder and stronger from her throat. *I won't let Breeze's silence distract me. This is a joyful moment. The pups' first Howl. I won't let any dog spoil that!*

Around her the sound rose higher, and higher. The Moon-Dog filled her vision, shining and silver, and she felt Pack-strength sing in her blood. *Not all of them, though . . . not all of them . . .*

No! I will think only *of the Howl and the Moon-Dog.* Squeezing her eyes tighter, Storm howled till she drowned out even her own racing thoughts.

The Howl's echo had barely died away, and already the rest of the Pack was quarreling again.

"What was that about?"

"What were you thinking, Breeze!"

The angry voices penetrated Storm's hazy thoughts, and she shook herself to attention. *Something's wrong. . . .*

"Rake didn't howl either. I watched him!" Beetle sounded livid.

"Or Woody," snarled Thorn. "Twitch, what have you got to say about your Pack's behavior?"

"They're not *my* Pack," Twitch corrected her mildly. "We're all one Pack, and that's Alpha's. And the Howl isn't compulsory, after all. If a dog doesn't want to howl, then they shouldn't be expected to fake it."

"Why wouldn't they want to howl?" snapped Moon.

"Perhaps they just weren't in the mood? Surely the Moon-Dog would know if a dog wasn't howling sincerely." Twitch hunched his shoulders. "That would offend her much more than a dog simply not joining in."

"That's not the point!" growled Bruno, his tail lashing furiously. "The Howl is supposed to be about togetherness. It's about unity *whether you feel like it or not.* But your friends, Twitch—they've always kept themselves separate, ever since they joined us. They're still outsiders! They still believe in the Fear-Dog! They don't even *try* to be part of our Pack!"

"How can we consider ourselves part of your Pack?" barked Rake.

"That's right!" put in Woody, showing his teeth. "There's always such favoritism shown to the half wolf's Pack. How is that unity? Eh?"

The argument had been bad enough, Storm thought—but that mention of the old half wolf Alpha sent a frisson of cold dread through her hide. Every dog knew that the half wolf had been untrustworthy at his core—that he'd ended up betraying his own Pack and siding with Blade and her Fierce Dogs. Were Rake and Woody dragging him up because they wanted to imply *none* of the old Wild Pack could be trusted?

"Packmates!" Their current Alpha's commanding bark rang out, silencing the commotion. Cowering slightly at her tone of reproof, the dogs looked toward her.

She stood with her head high, staring at them all with contempt. "This was my pups' first Great Howl. You will *not* tarnish it with your petty squabbles."

Storm's hackles rose. *There she goes again,* she thought bitterly. *It's always about her pups! It's her whole Pack that has the problems, not her litter!*

But again she kept her jaws shut, and not one of the other dogs dared to bark back at Alpha. They exchanged glances, or stared at the grass; at last, shamefaced, they turned one by one and trooped off toward their dens.

Her tail pressed between her hind legs, Storm plodded down-heartedly to her own sleeping-place. She hadn't taken any part in it, but the quarrel had been such a dispiriting way to end the Great Howl. No wonder Alpha was angry. Perhaps the Moon-Dog was, too, though she still shone full and bright in the black sky.

O Moon-Dog, perhaps it was a huge mistake for our Packs to join. Maybe even a fatal mistake . . .

Miserably, Storm trod her sleep-circle, then tried to settle on the fresh bedding Sunshine had laid out so carefully. Somewhere in the distance, far beyond the clearing, she could hear other dogs howling.

She pricked one ear, straining to listen. The howls were dis-tant, but she could hear the joy in them. It was a beautiful sound of perfect harmony, quite unlike the Howl the Pack had just offered.

Bella and Arrow, Storm thought. *They're howling together. They truly are one, in a way this Pack is not.*

An urge stirred in her belly, bringing her halfway to her paws.

Her hide tingled as an echoing howl rose in her throat. Suddenly scared she might bay and howl aloud, she clamped her jaws tightly shut and squeezed her eyes closed. *I mustn't sing with Bella and Arrow. I mustn't. But I so want to. . . .*

She forced herself to lay flat again, as the eerie and beautiful sound echoed in the distance. *A true Pack, even if there are only two of them.*

It took Storm all her strength and will not to leap fully to her paws and join her longing howl to theirs.

CHAPTER THIRTEEN

Dew sparkled on the grass of the clearing, and feathery white clouds scudded in the breeze as the Sun-Dog climbed up the pale-blue morning sky. Storm stretched out her forelegs, clawing the soft ground. Then, as she straightened, her ears pricked. Something was behind her; something was stalking her. She could hear the quiet crunch of paws that were trying too hard to be stealthy. Another blade of grass rustled, and the sounds stopped. After a pause, the hunter crept forward again.

No. *Hunters.* Because more than one dog was stalking her. Even through the whisper and rattle of the wind in the leaves, Storm could hear their flanks bump together; they were clustered too tightly instead of spreading out to attack. *Amateurs.*

Narrowing her eyes, Storm tensed. When the next pawstep fell, she spun on her haunches and snarled.

Four small pups yelped with delight and tumbled backward, falling over one another as they scrambled to escape. They didn't run far, though, bouncing back to crouch and wag their stumpy tails and bark high-pitched challenges.

As Storm's heartbeat returned to normal, she let her tongue loll. Lowering her own forequarters, she feigned indignant fury, snapping at thin air just in front of the pups' noses and then scuttling back as if terrified of them.

They're so tiny, she thought with amusement, *and I'm so big. Pups like these should be running a whole deer-chase from me, but they're not scared at all. Because they know me. And they trust me.*

And after all the jibes about Fierce Dogs, she realized that felt very good.

Pouncing suddenly, she pinned Tumble down with her forepaws; when his sisters squealed and rushed to his rescue, she managed to corral all of them under her paws. Grinning down, she watched them squirm and giggle and bark, batting their little paws at her.

"You little rogues," she growled. "I'll teach you to hunt a great big Fierce Dog like me!"

"Bad Storm! Grrrr!"

"Yipe!" Feigning terror, she jumped away from Tumble's baby

teeth. As she rolled onto her back, all four of them promptly piled on top of her belly, yelping with glee as she howled.

"Pack!" The gruff, grown-up bark interrupted their game, and the four pups pricked their ears and looked around for their Father-Dog. Lucky stood at the entrance to his and Alpha's den, the breeze ruffling his golden fur.

"The morning hunting party has returned," he announced when he had every dog's attention. "But before we eat, you all need to gather round. Assemble here, please."

Startled, Storm pricked her ears forward, letting the pups tumble off her and bound happily back to their Father-Dog. She followed them, rather more hesitantly. It was unusual for Alpha or Beta to call a Pack meeting at this hour, and given what had happened at the Howl last night, the reason couldn't be anything good. With trepidation Storm watched Alpha emerge from her den.

She glanced around her at her Packmates. Every dog looked much as she felt: hungry, and nervous. Alpha was watching them all with studied calm and did not speak until every dog was gathered around her. When they had stopped muttering questions to one another and had finally fallen silent in expectation, she raised her head.

"I didn't sleep well last night," she told them, "and I suspect neither did many of you. Our Pack can't continue to be divided like this. We all need to sort out our differences so that we can get back to working together, for the good of all dogs. Working as a true Pack. *Surviving.*"

"I agree that we need to survive, Alpha." To Storm's surprise, it was Rake who stood up, his eyes hard. All the other dogs turned to stare at him, too, their ears pricked forward in astonishment.

Rake gazed around at them all, a tinge of contempt in his eyes. "In fact, we all agree: surviving isn't possible in this situation. This Pack isn't working." He turned to study all the other dogs who had once been in Twitch's Pack—Breeze, Woody, Ruff, Chase, and Twitch himself—and his muzzle curled with what looked to Storm like glee.

"So," he went on, "Woody and Ruff and I have decided we're going to leave."

"No!" exclaimed Snap. Daisy whined with shock, and Mickey growled in disbelief.

"We can't be part of this Pack anymore," said Rake. "We don't feel welcome. Dogs of Twitch's Pack are never favored. And who can we trust? No dog knows who might be working against them."

He glared around again, and Storm realized the usually taciturn dog must have been preparing his bitter words for some time. "Any dog who wants to come with us is welcome. We're going to seek out new territory and establish our own Pack. One where things will be run fairly, where every dog will have a say in the decisions of the Pack."

For a long moment, there was stunned silence in the clearing. Then Twitch stepped forward, facing Rake squarely.

"This is the wrong decision, Rake. You are making a huge mistake. Three dogs can't survive in the wild by themselves— that's not a *Pack*."

"Four dogs," said a quiet voice.

Stunned, Storm watched Dart rise to her paws. "I'm going with them," said the skinny dog. "Rake, Ruff, and Woody are dogs I feel I can trust. I know for sure that none of them has sabotaged our prey, or tried to undermine the Pack. I know none of these dogs killed Whisper. And I can't say that about most of the dogs here. I'm sorry."

Storm gaped at her. *A dog of our own old Pack, defecting? I can't believe this is happening.*

Rake did not avert his eyes from Twitch's, but stared defiantly back. "Are you really happy here, Twitch? Being no better than Third Dog? Are you, Chase? And you, Breeze." He turned to the gentle-eyed brown dog. "You're one of us, and you deserve a much higher rank than you have in this Pack. Come with us."

Storm found she was holding her breath. Would Twitch, Chase, and Breeze leave them too?

"I am loyal to our Alpha," snapped Twitch, and Storm breathed again. "There are good dogs in this Pack. And Alpha took in all of my former Pack without worrying for a moment about the extra mouths that would have to be fed. She has been generous to us, and all this about the half wolf's Pack being favored is nonsense! I owe her my loyalty—as do you, Rake, and you two." He glared at Ruff and Woody.

"If Twitch is staying," barked Breeze, "then so am I. Besides..." She glanced at the four trembling pups at Alpha's paws. "I have another reason to stay around."

Alpha gave her a grateful look. She said nothing, having clearly decided that this was a moment to let every dog decide for herself or himself, but Storm could see the anxiety behind her dark eyes.

Chase was the last dog of Twitch's old Pack to speak, and she looked agonized. Blinking rapidly, she licked her chops, looking neither at Alpha nor at her old Packmates. At last she coughed, and looked directly at Rake.

"I'm staying," she said hoarsely. "Twitch has a point. And this Pack offers the best chance of survival."

"Very well." Rake wrinkled his muzzle in disappointment, but he nodded. "We'll leave right away; there's no point lingering." With a twitch of his tail he turned and paced off into the woods, Ruff and Woody at his heels. None of them looked back, except for Dart, who paused. She eyed them all.

"I hope I'm wrong, you know. About the murderer being one of you. You should all be very careful." She looked straight at Storm, let her stare linger for a horribly long moment, then spun around and disappeared after her new friends.

Storm couldn't speak. Anger gathered in her throat, almost choking her. *Did Dart really just imply that* I *killed Whisper? Am* I *the real reason that she wants to leave?*

When the four dogs had vanished into the trees, there was a heavy silence. Storm could feel some of them watching her, perhaps thinking about what Dart had said, but none of them spoke. She swallowed hard and looked around at the Pack—or at what was left of it. And suddenly the pangs in her belly had nothing to do with her hunger.

Without a word, Alpha stepped forward and tugged a fat hare from the prey pile. She rested her paw on it and lifted her head to look at each dog in turn.

"We've lost some good dogs today," she said at last. Her voice was slightly hoarse, but firm. "Our Pack is now smaller. But this does not need to be bad for us. Remember, there are four fewer bellies to fill now. Every dog here will be a little less hungry."

For today, thought Storm with some trepidation. *But when there are fewer of us hunting . . . ?*

Clearly Alpha would not stand for negative thoughts. "Today this Pack will eat better than it has for many journeys of the Moon-Dog. This is as hungry as we will ever be again."

Baring her teeth, the swift-dog took a bite from the hare's flank, tearing off a substantial hunk of flesh. Around her, the other dogs murmured in agreement, and Storm thought she could hear a more cheerful note in their voices. But she couldn't share their optimism.

First Bella and Arrow; now Rake, Woody, Ruff, and Dart. Our Pack is vanishing before our eyes.

And Alpha might vow that they would eat this heartily every day, but they had fewer hunters now as well as fewer mouths to feed. And suddenly, they had competition for prey. Storm couldn't help feeling acute trepidation.

There are three Packs now. The forest has suddenly gotten a lot more crowded. . . .

CHAPTER FOURTEEN

The worst thing, thought Storm the next morning as she watched the other dogs wake, was that she didn't know. She didn't know if one of these dogs, the ones who had stayed, was the one who had murdered Whisper—or if the killer was roaming the forest now, a member of another Pack. There was no way to be sure.

I'll only find out when the dog strikes again. When the Pack's home is sabotaged . . .

. . . or when another dog is killed. Storm shuddered with horror at the thought.

It was hideous to think that it might happen again, but gradually her sense of dread began to be overtaken by anger. *I hate this feeling—that there's nothing I can do to stop this unknown dog. I hate it!*

Across the clearing, Moon was organizing some of the remaining dogs into patrols for the day. She was usually such a calm

185

leader, but today the white-and-black dog looked flustered, and no wonder. It hadn't been all that easy to arrange patrols before, but now her pool of available dogs had been reduced to four—and that included Moon herself, as well as Third Dog Twitch.

"What about Daisy?" Twitch was asking.

"Daisy's been on patrol all night—she's worn out." Moon nudged the little dog, who did indeed look exhausted. "Daisy, go to your den and sleep for a bit. You aren't alert enough to patrol again, anyway."

"It's really my turn to take High Watch," pointed out Breeze helpfully.

"I know," said Moon patiently, "but you're a scout dog. Twitch can't do that for the hunters, so they need you."

The watching hunters were following Moon's decisions with quiet interest. Mickey scratched at his ear with a hind leg.

"I was already worried about feeding the Pack when we lost Bella and Arrow," he sighed. "Now we may have fewer mouths to feed, but we could easily miss the signs of an attack. We could start to lose territory, and we can't afford that."

"And it's not just strange dogs we have to worry about," agreed Bruno. "We could lose territory to foxes, or coyotes—we just don't have the strength of numbers anymore."

Privately, Storm thought that strange dogs and other animals weren't the real problem. She was more worried about losing territory to the very dogs who had just abandoned them. She'd been confident that Bella and Arrow would respect the boundaries of the Pack's territory, but she wasn't nearly so sure that Rake's group would do the same.

This problem might be one I can help solve, though. . . .

Storm padded up to Moon, clearing her throat to get the distracted dog's attention. "Moon? I'd like to volunteer to patrol."

Moon glanced around, surprised. "That's good of you, Storm. But to be honest, we need a more permanent solution. Only Alpha can fix this."

With that, Moon walked over to where Alpha and Beta were watching their pups clamber out of their den into the sunshine.

"Alpha," she said firmly. "Beta. I need to talk with you both."

Alpha swiveled an ear and raised her brows. "Yes, Moon?"

"The Pack is out of balance." Moon sat back on her hindquarters and fixed Alpha with her steady blue eyes. "Some dog must become a new Patrol Dog, or we will stand no chance of protecting our territory. It's fundamental to our survival here! It's all very well having fewer dogs to feed—but if we can only hold on to a small territory, we'll still run out of prey!"

Alpha seemed to be thinking hard. Then, to Storm's great relief, she nodded.

"You're right, Moon. We need to be adaptable, don't we? The Pack has changed a lot in the last few journeys of the Sun-Dog; we must also change the way we do things." She frowned, then shook herself, looking brighter. "What we'll do is send out three smaller hunting patrols."

"All at the same time?" asked Moon. "I don't see how that helps the patrol situation."

"Yes, all at once. There will be two hunters and a scout in each patrol. But they'll have to combine hunting *and* patrolling. The smaller groups will be able to cover more ground between them and check our boundaries even as they stay alert for prey scents."

"There won't be much chance of catching big prey," said Lucky doubtfully.

"No, but there should be plenty of opportunity to find smaller prey—mice, voles, perhaps even an occasional rabbit. It's just going to be important for them to check for scents of other dogs, too—and enemies like the foxes. I think it can be done, don't you?"

Moon nodded slowly. "It's worth a try."

Thoughtfully Alpha gazed around the remaining Pack. "All right. Lucky and Storm can go out with Daisy, when she's rested.

Thorn and Beetle should go with Breeze—you two have been doing well at your practice, and I'm sure you can manage a hunt of your own, with a good scout dog."

Beetle and Thorn drew themselves up, looking proud and pleased.

"And Bruno and Snap," finished Alpha, "you go with Moon."

"But that's all the Patrol Dogs except for Twitch," Moon pointed out hesitantly. "Shouldn't I patrol the whole territory boundary, while he takes High Watch?"

Alpha's gaze chilled, and her facial muscles tightened. "Are you contradicting me, Moon? I've already considered that." Her tail tapped the ground brusquely. "Even though it's beneath an Alpha's rank, I myself will run the boundary this morning. I'm far faster than any of you, especially now that Dart has gone. And besides, I want to stretch my legs. Twitch and Mickey can stay with the pups while I'm gone."

Moon dipped her head in resignation. "All right. I apologize, Alpha. I didn't mean to challenge you."

Alpha gave her a curt nod. "And another thing. All dogs will take turns on High Watch from now on. That includes Patrol Dogs, hunt dogs—and even Beta and myself. I appreciate that the Patrol Dogs are stretched thin, Moon, and we don't want to give you more burdens than we have to."

There was a murmur of agreement among the dogs, and Storm felt a sweeping sense of relief. For a moment she'd been worried, but now she had a renewed surge of respect for Alpha. She'd handled that so well—even when she'd had to scold Moon.

Alpha was willing to bend the rules when the Pack needed her to, after all. That was something the half wolf had never done—and his insistence on rigid control, even when he was in the wrong, had been disastrous.

And I can't imagine the half wolf—or Blade—ever deigning to run a patrol themselves, so that lower-ranked dogs can go hunting! I was wrong about Alpha. She has more sense in her left ear than the half wolf ever had.

This Pack will survive, even with our reduced numbers, thought Storm hopefully. *We have an Alpha who will make sure of that.*

As well as being able to combine hunting and patrolling, there was another unexpected advantage to the smaller hunting parties, Storm found: she had a chance to hunt with Lucky, just the two of them. It was something they'd never had the opportunity to do before, and Storm realized very quickly that they made a good team. Perhaps it was the fact that she'd grown up with Lucky as her foster-father but she found she knew instantly what he was thinking and planning, and that he too could anticipate her moves.

It's not just efficient, she thought with pleasure. *It's fun!*

Daisy was a nimble and quick-witted scout dog, too, darting off frequently to search for signs of prey and returning with useful reports. She came running back now, just as Storm looked up for her: a fast small dog dodging between grass tussocks and tree stumps.

"Rabbits!" Daisy panted. "I know there are only two of you, but I can help. The warren's just over this rise!"

"Excellent work, Daisy." Lucky's eyes gleamed. "Let's take it slowly, Storm. We can't set up much of an ambush, but I think Daisy's right—if we're careful, we can get one of them."

It turned out even better than Lucky predicted. The dogs had come upon the warren downwind, and the rabbits were taken almost completely by surprise. With Daisy watching from a distance and telling them how far away the rabbits were, Lucky and Storm could keep low until the very last moment. When Storm and Lucky finally sprang, Daisy was able to run barking from the opposite direction, sending the rabbits into a frenzied panic.

They fled and darted, white bobtails flashing, but Lucky and Storm were almost on top of them right from the start, and the creatures were too afraid of the ferocious smaller dog; Daisy darted and dodged in all directions, confusing the creatures and blocking their way to some of the holes. It was a wild frenzy of running, grabbing, and snapping, but by the time the last rabbit had vanished beneath ground, Storm and Lucky found themselves panting, flanks heaving, over three plump dead rabbits.

"That was fantastic!" Storm barked as she got her breath back.

"Yes—terrific teamwork!" Lucky's eyes shone with satisfaction.

"Lucky! Storm!" Daisy was bounding back to them across the lumpy grassland, but she didn't look as thrilled as Storm felt. In fact, her sweet face was twisted in concern.

"What is it, Daisy?" Lucky frowned.

Daisy panted and sat down on her haunches. She let her ears droop. "I smelled something, Lucky. A familiar dog." Her voice grew softer. "I think it might be Bella."

Lucky drew in a breath. "Bella? And Arrow?"

"I don't know but I . . . I think so. What should we do?" Daisy lifted pleading eyes to Lucky's. "Should we try to avoid Bella? Do we have to drive her off our territory, if she's hunting here?" The little dog swallowed hard, and Storm realized that driving Bella away was the last thing Daisy wanted to do. Storm glanced at Lucky.

Daisy and Bella were Leashed Dogs together long before the Big Growl; they were friends. It must be so hard for her to try and think of Bella as an enemy!

Yet somehow, I can't imagine Lucky making Bella do anything she doesn't want to do. Lucky knows as well as I do that she's . . . determined.

Before Lucky could voice any decision, though, it was taken out of his paws. A chaos of furious barking echoed from beyond the next shallow ridge. Lucky bolted toward the noise, and Storm raced behind him, leaving Daisy to run gamely in their wake, trying as hard as she could to keep up.

As soon as they crested the ridge, Storm's heart sank. Bruno and Snap stood there, facing down Arrow and Bella over the crumpled body of a weasel. Fangs were bared, hackles were raised, and the air crackled with fury.

"You should have left our territory by now!" barked Snap. "It's time you found your own!"

"Yes," snarled Bruno. "Why are you still here? That weasel is rightfully ours! Not only is it on our land—we saw it first!"

"I made the kill!" Bella barked. "You scared it into my path. That carelessness makes it *mine!*"

Snap twisted her head at the sound of Lucky and Storm's arrival, and her eyes gleamed with triumph. She turned back to Bella. "Reinforcements are here, Bella! You two had better get off our territory *right now!*"

Arrow stepped forward menacingly. He lowered his head, his hackles erect, and his muzzle wrinkled to display his gleaming fangs.

The growl Arrow gave was low, and he spoke no words, but it was far more terrifying than any of the frantic barking they'd heard so far. It rumbled in his throat like the thunder of the Sky-Dogs, and the glint in his eyes was murderous.

Despite her own Fierce Dog blood, Storm felt a shiver of fear go through her hide. Now that he was out in the wild with Bella, Arrow sounded far more threatening and dangerous than he ever had when he was living with the Pack.

He's been keeping his temper all this time, she thought, *but now he has nothing to prove to any dog. . . .*

Storm knew that he wouldn't physically attack Snap and Bruno—she didn't know how she was so sure, but she felt it in her bones. But clearly, Snap and Bruno didn't know that. They cowered, cringing and shivering, their heads on the ground and their ears pressed close to their skulls.

"He was savage all along," said Bruno in a strangled whimper.

That's not fair, thought Storm. But before she could open her jaws to argue, Snap finally gathered her courage. She sprang upright and jumped toward Arrow, yapping furiously. At just that moment, Moon appeared, and when she saw Bella and Arrow, she broke into a run and raced forward to Snap's side.

"What's happening here? What are you two doing on our territory?" barked the white-and-black dog.

Now Bruno had recovered his dignity, too, and was on his four paws growling at his two former Packmates. Storm stared at them all, aghast. Despite Snap's diminutive size, Storm knew she was a fierce and merciless fighter, and Moon was well accustomed to defending the Pack with her claws and teeth. Arrow and Bella might beat them in the end, but it would be a bloody and pointless combat. Dogs could die—dogs who Storm knew and loved.

I have to stop this fight!

But how? If Snap, Moon, and Bruno thought she was coming to the defense of exiled Pack members, her loyalty would be questioned.

They might throw me out of the Pack too!

As she hesitated, anguished by indecision, Lucky took a bounding pace forward, shoving himself between the quarreling dogs. He glared at one side and then at the other, his muzzle curled back in contempt.

"You," he snarled at Snap and Bruno. "Have you forgotten that these dogs were your Packmates? Just a few journeys of the

Sun-Dog ago? Surely you can resolve your differences now without violence!"

Storm was afraid they might accuse Lucky of going soft, or of taking his litter-sister's side against his own Packmates. But Snap only looked taken aback, and Bruno downright astonished. It gave Lucky the time he needed to turn to Bella.

"Get out of here," he growled. "And fine, take the weasel with you: you killed it. But leave our territory. You can't hunt here anymore."

Bella gave a low, rumbling growl, then regained her dignity and sniffed disdainfully. "Why? Your Pack has fewer dogs without Arrow and me. Why shouldn't we share the hunting grounds?"

"Because this territory is *ours*," growled Lucky, "and you chose to leave the Pack!"

"Hmph." Bella curled her lip. "The real trouble is, we're better hunters. Isn't that right? Are you scared we'll find the best prey before you get near it?"

Lucky's hackles sprang up. Storm was surprised to see him bare his fangs in a truly threatening snarl. His voice was silky but cold.

"It doesn't matter how many dogs we have," he said. "The

territory belongs to *the Pack*. You and Arrow *will* go and hunt elsewhere. And stay there."

"You're going to drive away your own litter-sister?" With a growl, Bella laid her ears back.

"Don't force my paw, Bella." Lucky didn't drop his eyes from hers. "You're my litter-sister, and I would never want to hurt you or see you go hungry. So *find. Another. Territory.*"

Storm felt sick in her stomach. The two littermates' eyes met in a ferocious glare, and she had no idea what might be about to happen. *I don't want to see them fight. I don't want them to hurt each other.*

In the tense, dangerous stillness, Arrow stepped forward. "Bella. Come with me." He gave Lucky a brief nod. "We should go."

He picked up the weasel, ignoring Bruno's angry growl. Bella hesitated a moment more. Then, with a huff of disgust, she turned and followed her mate toward a curving outcrop of rock.

Before Storm could even bark a farewell, they were gone.

CHAPTER FIFTEEN

The confrontation with Bella and Arrow had stolen some of the Sun-Dog's light from the day, thought Storm unhappily as she padded back toward the camp boundary. The hunt had been so successful, she had dared to hope that life for the Pack might turn out all right, but the hostile encounter had sent her spirits plummeting once more. Beside her, Lucky and Daisy looked no happier than Storm felt, despite their excellent haul of rabbits.

On the outskirts of camp she saw Snap, Bruno, and Moon returning, too, from the direction of Sun-Dog's rising. In their jaws they carried a few mice and weasels, but none of the weasels looked as big or tasty as the one Bella had taken.

All the same, we'll eat tonight, thought Storm. *Look on the bright side. And maybe even Beetle and Thorn managed to find some prey.*

But as the older dogs laid their catches on the prey pile, she heard the sounds of argument nearing the camp. Beetle and Thorn crashed into the clearing, followed by a downcast Breeze. The litter-siblings' growls were high and aggressive, and they were barking over each other in their efforts to get the last snarl.

Unsurprisingly, thought Storm with a sigh, the two novice hunters had not brought home a single kill.

"You were too loud!" snapped Beetle. "You scared off all the prey, stupid!"

"Don't call me stupid!" yelped Thorn in fury. "If you weren't so clumsy, we'd have had that squirrel!"

"The squirrel was long gone because you can't stalk without breaking every twig in the forest!"

"You're the one who slipped on leaves and *missed it*. And I thought you'd learned about gophers. You've got a short memory, that's your trouble!"

"Yeah? Then why can't I ever forget how *annoying* you are?"

Oh, Sky-Dogs, thought Storm in exasperation. *Littermates bicker, I know as well as any dog—but that's for sitting in camp, or arguing over sleeping spots. Not on hunts!* Now the siblings' sniping was actually interfering with the Pack's ability to eat. Storm glanced at Breeze, who looked mortified and fed up. The brown dog rolled her eyes, then hunched her shoulders in apology.

It's really not your fault, Breeze, thought Storm sympathetically. Breeze might be the most responsible of the three by a long way, but a scout dog didn't have the authority to boss around two hunters.

"How did the hunt go?" said a familiar voice.

Storm turned her head to see Twitch padding over, his expression stern. *He can obviously see exactly how the hunt went. . . .*

"It's not my fault, Third Dog!" began Thorn. "If Beetle took the hunt more seriously—"

"Me?" interrupted Beetle with a dangerous growl. "I'm not the one who can't stalk a snail."

"Quiet, both of you!" Twitch's uncharacteristic sharpness silenced both young dogs, and they lowered their ears and tails. "I don't care whose fault it was; you're supposed to be a team. Now, since you haven't brought any prey, you can make yourselves useful in other ways. Beetle, go and see if Omega needs any help. Thorn—" Twitch glanced around in the opposite direction, then nodded. "The camp boundary needs re-marking over there. See to it at once."

Shamefaced, the two dogs slunk off in different directions to their respective tasks. Twitch turned to look at Alpha, who had emerged to stand outside her den, her head tilted and thoughtful.

He said nothing, though. Storm licked her chops. *Now I know why he came up and challenged Thorn and Beetle; it was just to draw Alpha's attention to what happened on the hunt.* Storm had a feeling that Twitch would like to snap *I told you so, Alpha*—but that wasn't the gentle dog's way. He'd shown Alpha the problem; he'd leave her to deal with it.

Well—for now, at least, thought Storm gloomily. *He won't be able to hold his tongue forever. And this is partly Alpha's fault. Beetle and Thorn weren't ready for this responsibility, and every dog knew it.*

With a sigh that was audible even at a distance, Alpha raised her head. "Breeze," she barked softly. "Could you watch the pups for a moment, please?" She turned back to her den. "Lucky, come with me?"

Looking relieved not to be involved anymore with the litter-mates' squabble, Breeze nodded and trotted eagerly toward the den, where the four pups were just emerging. They greeted her with sleepy yaps. Lucky followed them from the den and fell in next to Alpha as she paced purposefully over to Twitch.

"We should go for a walk," Alpha told the Third Dog. "The three of us have things to talk about."

Storm licked her jaws. Surely Alpha wasn't going to repri-mand Twitch, or punish him for insolence? *He stayed loyal to this*

Pack, even when half his closest friends left.

But the swift-dog's expression softened as she approached Twitch and licked his ear. "I owe you an apology, Third Dog. Let's discuss it outside camp."

With a strong sense of relief, Storm watched the three senior dogs pad out of the clearing together. *Thank the Sky-Dogs. We don't need any more confrontation in this Pack.*

Back at the entrance to Alpha and Lucky's den, Breeze was gathering the pups around her, licking their small heads and nudging them gently into position. "Would you like another story, pups?"

Storm's ears pricked up. She would never admit it aloud, but she rather enjoyed Breeze's stories herself. With a twinge of affection she turned and trotted over to the little group, settling down a short distance away so as not to distract the pups.

Not that they'd be distracted by me anyway, she realized with amusement as she laid her head on her forepaws. The four little ones were squirming and fidgeting and yipping with excitement. Tumble batted Fluff into silence, placing his paws firmly on the back of her head and squashing her down. "Go on, Breeze. Tell us a story!"

"Yes," mumbled Fluff with a scowl as she wriggled. "'Story!"

"Please! Please!" chorused Nibble and Tiny.

"Yes, yes," laughed Breeze. "Didn't I say I'd tell you one? Now, settle down." She licked Tumble into submission. "This is a story of the Sun-Dog."

"I love Sun-Dog stories!" yelped Tiny.

"This one is also about a brave young Wind-Dog pup," Breeze told her.

Storm smiled to herself. Breeze hadn't known about the Wind-Dogs till Alpha told her about them, so how could she know the stories? She must just be making these ones up for the pups. *Breeze is so good at stories.*

"What was Wind-Pup's name?" squeaked Nibble.

"His name was . . . Whoosh!" said Breeze, nuzzling her.

"That's a good name for a Wind-Dog," said Nibble approvingly.

"Yes, it is," agreed Breeze fondly. "Because he was a good pup! And a brave one. Whoosh wanted to know where the Sun-Dog went to sleep at night. He was a very curious pup, and he knew he wouldn't rest until he'd seen the Sun-Dog's sleeping-den. So, one evening, as Sun-Dog was yawning and loping down the sky toward his rest, Whoosh crept away from his Pack and followed him."

"That's naughty," pointed out Tiny.

"Yes," said Breeze with a smile. "But he *was* a very curious and brave little pup. So he followed the Sun-Dog over hills and through forests and down into deep valleys. He followed him across a stream and down a rocky cliff, and even when he saw that Sun-Dog was running down behind a lake, he kept running to catch up with him. In fact, Whoosh ran so fast, he ran right across the lake without sinking!"

"Wow," murmured Tumble.

"Did Whoosh's paws get tired?" asked Fluff, wide-eyed.

Storm crept closer, enchanted. *I'm not a pup, but I can still enjoy a story,* she thought. *And it's so much fun to watch the pups' reactions!*

"Oh yes, Fluff!" Breeze was saying now. "Whoosh was very tired, but he was determined to see the Sun-Dog's den—so he kept on running and running across the lake till he reached the other side. The Sun-Dog was just curling up in his sleeping-spot, and he'd turned the sky to red and gold, the way he always does to guide the Moon-Dog. Well! What a surprise he got when he saw a little pup appear at the edge of the world, looking down into his den!"

"Was Sun-Dog angry?" asked Tiny nervously, as Storm came closer still and settled down beside her. Breeze glanced at Storm, her eyes warm.

"He wasn't even a little bit angry," Breeze reassured the anxious pup, nuzzling her ear. "Whoosh was worried he might be angry, of course. But instead, the Sun-Dog was very impressed and pleased that such a little dog had run all that way, and just to see his sleeping-den! 'Always be inquisitive and brave, young dog,' he told Whoosh, 'and you will be a fine member of your Pack!' And Whoosh promised always to be as brave as he was that night, so what do you think the Sun-Dog did?"

Tiny shivered against Storm's flank, but, "We don't know!" squeaked Tumble and Fluff together, breathless with excitement.

"He gave Whoosh a bone"—Breeze turned to point her nose at the edge of the clearing—"and it was the size of that pine trunk!"

"Wow!" barked Tumble, spinning in delight.

"Good story!" yelped Fluff, rising to hop from paw to paw.

"Oh, now, now!" Laughing, Breeze licked their heads to settle them again. "I'm supposed to be calming you down, not getting you all excited."

Storm felt a nudge against her flank and dipped her head to see Tiny snuggling tighter against her. An odd twinge of emotion tugged at her gut, and her heart skipped a little.

It was a nice story, she thought. *I wish I could tell stories like that to the pups.*

Well, she might not be the best pup-sitter in the world—as even Lucky had acknowledged—but that didn't seem to matter to Tiny. *And even my being a Fierce Dog doesn't seem to be an issue. They see me and like me for who I am without worrying about that.*

Storm slipped between forest trees, approaching the edge of the meadow. Night scents were all around her, the shadows deep and dark. This was where Bella had caught the weasel, where Snap and Bruno and Moon had angrily challenged her. Where a lethal fight had almost broken out between former Packmates . . . But it hadn't been night when that happened!

What's going on? This happened already. It wasn't pleasant, but it's over. It was over. . . .

Light from the Moon-Dog silvered the grass of the meadow as she stepped out into it. The glow was eerie and somehow unnatural, and it made the shadows between the pines seem even more impenetrable. She'd thought this horrible place was silent, but now she could hear dreadful sounds: barking and snarling, the sounds of dogs hurling hate at one another.

She crested a low rise, and there they were: two groups of dogs facing each other down, hackles raised, muzzles curled back to show gleaming fangs. They looked as if they would attack one another at any instant. Bella and Arrow were there, just as they had been when their Packmates turned on them. But it wasn't just Snap and Bruno who were lined up to attack them. So were Lucky and Daisy. Storm had never seen the little white dog look so enraged, so full of spite and hatred. Daisy's face was contorted in a snarl of loathing.

Storm was seized by an urge to fling herself between the dogs, to drag them apart by their scruffs if she had to. But before she could make a move, the earth shuddered beneath her paws. She staggered, trying to keep steady, but with a dreadful ripping noise that hurt her ears, the ground beneath her split and parted. With a yelp of terror, Storm jumped back in time to see a great fissure open in the earth. The crack raced between the dogs, separating them with the speed of Lightning, opening bottomless chasms between each of them.

The furious dogs seemed not to have noticed that they were now separated. They carried on barking and snarling at one another across the fissures.

Storm leaped back from a new crack as it appeared between her paws. What was wrong with those foolish dogs? Why wouldn't they see, why wouldn't they listen? She tried to bark a warning at the top of her lungs, but they couldn't hear her: her howls were drowned out by the roaring and crashing of the Earth-Dog as their world tore itself apart.

Black shadows flowed up from the chasms, spilling out like a river in flood. As Storm watched, horrified, liquid darkness engulfed the oblivious dogs, swallowing them up.

Storm's helpless terror was like cold teeth in her heart. All she could do was *back away slowly, then much faster, until at last she turned, her tail between her legs, and fled. . . .*

Storm jerked awake. She was still running from the terror of the dream, and for an instant she reeled, staggering, looking desperately for the cracks beneath her. Instead, there was solid ground beneath her paws. Trees stretched above her head. She was in the forest. At last the thrashing of her heart calmed, and she could breathe again. Storm let her tongue hang from her jaws, panting for air.

I've done it again. I've walked in my sleep.

She'd been so sure this trouble was over. For a moment, crushing disappointment swamped even the lingering horror of the nightmare. *And I don't even know where I am! I don't know these woods.*

Lifting her muzzle to snuff at the air, trying to calm herself, Storm closed her eyes. *How far could I have walked?* A faint trace of something familiar touched her nostrils like fine rain: something salty and pungent.

The Endless Lake . . . I can smell it. If I go toward it, and find the shoreline, I can find my way home.

She took a few tentative paces, her muscles still shivering. The shadows around her were ordinary shadows, she told herself. They weren't going to flood out from every gap and hollow and eat her alive. *This is the right direction. I'll find the Lake, find the beach, make my way back to the clearing. . . .*

The voices of dogs made her jump. Her heart raced back into a pulsing throb, and she swallowed hard. *Who's that?*

It took Storm only a moment more to recognize the soft growls. *Bella and Arrow!* They spoke quietly to each other, but in the still air they were perfectly identifiable. *I'm right beside the old Fierce Dog cave! I walked a long way in my sleep. . . .*

Creeping through the undergrowth, Storm nervously approached the cavern mouth. She could make out their shapes now: Bella and Arrow lying close together, their flanks touching, their faces upturned to the starry sky. As Storm watched, Arrow gave a great contented sigh and lowered his muzzle to rest on Bella's shoulder.

Storm's sleepwalking panic, and her instinctive fear of the Fierce Dog cave, were overcome for a moment by embarrassment. She felt suddenly that she'd intruded on a private, peaceful moment, and she cleared her throat. But Bella's ears pricked up in delight, and she rose to trot over and greet Storm.

"Storm! It's so good to see you." The golden dog licked her jaw happily. "Welcome!"

Storm could only nod. Bella's delighted greeting had tilted her a little off-balance. Why was Bella so pleased to see her in the middle of the night?

"Have you left the Pack? Have you come to join us?" Bella's tongue lolled in a cheerful smile, and Storm was so taken aback she couldn't protest. "Arrow had a feeling you might come with us. I wasn't sure, but I'm so happy he was right!"

"Bella, I—"

"You're the perfect dog to have with us," enthused Bella, giving her no time to interrupt. "You'll help our Pack to thrive. It's funny, but maybe it's because of the relationship you had with Lucky—I've always felt you were my younger litter-sister, in a way! This feels so natural, doesn't it? You belong with us!"

At last Bella had stopped talking and was gazing at Storm with an open, questioning expression. Storm licked her jaws.

I actually wish I could tell her she's right. I wish I really was joining them.

After all, would it be such a bad idea? Of all the dogs she knew, Bella and Arrow were the two she was most certain of. Neither of them, she was sure, had had anything to do with Whisper's death, or with the other chilling acts of sabotage against the Pack. She could trust both of these dogs with her life. And unlike the rest of her Pack, Bella and Arrow seemed to trust her without question.

But...

A muscle in her flank quivered as she remembered little Tiny snuggled up against her, trusting and secure. How could she abandon the pups, just when she'd realized how much she adored them? They needed their Pack to protect them. How could she take away yet another dog from it?

I simply couldn't do this. Deep down, I know I can't betray my Pack.

"Bella, I . . ." She cleared her throat again and glanced from Bella to Arrow. "I'm sorry, I haven't come to join you. I came here—well, it was an accident. I came by mistake."

Bella's brow furrowed. "How—I mean, how could you come by accident, Storm?" Behind her, Arrow got to his paws and regarded Storm with his head curiously tilted.

"I just . . . well, I couldn't sleep, and I went for a walk," Storm gabbled. "And I walked a bit far. And I got lost. And I ended up here." She blinked. "That's sort of how it happened. I'm sorry."

"That makes no sense, Storm." Arrow narrowed his eyes to study her. "A dog with your eyes and nose? You don't get lost! You couldn't if you tried."

"There's a first time for everything . . ." Storm began lamely.

Arrow shook his head, looking a little amused. "No, Storm,

you couldn't. So why did you really come here, if not to join us?"

Storm lowered her eyes, licking her jaws. Her tail flicked nervously. *What was I just telling myself, only a moment ago? That I trust these dogs. That I could rely on them for anything. Bella and Arrow have always believed in me. So why am I hesitating now? Maybe it's time to prove I really do trust them. Even if they're not my Packmates anymore . . .*

She lifted her head, clenching her jaw against her nerves. "All right. I'll tell you the truth. I . . . I walk in my sleep."

"You do what?" Arrow's ears pricked forward in surprise.

"It's true. I've been doing it for a while. I can't help it." A soft whine escaped her throat. "I'll just wake up and find myself far from camp. And I never have any memory of how it happened."

"Oh, Storm!" Bella's soft eyes were full of sympathy and shock.

"Please," Storm said desperately, "don't tell the others? If you see them, I mean. Not even Lucky!"

"They don't *know*?" Arrow looked startled.

"No! I can't tell them. Don't you understand?" Storm gave them each a pleading look. "If the Pack knew about this—if they ever suspect that I do things, go places that I have no memory of— they might think I'm the bad dog. They might think I'm crazy, or—or just that I do terrible things without meaning to. I *know* now that I didn't kill Whisper—I thought for a while that I might have, but I don't anymore; I'm sure I didn't—but what if the Pack thinks I did?"

"Storm!" Bella darted forward to press her head against Storm's. "Of course you did no such thing!"

Storm felt Arrow's warm tongue lash her ear. "Bella's right— there's no way you could do that. We know you, and we know you never would have done anything to hurt your Packmates!"

For a long moment, Storm closed her eyes and let them comfort her. Deep inside her chest she felt a stirring warmth. *They trust me. They believe me. It's so good to tell the truth ... and still be trusted and loved. I never even thought that was possible.*

"Thank you," she managed to croak at last, and the two dogs stepped back with a parting nuzzle. "That means a lot. Thanks."

"If you don't want the Pack to know," murmured Arrow with a glance at the horizon, "then you'd better be getting back. It's been wonderful to see you, Storm, but I think your instincts are right. It's best if the Pack doesn't know you were gone tonight."

Bella nodded. "Arrow's right. Why don't I walk back with you as far as the outskirts of your territory, Storm?"

Storm licked her gratefully. "I'd like that. Thank you."

Bella turned back to nuzzle Arrow. "I'll be back soon, my love."

"I know. Take care." Gently he licked her jaw.

Storm turned away, a little embarrassed, and waited for Bella to join her. *I'm fond of them both, but I still don't know how two big strong dogs can be so wet-eared about being apart for a few moments. . . .*

Storm soon forgot her awkwardness as Bella walked beside her toward the camp. This felt so natural, she realized. Whether she was still a Packmate or not, Bella was her friend, and it was good to be in her company; they didn't even have to talk. And the same was true of Arrow. When at last they reached the Pack's first scent-mark, Bella halted.

"I should turn back here. Good-bye, Storm."

"I'll see you both again soon, I hope." Storm butted her neck.

"I hope so. And remember: you'd always be welcome with me and Arrow. It's a very little Pack, I know, but we'd be so happy to have you, especially now that . . ." Her voice trailed off.

"Especially now?" Storm cocked her head.

Bella shook herself. "It doesn't matter. You should get back to your own Pack, Storm. But don't forget what I said!"

"I won't, I promise." With a final lick and a wag of her tail, Storm turned away from Bella and headed back to the camp, picking up her pace.

It was curious, though, Storm thought as she threaded her

way stealthily through the trees toward the hunters' den. Bella had been so welcoming, and so friendly, but something about her behavior had been odd. She'd seemed preoccupied. . . .

But happy, Storm thought. *And that's what matters most. Whatever else is happening, and however difficult it is for them, at least I know Bella and Arrow are happy.*

But I would like to know what mysterious thing is going on. . . .

CHAPTER SIXTEEN

A breeze blew steadily over the headland, bending the stiff sea grass, but the Sun-Dog's rays were warm enough to keep any chill at bay. Half closing her eyes, Storm reveled in the sensation of the warm air ruffling her fur. It wasn't so bad taking her turn on High Watch, especially when she could free up one of the others to patrol the territory boundaries. Even though she was a little bored, she was content. She could gaze out over the Endless Lake, which was dark blue and flecked with whitecaps, and enjoy the vast view without much disturbance.

It was a beautiful place to be, but Storm knew that any threats to the Pack would probably not come from this direction. They would be more likely to come from the forests and hills on the other side of the clearing.

Unless danger comes from within the camp itself...

She didn't want to dwell on that. Scanning the landscape below, Storm watched small dots of tan and gold, white and gray, moving away from camp: *the hunting patrol,* she guessed. By the look of them, she reckoned that was Alpha and Lucky, and she rather envied them. High Watch might be a pleasure in this weather, but she'd still rather hunt, Storm decided: her paws itched to run and chase down some prey. *Moon never gets bored when she's patrolling. Nor do the other Patrol Dogs. But I can't help it.*

A white lake bird flapped down to the edge of the cliff, and Storm made a pounce for it, but it evaded her easily and took off with leisurely wing beats. It wasn't the first bird she'd tried to catch, she thought with a sigh, and it wouldn't be the last; there was nothing else to do up here. Blinking and yawning, Storm surveyed the horizon again.

Something caught her eye, moving across the surface of the Endless Lake. Stiffening, Storm narrowed her eyes. It was drawing closer to the shore . . . another floatcage.

She watched as it came slowly closer. *Is it going to come right up onto the beach? Can floatcages run on land, the way loudcages do? I wish I could ask Lucky.* What if the longpaws that rode it could dismount and come up onto the land? What might they do? The Pack's camp was so close to the shore. . . .

Should I howl for help? Should I run and get Alpha or one of the others? In an agony of indecision, Storm licked her chops and stared at the floatcage. It didn't seem to be moving any closer; it had paused on the lake surface, and now she could make out the longpaws on its back. They were throwing their trap-meshes into the water again. Storm breathed out a sigh of relief. It seemed the longpaws were simply hunting for fish, and that they weren't interested in exploring the shore. *I'll report to Alpha later, then. There's no emergency.*

In fact, it was almost relaxing to watch the floatcage, now that she wasn't afraid of it. It was close enough that she could see its motion as it rocked gently on the lake waves, and there was something fascinating about the repetitive work of its longpaws as they threw the trap-meshes and retrieved them. Storm had begun to feel almost drowsy when a shrieking, deafening sound rose up from somewhere near the camp below.

Shocked out of her reverie, Storm tensed and sprang toward the cliff path. She could still hear the echo of that awful sound in her ears, like a dog howling in pain and fear. But it wasn't a normal voice; there was something chilling about it, something that sent shivers through her bones so that she almost tripped as she ran. *Some dog's in real trouble!* Her hide prickling horribly, Storm didn't think twice about abandoning High Watch and dashing down the steep path.

The noise had stopped by the time she thundered into the camp. *What happened? What happened to that dog? What silenced it?*

She skidded to a halt, sending up a spray of dry leaves, panting desperately. *No!*

There was blood everywhere. Across the grass, spattered on the boundary bushes, spilled at the den entrances. A great splash of it had been flung across the stump in the center of the clearing, and even the pine trunks bore deep red stains.

Panic clutched at Storm's heart. Raising her head, she let out a soaring howl of distress.

Daisy came scrambling out of her den, racing up to Storm on her little legs. Beetle appeared too, barking in alarm. Seeing them alive made Storm tremble with relief, but where were the others?

"What's wrong?" barked Daisy, her eyes wide. She stared around at the blood. "Oh. Oh, Sky-Dogs!"

Beetle was panting. "I was supposed to be on guard," he stammered, "but it . . . the Sun-Dog was warming me and . . . oh no! I dozed off. Oh, Storm! What happened here?"

"I don't know!" Storm's throat was constricted, her voice hoarse. "I heard an awful sound from up on High Watch—some dog in trouble. Who was it?"

"I don't know. I heard it, and I was too scared and surprised to move until I heard you howl," whined Daisy. "We've got to find out!"

She, Storm, and Beetle darted to every corner of the clearing, snuffling and scenting, hunting through the undergrowth. Storm's heart was thrashing in her rib cage. *What happened and who did it happen to? Please, please, Sky-Dogs, don't let it be something as terrible as Whisper's murder. . . .*

But as the three dogs gathered again in the center of the clearing beside the bloodstained stump, their ears and tails were drooping.

"I don't understand," whined Beetle. "There's nothing."

"Where did the blood come from?" Storm shook herself. A hideous thought froze her muscles for a moment. *The pups!*

Almost unable to breathe with fear, she bolted for Alpha's den. She was at the entrance when a dog emerged and collided with her.

"Breeze!" Storm recovered, trembling.

"What's going on?" Breeze demanded. "What's all this racket? You know the pups are sleeping!"

Shoving past the brown dog, Storm barged into the den. In a corner, piled together, were all four pups, their little flanks rising and falling. But they weren't asleep now; they huddled together wide-eyed and terrified, staring at Storm.

"Storm?" squeaked Nibble, her eyes huge.

"It's all right." Storm's voice was shaky. "Don't worry, pups, it was just a loud noise. Nothing's wrong." She wasn't sure it was true, but what else could she tell the pups? "Go back to sleep now, all right? Don't come out just yet."

"Why, Storm?" demanded Fluff.

"Never mind. Just, er . . . stay here. Where it's quiet. And you can sleep. Breeze is right here, and so am I."

Weak with relief, Storm backed awkwardly out of the den once more. She expected Breeze to snap her nose off about waking the pups, but instead the brown dog was staring open-jawed around the blood-spattered camp.

"Storm, what happened?" she whispered. "Where are the others? Who's been hurt?"

Storm shook herself helplessly as Beetle and Daisy whimpered with nerves. "I don't know, Breeze. I don't know! I came down from High Watch and found it like this."

With a crash of bracken and a loud rustle of brush, more dogs raced into camp. Snap and Bruno slithered to a halt, staring. Mickey and Moon looked at each other, then at the blood. Alpha bounded into the clearing, Lucky at her heels.

"What's wrong?" demanded Alpha. "We heard a terrible sound." She glanced around, her dark eyes taking in the gory scene, and then sprinted for the den, Lucky close behind.

"It's all right," barked Breeze. "Don't worry, they're safe!" But Alpha and Lucky took no notice, disappearing into their den.

"Storm!" Snap came close to inspect Storm for wounds, her face full of concern. "What in the name of the Forest-Dog is going on?"

"And where did all this blood come from?" Moon's hackles were erect, and she loped over to stand protectively beside Beetle.

"We don't know!" Storm told her, despairingly. "And we don't know who howled, either. I was up at High Watch!"

"Where's Thorn?" demanded Moon suddenly.

Silence fell at once, and the dogs looked at one another, then turned to stare at every corner of the camp.

"And Twitch," pointed out Bruno. "He's not here either. And neither is Sunshine."

It was true, Storm realized with horror. The little Omega was nowhere to be seen. "Where are they?"

Moon's voice was trembling. "Thorn and Twitch were hunting together. But why didn't they come back when they heard the noise?"

"I don't know where Sunshine is," added Breeze.

Alpha emerged from her den, and every dog turned toward her, their eyes pleading. She gazed around at them all, worried and solemn.

"All of you—we have to find the missing dogs. My pups are fine, but if any dog has been hurt, we have to help them immediately." She gazed beyond them all, at the awful bloodstains spattered around the camp, and she swallowed hard. "And we have to discover who did this!"

"Wait." Storm's heart was calmer now, and her breathing had almost returned to normal. She could think again. Padding across to one of the biggest pools of blood, she sniffed delicately at it. She furrowed her brow.

"This isn't a dog's blood," she told them, lifting her head. "It's from a rabbit!"

"Are you sure?" Daisy's voice was high-pitched with fear.

"I'm sure, Daisy." Storm nodded at the blood. "This is a horrible sight, but it didn't come from a dog." She felt light-headed with relief.

Mickey frowned. "Can you rely on your senses right now, Storm? We're all shocked. . . ." But he walked to her side and bent his muzzle to the blood, and Bruno and Chase joined him.

They've got a point, thought Storm. *But I'm pretty sure it's rabbit—I've caught enough of them.* Patiently, and feeling far calmer, she waited for their verdict.

Bruno lifted his head. "It's rabbit, all right. Thank the Sky-Dogs."

Moon closed her eyes in gratitude. "But who could have done this? Killing a rabbit—or even three!—wouldn't make this mess."

"Some dog did this deliberately," growled Storm. "Look at it. It's as if a rabbit's been killed and then dragged all over the camp, to leave as many bloodstains as possible."

"That's crazy," muttered Chase.

Daisy whined miserably. "Why would any dog do such a thing?"

"It does seem crazy," Storm agreed, blinking at Chase. "But I think I know why it was done. There's only one reason it *could* have been done. To scare us."

"What?" said Bruno. "But why?"

"I don't know." Storm shook her head. "But everything that's happened to this Pack lately—the broken clear-stone in my bedding and in the deer, the poisoned prey in the pile—it can only have been done to fill the Pack with terror, make us distrust and fear each other."

Even Whisper's death, she thought grimly. But she wouldn't mention that, not when so many of her Packmates still insisted foxes had killed him. *It's all connected, I'm sure of it.*

"But that doesn't answer the important question," pointed out Daisy in a shaky voice. They all glanced toward her, and she sat down. When she spoke again, her voice was calmer, level and cool.

"Who would even want to scare us? Who would do such a thing?"

CHAPTER SEVENTEEN

Snap gave a whimper of distress, and Moon was trembling with anxiety as Beetle tried to comfort her. All the dogs looked shaken to their core, thought Storm: and no wonder. *Well, I'm not going to play this dog's game. I'm not scared; I'm angry!*

"I'm not going to do what this enemy wants," she snarled into the silence. "This might have been frightening, but that doesn't mean I have to be frightened, and neither should any of us." She decided not to voice her next thought: *If there's an advantage to being a Fierce Dog, surely this is it!*

"I agree," said Alpha firmly. "This blood looks bad, but we know it isn't dog blood. We all need to stay calm."

"But what about the missing dogs?" barked Daisy. "What will we do?"

"Look!" Chase gave a yelp of relief as she pointed with her snout. "It's Omega!"

Storm whirled round to see the little white dog approaching the camp through the trees. "Sunshine!" She was dizzy with relief. "You're all right!"

There were growls and murmurs of delight from the other dogs as Alpha padded forward. Sunshine grunted a muffled greeting through a mouthful of fur; Storm saw that she was dragging a piece of prey almost as big as she was.

But it didn't look fresh. As Sunshine dropped it, shivering, Storm took a step closer. The creature was limp and sodden, and so badly torn it was almost unidentifiable. Even its long ears had been ripped away. If it hadn't been for its lingering, slightly rotten scent, Storm wouldn't have been able to tell it was a rabbit.

"What's this—" began Alpha, but Sunshine didn't seem to hear her leader. She was staring around the camp, her little jaws open in horror. She let out a high howl of misery.

"What happened?" she wailed. "How did the camp get into such a mess? Is that . . . is that *blood*?"

She scampered under Storm's belly and crouched there, shivering. Storm twisted and lowered her head to offer her a reassuring lick. "It's all right, Sunshine. No dog has been hurt."

Lucky blinked gratefully at Storm, then padded carefully over with Alpha to examine the soaked and mutilated rabbit. "What's this, Omega?" he asked gently as Alpha sniffed it with disgust. "Where did you find it?"

"I . . . I . . ." Sunshine gulped; Storm could feel that she was still trembling. "I found it in the pond," she managed finally, in a tiny voice. "It was just floating there. It hadn't been there long, I'm sure it hasn't poisoned the water—but . . . I thought I should get it out. And bring it. To show you."

"That was good, Sunshine," Lucky told her. "Well done for getting it out of the water as soon as you saw it."

"It must be the rabbit that was used to do this to the camp." Storm pricked her ears at the mess in the clearing. "See, Sunshine? It's not a dog's blood. We think some dog dragged a dead rabbit around, to stain everything and frighten the Pack."

"But . . . . *why?*" Sunshine was shaking even more.

"We don't know, but you see?" Storm bent down and cocked her head at Sunshine. "It's nothing to be scared of. It's just the blood of a dead rabbit!"

Sunshine gave a sound that was something between a moan and a squeak of helpless terror. Beneath Storm's belly she swayed, dizzily, and before Storm could grab her scruff, she thudded over onto her side, paws quivering. Storm stepped quickly away and turned to nudge her gently with her nose.

"Is she all right?" asked Daisy in alarm.

Storm growled anxiously, then licked Sunshine's flank with relief as the little dog blinked and struggled to get back on her paws. "Yes. She just fainted, I guess."

Lucky was sniffing at the wet rabbit corpse, his teeth slightly bared and his muzzle wrinkled. "I think I know why this was thrown in the pond," he said darkly. "I can't smell any dog on it now. The scent must have been washed off it."

Storm lowered her ears in disappointment, but she wasn't surprised. "So it was deliberate. It's obvious this enemy's clever and cunning."

"Yes," agreed Alpha, narrowing her eyes. "This dog, whoever it is, managed to sneak into our camp without our Pack seeing or hearing or smelling a thing." She raised her head, looking angry and determined, but calm. "Some dog here may have seen something, even if they didn't realize it. Some dog here may have done this. Every dog, think hard about what you saw and smelled today. About anything odd or out of place you might not have noticed at the time."

"We all heard that horrible howling," said Storm. "But I didn't hear or see anything else."

"I might've heard a noise this morning!" barked Beetle.

"Wouldn't that have been before anything happened?" yapped Daisy.

"There was an odd shadow, though," added Bruno, drawing himself up. "I saw it just as I came out of my den."

"I might have heard cracking and rustling," said Breeze, "though the pups are noisy sometimes."

"I didn't see anything," barked Mickey. "I'm sure I didn't."

"Me neither," agreed Daisy. "Nothing odd happened today."

"Something did!" argued Beetle, and Bruno barked in support. "And I'm sure there was a lot of barking before we saw the blood."

"Of course there was," snapped Mickey irritably. "We all heard Storm raising the alarm!"

"Enough!" Alpha's deep, echoing bark silenced them all. "Be quiet, all of you! All this barking and yelping won't get us anywhere. I want you all to calm down and think carefully about where you were, and what you saw—especially which dogs you saw, and when. Once you've collected your thoughts, I want every dog to come to my den, one by one. Lucky and I can talk to you there

in peace, and try to figure out together what happened here."

"Shouldn't some dog go find Twitch and Thorn?" Daisy asked.

"No," Alpha said firmly. "I want us all to stay together for now. I'm sure Twitch and Thorn will be here soon."

The dogs, sharing glances, wagged their tails uncertainly. "That makes sense," growled Mickey at last. "All right, Alpha. We can do that. Right, everyone?"

"Absolutely," agreed Bruno, as the others began to sit and lie on the grass, looking as if they were already thinking.

"But don't any dog relax yet," warned Alpha, and they all scrambled back to their paws. "This camp is in chaos, and it's not fair to expect Omega to clean it all up. Work as a team and do what you can to clean the blood away. Now, Mickey: you're the calmest dog here. You come to the den first."

The Pack split up at once to hurry to the worst of the drying blood, clearly eager to obey their Alpha's stern command. Storm headed for the stump, where she began to lick at the dark stain. *This was never going to be a pleasant job,* she thought dismally as her tongue rasped across the surface, *but it's surprising just how nasty it is.* For once, rabbit didn't taste enticing at all. Maybe it was the circumstances, but the blood was sharp and sour on her tongue. Storm stepped back, shook herself, and then set to work again.

Around her she could see her Packmates working on their own spots, and they all seemed to be having the same reaction. Snap's face was twisted in disgust, and Bruno's muzzle was set in a silent snarl as he licked at a patch of dark grass. They weren't making much impact on the mess, either, Storm realized: it was a harder job than it had seemed, especially where the drying blood had seeped into cracks or soaked into the soil.

A little white shape appeared at her side. Sunshine had recovered herself and had the sense to gather a bunch of wet moss. Holding it in her jaws, she scrubbed diligently at the blood. It was more effective than licking, and must also have tasted a bit better, but it still didn't make a big difference.

Mickey emerged from Alpha's den and barked to Bruno. The big dog looked relieved as he stopped what he was doing and trotted to the den to give his own story, while Mickey joined the cleaning party. When Bruno came out again, it was Snap's turn, and then Sunshine's. One by one, each dog trooped into the leaders' den to tell their tales.

Storm licked disconsolately at her claws. Much of the spilled blood was still wet, but it was sticky and clotting, and it wasn't pleasant to have it on your paws. Storm sighed. Whoever had done this had caused all kinds of problems besides fear. The Pack had more than enough to worry about without wasting a day on this horrible work. Every dog looked dejected and tired. Moon and Beetle were especially silent, and, Storm thought, looked as if worry were gnawing a hole in their insides.

Storm glanced up as Snap gave a sharp, encouraging bark. The hunt-dog had paused and was looking around them all, bright-eyed.

"We mustn't let this get to us," she declared. "This was done deliberately, to get into our heads and disturb us. So let's not let that happen! No dog was hurt, after all."

"But the mess . . ." began Sunshine querulously. "Our beautiful camp . . ."

"It'll all wash away in the next rainstorm," said Snap. "Don't you worry, Omega. We might have to live with it for a bit, but the Sky-Dogs and the Earth-Dog will take care of it eventually."

Sunshine brightened. "That's true."

"Snap has a good point," agreed Mickey. "We won't let this drag the Pack down."

"Right!" said Chase. She got back to her work on a pine trunk with more enthusiasm.

"I wish I had seen something useful, though," murmured Bruno. "There was nothing I could really tell Alpha after all."

"I know," sighed Breeze. "All the shadows and noise: they were just normal forest shapes and sounds, when I thought about it more."

The dogs returned to their cleaning projects, but now they seemed more relaxed, Storm was glad to see, and more cheerful. In small groups they were discussing what they'd told Alpha— which didn't seem to be much, sadly, but at least the atmosphere was more positive now. *There's a real sense that we're in this together, that we're going to deal with it.*

"Thorn!" Moon's delighted yelp made all the dogs stop what they were doing and look up. Sure enough, Thorn was trotting into the clearing with Twitch. They both paused to stare around in disbelief, just as their Packmates had done. Moon and Beetle bounded up to greet Thorn, covering her muzzle in welcoming licks, as Twitch limped slowly around the glade.

"What in the name of the Earth-Dog?" he muttered.

Snap butted his head gently, clearly delighted to see her old friend. "We're all safe, that's what matters. I'll tell you everything." She and Twitch settled at one side of the camp.

"Yes," yelped Moon happily, nuzzling Thorn's neck. "We're so glad to see you—both of you. Now we know every dog is safe, and we can get back to clearing up the camp."

"Yes." Thorn was still staring at the mess, her eyes wide. "You'd better tell me what happened while we work, Beetle."

At least the Pack was all calmer now, Storm thought, and they could tell the strange story without hysterical yaps. Idly she listened to Thorn's gasps of disbelief as her litter-brother explained what they'd found on their return from patrol. At last, Storm realized she'd done as much as she could with the stump. Moving on to a clotted puddle of blood beside the hunters' den, she passed closer to the two litter-siblings.

"It's my fault, that's the thing," she heard Beetle say softly. He sounded miserable and guilty. "I was supposed to be on guard, Thorn. I should have seen what happened—but it was a warm day. I fell asleep. I'll never forgive myself."

"It's not your fault, Beetle." Storm stopped to give him a reassuring lick.

"It is. I was meant to be watching, Storm, but I didn't see or hear a thing, not till that awful scream. And then you came running back, and so did the others."

"No other dog saw anything either," Thorn pointed out. "Not even the ones who were on the scene straightaway."

"But at least they were doing other useful things," said Beetle miserably. "Some of them were patrolling and some were hunting, like you and Twitch."

"Really, Beetle, try not to worry." Storm bumped his jaw with her nose. "The dog who did this was very cunning. I've no doubt they would have waited till they could be absolutely sure of being unseen."

"Storm!"

She turned her head at Lucky's summons, then trotted over to Alpha's den. The scents inside were a mishmash of all the Pack dogs, with a distinct tang of nervousness that lingered in the nostrils. *I wonder if Alpha's discovered a single useful clue?*

"You were alone, Storm?" Alpha studied her face as she entered. "I believe you were up on High Watch by yourself?"

Storm inclined her head. "Yes, Alpha. I ran straight down, as soon as I heard the strange howl."

"And there were no other dogs here when you arrived in the camp?" Alpha twitched a curious ear.

"That's right. Well," Storm added, "there were dogs here. But Breeze was napping with the pups, and Daisy was sleeping in her den, and Beetle was outside the camp. I was the first to find the blood."

With a deep sigh, Alpha closed her eyes. "The fact is, no dog can prove where they were when this happened. Every dog was off alone, or in twos and threes, and not one Pack member saw any other dog in the camp. You were the first dog they all saw."

Storm's ears pricked up in alarm, and she felt her heart turn over. "What are you saying, Alpha? Are they blaming me? But I was the one who howled for help!"

"No, Storm, no!" Alpha assured her quickly. "No dog thinks you were responsible—at least, not many of them. And whatever they thought, I would never believe it was you who did this."

Storm breathed out once more, trying to calm her heart. *Alpha believes me, and that's what matters. Even if some of the Pack think I'm to blame.*

"The trouble is," said Lucky, "nothing we've heard today has helped. We don't have any idea yet who could have done this. The culprit was quiet, obviously, and very, very sneaky—and any dog could have taken an opportunity and crept back into camp."

"It's true," agreed Alpha glumly. "We're no further along than when we started."

"There's something else." Lucky scratched his ear with a hind-paw. "It might not have been a dog who is still in the Pack. The dogs who have left—well, their scents are still all over the camp. Between their old scents and the reek of that dead rabbit, we wouldn't know if one of them had snuck back in." He gave Storm a long look. "But Alpha's right. We certainly don't suspect you, Storm."

"But we did want you to be fully aware of what's going on," said Alpha. "The fact is, you're most in danger of being accused. That's not fair, but it's the way things are. We don't suspect you—but without more evidence, we can't prove your innocence to the rest of the Pack."

Storm's heart sank, and she felt a twinge of terrible sadness in her belly. "Thank you, Alpha, and Beta. I appreciate it." *But it's awful to know other dogs believe I'm guilty. It feels . . . bitter, and so disappointing, too. Don't they know me yet?*

More dejected than she'd been before, Storm squeezed out of the den and blinked in the sunlight. The Pack was all together in the center of the clearing, deep in argument. Storm padded closer, cocking an ear to listen.

". . . and that's what I told Alpha," Bruno was growling. "So you see, there's no way I could have made this mess."

"Well, it certainly has nothing to do with me," declared Snap. "And I think we can all agree Daisy can't have been responsible, either."

"Or Beetle, or Thorn," snapped Moon.

"Though they *were* separated," growled Snap, half under her breath.

Moon had taken a breath to bark in anger, but Daisy interrupted. "Did it have to be a dog at all? Foxes could have gotten into the camp. Or coyotes!"

"I'd have smelled *that!*" yelped Beetle indignantly.

"Beetle's right. There's no scent of foxes or coyotes," growled Chase. "That's the one thing we can be sure of."

"Yes, don't be silly, Daisy!" snapped Moon. "Storm was right all along—this was a dog's doing."

"Yes, obviously," said Mickey—but he shot Moon a look of rebuke and moved protectively closer to Daisy. "Whoever it is, they have to be stopped before some other dog gets hurt."

At least they all believe me this time, thought Storm sadly. *But I wish I was wrong, to be honest. They all agree a dog is to blame—but what will that do to the Pack?* The cleaning work had turned them back into a team for a while—but now morale seemed to have plummeted once again, and dogs were growing snappy and bad-tempered. *Soon loyalties might start to break down altogether....*

"We mustn't let the traitor get to us," Storm declared, easing her way through the throng of dogs. "That would mean they'd won. We have to stay united!"

"I agree," said Breeze, blinking her dark eyes. "Especially since it's quite likely it wasn't one of *us*. It's much more likely to have been one of the dogs who left, isn't it? Bella and Arrow weren't happy about being driven away like that. Or—I hate to say it, but it could even have been one of *my* old Pack. The ones who left us—Rake, maybe, or Ruff."

"I still don't believe that," said Bruno stubbornly. "I'm sure there would be stronger scents of them around, if they'd been here so recently."

"I agree," put in Beetle. "I'd have *smelled them*."

"And I feel guilty about accusing Arrow," muttered Snap. "Right now it looks like he's one of the few dogs who's definitely innocent!"

"But then it must have been one of us," said Daisy with a doleful whine.

"Well, Storm was the first dog to get here." Bruno pricked his ears at Storm, and her insides shrank with dread.

"Yes," growled Mickey, "but that means nothing. No dog has proof of their innocence."

"I agree," said Moon firmly. "Storm's under no more suspicion than any of us." Storm breathed more calmly: at least Mickey and Moon still believed in her.

"Beetle would have had the opportunity, because he was on guard," pointed out Snap. Seeing the look in Moon's eye, she added hurriedly, "And Daisy was here too, and Breeze."

"Breeze was with the pups, though," said Storm, as Breeze gave her a grateful growl, "and they'd have woken up and started whimpering if she'd left them alone for long. Knowing them," she added drily, "they might even have wandered off." Breeze chuckled in agreement.

"And I'm sure it wasn't Storm," announced Beetle defiantly. "As far as I could make out, the howl came from *outside* the camp— I'd say near the pond, if I had to guess, and that's where the rabbit was found. Storm was far away from there, on the cliff side of the camp."

Storm reached across to give him a nudge of thanks. But his words had woken the memory of that awful howl, and she couldn't suppress a shiver.

We're all sure it was a dog, she thought. *But that awful cry didn't sound like a dog at all.*

At least, she realized with a chill of dread, *not like a sane dog. . . .*

CHAPTER EIGHTEEN

The clearing felt almost eerily calm, given the horrors of the day. The breeze had died down, and the air was still, scented with the leaves and earth of the forest—and with the lingering tang of blood. The Sun-Dog sent rays of hazy red light through the tree trunks, though he was low in the sky and close to his night's rest. *Even the colors of the Sun-Dog are making me think of blood tonight,* thought Storm unhappily.

Except for the small patrol out hunting, the Pack had settled down in their familiar places, trying to relax and get some rest after the anxious hours of the day. For all the argument and discussion, they were no closer to identifying the saboteur. Storm sighed through a mouthful of fresh leaves, and Sunshine gave her a worried glance.

"Are you all right, Storm? If you're tired, I can do this myself. You don't have to help, really you don't. . . ."

Storm shook herself briskly. "No, Sunshine, of course I want to help. That's one of the reasons I offered—it takes my mind off things." She ducked her head to nudge the little Omega with her nose.

In a way I wish I was out hunting with the patrol. But Alpha was right to send the dogs who are most upset and distressed. A good run will help them feel better.

And she was glad she had offered to help Sunshine. This might not be a hunter's work, but it was worthwhile all the same—and she'd felt so sorry for the little white dog, who was still visibly shaken by the sabotage of the camp. Even now, her fluffy tail drooped and her fur trembled.

"Storm." Lucky approached at a brisk pace, and for a moment Storm thought he was going to scold her for helping with Omega work. But he nuzzled Sunshine fondly, showing no sign of annoyance, and then turned and spoke to Storm in a low, conspiratorial voice.

"I think we should go out for a hunt."

"Right now?" Storm blinked.

"Yes. It's good to spend time with friends." Lucky was looking very intently into her eyes, and Storm had to bite back a bark of understanding.

"Ah—yes. Yes, we should go, then." She set down the leaves. "Will you be all right, Sunshine?"

"Of course I will," said the little Omega cheerfully. "It was kind of you to help, Storm. Have a good hunt!"

Storm didn't feel guilty about leaving Sunshine with the bedding work, but she did feel a little bad about misleading her. It wasn't a hunt Lucky wanted at all, she knew. He wanted to visit his litter-sister again. But perhaps it was better for Sunshine not to know the truth, Storm thought as she followed Lucky out of the clearing. The little dog didn't need even more anxieties piled on her existing ones.

"You don't think . . ." Hesitating as she followed her Beta through the trees, Storm licked her jaws. "Lucky, you don't think Bella and Arrow could have been responsible for the mess in the camp?"

"No, of course not." There was such absolute certainty in his voice, Storm felt immediately reassured. She hadn't thought so either, of course—but it was good to know Lucky harbored no suspicions.

"I'm glad," she told him, letting her tongue loll. The free air out here tasted so good, untainted by the blood and treachery that had infected the camp.

"It's possible, though, that they heard or saw something," Lucky went on. "If they have information, it could really help us."

"That's a good point," said Storm. *I think there's more to this expedition, though. Lucky's probably worried about his litter-sister and her mate. After all, if there's a bad dog around, there's no reason Bella and Arrow would be immune to their viciousness.*

As the two of them padded through the woods on the approach to the old Fierce Dog lair, Storm realized with a start that her worries might be justified. A clamor of barking and snarling and yelping reached their pricked ears, and with a glance at each other, Lucky and Storm broke into a run.

Has our own Pack found out that this is where Bella and Arrow are living? Have they mounted an attack? Storm sprinted faster, alarmed. *Oh please, Sky-Dogs, don't let this be a battle between old friends—*

"Bella!" Arrow's bark rose above the chaos. "Watch your back!"

"Better do!" came a hideous, high sneer. "Bad dogs best watch out, best run, best flee!"

Storm recognized the strange not-dog voices at once, and she curled her muzzle in a snarl. *Coyotes!*

She didn't even hesitate as she broke out of the trees. She flung herself into the fight, biting and scratching at yellow rumps and throats; behind her she heard Lucky's furious snarls as he too joined the battle. Beyond the coyotes, she saw Arrow's head jerk up and his eyes widen in relief.

"Youse!" screamed the lead coyote, ducking from Storm's swiping claws. "Youse not them-friends no more! Youse have own Pack, not this Pack!" He rolled onto his back to avoid her teeth and scrambled up.

Storm didn't bother to reply, lunging for his throat as he dodged and yelped. Lucky had one by its scruff now, shaking it violently. Arrow, now that the odds were much fairer, was attacking the rest with renewed vigor, but even in the turmoil Storm could see that Bella was hanging back. It wasn't like her—but Arrow stood in front of his mate as if she was somehow fragile.

Storm didn't have time to wonder at their odd behavior, though. A coyote darted in to nip her hind leg, and she spun to bite its muzzle hard.

"Back, cohorts!" squealed the leader. "Too many dogses. Back for now." With a hoarse and high-pitched snarl he bolted for the woods with his tail between his legs, and his pack swiftly doubled around and followed him. Arrow still gripped the last and skinniest coyote in his jaws, and he dropped it with contempt. It scrabbled to its paws and fled with a long, whining howl.

Panting, the dogs watched them go. Arrow turned to Bella, and she pressed her head to his, closing her eyes. Their ears and tails drooped despite the victory, and Storm thought they looked sadder than she'd ever seen them, sadder even than when they'd left the Pack.

"What is it? What's wrong?" Regaining his breath, Lucky padded up to Bella and licked her ear quizzically. "Besides a coyote attack, I mean." He gazed at her, his tailtip flicking slightly.

"Oh, Lucky." Bella gave a sigh and turned her head to him, though she kept her shoulder pressed to Arrow's. "We've been talking, Arrow and I. Just before the coyotes attacked, we'd come to a decision. And the attack only confirmed it."

"What?" Storm cocked her head, anxious.

"We're going to leave this place." Bella looked around at the little glade and the cave, her eyes regretful.

"Yes," Arrow confirmed. "It's not good that we're competing with your Pack for territory and prey. And when there are coyotes here too, and foxes, and longpaws . . ."

"Yes." Bella nuzzled him. "There are only two of us, Lucky. We need to find a place where it's safe to live and hunt, somewhere we won't be forever watching our backs and worrying. And," she added, "by Long Light, we'll be down to one efficient dog. Only Arrow will be able to hunt and fight well."

"What?" Lucky glanced at Storm, confused, then back at Bella. "Why?"

"That doesn't make sense," growled Storm in perplexity. "You're a good hunter *and* a good fighter, Bella."

"I won't be then." Slowly, a happy expression crossed Bella's face, as if she couldn't help herself. Her tongue lolled, and a soft fondness entered Arrow's eyes. "By Long Light, I'll be clumsy and awkward. I'm expecting pups, Lucky."

"What?" Lucky's jaw fell open, and his ears pricked up high. "Bella! Really? That's wonderful!"

"Uh . . . yes!" agreed Storm. *This seems like a bad time to become a useless hunter, but they look so happy. . . .* "That's good news, Bella."

"Yes. It's true," murmured Arrow, his tongue caressing Bella's head. "Our small Pack will be growing soon."

"It's tremendous news, and I'm happy for you, litter-sister— I'm delighted!" Lucky's ears drooped slightly, and he licked his jaws. "You won't go *too* far away, will you?"

"I don't know, Lucky." Bella shook her head slightly, sighing.

"We have to go wherever is safe. Wherever there's enough prey for our pups to grow strong."

"Oh, Bella." Lucky sat down, and his tail thumped the ground slowly, as if he was having to put a lot of effort into making it wag. "I found you again, and I don't want to have to say good-bye forever. And you're going to have pups, and . . ." He took a breath and raised his eyes to Bella's. "I don't want them to grow up not knowing me! And not knowing my pups, their kin. And not knowing our Pack . . ."

"I know, Lucky." Bella gave an unhappy nod. "I understand all that, but I don't think we have any choice."

Storm's ears twitched with unease. *I don't want them to go away forever either,* she realized. She stole a glance at Arrow. *If Arrow leaves for good, I'll lose my only true ally, the only one who really understands. I'll go back to being the only Fierce Dog. I don't know any others. And besides, I'll miss them. . . .* "I wish you'd stay, too," she blurted.

"We can't, Storm," said Bella softly. "We've made up our minds. This is the right thing to do."

"You won't reconsider?" pleaded Lucky.

"I'm sorry." Bella reached forward to lick his nose. "I truly am, but we can't change our decision."

"We know a little about what lies inland," said Arrow, pricking his ears in that direction. "And down the coast of the Endless Lake, toward the old longpaw town. Those aren't good places for us, I think, so we'll travel up the coast instead. We'll follow the shoreline past the tall house, the one with the light on its top. We'll head into the hills." Gently he pressed his face to Bella's again. "Perhaps a better life will be waiting for us there. A safer life."

"But . . ." Lucky looked so downhearted, Storm wanted to lick his muzzle till he looked happy again. "When will you leave?"

"Now," Bella told him quietly. "Right now, Lucky. I'm just glad we had a chance to say good-bye."

Lucky closed his eyes in pain, then lifted his head. "Oh, Bella. I'm glad too. But I'll miss you. We'll miss both of you."

"I know." Bella nudged him gently. "And we'll miss you, so much. But we have to do this."

Lucky swallowed; Storm saw a muscle in his throat jerk. "I do understand, Bella. And I hope you'll be happy. I wish you all the best."

"So do I," said Storm. There was a catch in her throat that took her by surprise.

The four dogs pressed their muzzles close together, murmuring final farewells. But at last Arrow drew away, nudging Bella's side.

"We should be going," he said softly.

"Yes." Bella turned, and Storm felt a twinge in her gut to see the joy and excitement in her eyes. *They're happy to be leaving. And I understand, I do. But it's breaking Lucky's heart.*

And mine.

The two mates loped from the glade at a run, without looking back. Lucky and Storm watched until Bella and Arrow had vanished altogether, into the shadows between the trees.

CHAPTER NINETEEN

The Sun-Dog was already heading for his rest, his glow lighting the horizon in pink and gold, as Lucky and Storm made their way back to the camp. Soon his light would fade altogether, Storm thought, and it would be the end of the last day they'd ever see Bella and Arrow.

Maybe not, she tried to tell herself. *It's still possible we'll meet again. It's possible. . . .*

At her flank Lucky was silent, seeming lost in his thoughts—and probably his grief, Storm realized. He was losing his litter-sister yet again, and this time there was little chance they'd be reunited. But as they crossed a short stretch of grass beyond a stream close to the camp, he spoke at last, his voice clear and determined.

"I'm going to find this traitor," he told Storm grimly. "Too much has happened on account of that bad dog. I'm going to make sure the Pack is safe, and my pups are protected. I'll make sure Whisper is avenged, too." He gave Storm a glance. "I swear the dogs of our Pack will trust one another again. Everything's going to be better." He drew a breath. "And then Bella and Arrow will be able to return. They'll have their pups with us, in the Pack, just as it should be. Our Pack will be whole and together again."

Storm hesitated, gathering her thoughts before she could reply. The last thing she wanted to do was discourage Lucky; it seemed like a noble and proper aim to her—in fact, one she wished he'd settled on several journeys of the Moon-Dog ago. Finally she licked her jaws and looked sidelong at her Beta.

"Will they want to come back?" she asked. "Bella and Arrow?"

"Of course they will," said Lucky. He picked up his pace, drawing a little ahead of her. It seemed the conversation was at an end already.

Bella invited me to go with them, Storm reminded herself sadly. *And I said no.*

Did I make the right choice?

She might have gnawed over her decision for much longer, but at that moment they heard an eruption of howls and barks from the camp ahead of them. Their eyes met, and without a word both dogs broke into a run.

What now? wondered Storm frantically. *Another act of sabotage? Another attack?* Her heart pounding, she increased her pace.

As they broke through the trees and into the clearing, though, there was no sign of an ambush. Dogs were rummaging in the bushes, sniffing the air and the grass for trails, hunting in and out of the dens with desperation in their eyes. As Lucky stopped dead, gazing around in consternation, Alpha raced up to him, her eyes wide and bright with panic.

"Lucky! The pups! They've vanished!"

Lucky gave a reflexive bark of horror. "What? How did this happen? Who was watching them?"

Daisy shuffled up, her belly on the ground, her ears pressed low. Her face was full of shame. "I was, Lucky," she whispered. "Alpha asked me to watch them while she ran in the forest. I was with them, but . . . but they fell asleep . . . and I dropped off too." She licked her chops. "And when I woke up, they were gone!"

Lucky said nothing, not even to howl his anger. He turned, staring at the Pack. They were running in circles now, panicking, yelping at one another.

"Bruno, didn't you see anything? You must have seen something!"

"How could I, Snap? And where were *you*?"

"Shut up, both of you!" That was Chase. "Keep searching!"

"Every dog calm down," barked Mickey, but he didn't look very calm himself, and Storm realized he was repeating it over and over again. "Every dog calm down. Every dog! Calm down!"

"Storm!" Snap ran up to her, panting. "Did you see anything while you were out of camp?"

"They must have passed near you!" barked Bruno, lowering his shoulders aggressively. "Did you take the pups somewhere, Storm?"

"How could she?" snapped Lucky. "She was with me the whole time. And she wouldn't do anything with the pups unless Alpha or I asked her to!" He glared at Bruno till the big dog averted his eyes, growling.

Despite the circumstances, Storm felt a rush of warmth toward Lucky. *Even though he must be beside himself with worry, he's sticking up for me.* "And we didn't see anything on the way back," she whined.

"We have to do something *right now*," commanded Lucky. "Split up! Cover all directions—they're so tiny, they could have slipped out of camp anywhere." Storm could hear the fear in his voice, but he butted Alpha's trembling shoulders gently. "It'll be all right, Sweet. We'll find them."

Storm hadn't heard him use Alpha's original name in a very long time, but it was clear that Alpha was too distraught to take command herself. Storm remembered how frustrated she had been with Alpha's leadership—but this time she understood completely. A Mother-Dog must find it hard even to think straight, if her pups vanished without warning.

Lucky looked calm and authoritative as he organized the search, but she could see from the tremor in his hide how afraid he was.

"All of you, fan out individually," he ordered. "The important thing is to cover as much ground as possible, so we have to split up. Howl for help if you get into trouble—but the most important thing is to *find our pups!*"

Each dog was quickly assigned a direction, and last of all Lucky turned to Storm. "You go—"

Storm realized something. "Lucky, no dog is covering High Watch. There's at least a chance they went up that way, isn't there?"

He nodded. "I suppose they could climb up there if they were determined. Good idea. Yes, Storm—go up there. Bruno's covering the section of the woods to your left, and Thorn and Beetle are searching to the lake side of you. You'll be able to smell them, and they'll know where you are if you need help. Don't leave any patch of ground unsearched!"

"I won't." Storm gave Lucky a last lick of reassurance before she bounded off.

The cliff path seemed steeper than ever, as if it were deliberately making her job harder, but Storm knew it was only because of her anxiety that she was so breathless, that her legs felt as if they were weighed down by stones. She bounded up, taking leaping shortcuts from rock to rock, until she at last scrabbled up onto the high plateau that overlooked both the camp and the Endless Lake. *Even if they aren't up here—and I doubt they really could climb all this way by themselves—I might be able to see them. It's such a good vantage point.*

Behind her and far below, she could hear the barks and howls of the Pack.

"Tiny! Nibble!"

"Pups! Where are you?"

"Tumble, come out. This isn't a game!"

Turning away from the edge, Storm bounded across to the customary post at High Watch. She could see no movement below, but perhaps that was only because the Sun-Dog's light was so blinding. He was curling up in his sleeping-place now, his rays flashing across the Lake surface, turning the water to gleaming silver and the horizon to an explosion of amber and gold.

It reminded her of something, something she'd heard only recently . . . she kept picturing a little dog on his own, following the Sun-Dog.

Breeze's bedtime story!

Storm's blood chilled as she craned over the cliff edge, peering down. How did the story go? Brave little Whoosh the Wind-Dog set off in search of the Sun-Dog's resting place. . . .

Whoosh ran so fast, he ran right across the lake without sinking. . . .

Desperately Storm scanned the beach, creasing her eyes against the glare. *There!* Her heart leaped as she made them out: four tiny dots, darting haphazardly across the sand.

"Tumble!" She threw back her head and bayed at the top of her lungs. "Fluff! Nibble! Tiny!"

They can't hear me! In despair she peered over the edge, wishing she could reach down right now to grab them in her jaws. "Pups! *Tumble!*" Her voice was lost in the brisk lake breeze.

Blinking, she could make out their outlines more clearly now; they were gamboling and leaping, chasing one another closer and closer to the edge of the lake. *No! Don't try to chase the Sun-Dog, pups!*

There was no way down the cliff here. She could do many things, but she couldn't fly! Frantically, Storm bolted back the way she had come. She leaped onto the cliff path, almost tumbling head over heels, and sprinted as fast as she could down the precipitous, winding trail.

There were shapes ahead of her and lower down the path— Thorn, Beetle, and Breeze must have heard her agonized barks—but she didn't even pause as she flew past them. Between desperate pants, she gasped, "The pups! Follow me!"

Without looking back, she knew they had all followed her; she could hear their pounding paws. She was still outpacing them as she sprang down the last incline and raced for the beach, but behind her they were yelping frantic questions.

"Where, Storm? Where are they?"

She managed to turn her head a little as she ran. "On the shore, Thorn! Close to the water!"

"Oh no!" Breeze gave a howl of anguish. Putting on a burst of speed, she overtook the flagging Storm and raced ahead of her toward the lake. *She feels guilty for telling them that story*, thought Storm, *and no wonder!*

She followed Breeze's haunches as the brown dog plunged through a stand of long yellow grass. Bursting out on the other side, both dogs skidded to a stop.

"Where are they?" yelped Breeze.

"There!" Storm pointed with her snout.

The four pups were still splashing in the shallow waves. Storm felt a surge of relief that they hadn't yet tried to run across the water to the Sun-Dog—but they shouldn't be in the water at all! She tensed to spring after them, but Breeze abruptly shouldered in front of her, ears pricked and tail stiff. Thorn and Beetle almost careered into their rumps before coming to a frozen halt.

"Careful, Storm." Breeze's voice was taut with fear. "There are longpaws!"

Peering past her, Storm saw that Breeze was right. A float-cage had swum right up to the shore, grounding on the sand about five rabbit-chases away from the pups. Longpaws were leaping out of its flanks, splashing into the water and wading ashore. They didn't seem to be paying any attention to the pups, but they were far too close. Thorn and Beetle gave low whimpers in unison.

"We have to risk it," Storm panted. "We have to get the pups!"

"You're right." A fierce look came over Breeze's face. "We must!"

"Yes." Beetle swallowed, dipping his head in agreement.

Thorn, though, was stepping backward, her tail tight between her hind legs. Her head and ears were lowered defensively. "I . . . I can't," she whispered hoarsely. "I can't!"

Beetle turned to her in surprise. "You have to!"

His litter-sister was trembling now. "Don't you see, Beetle? Those creatures killed our Father-Dog. We can't let them see us! If they killed a big, strong dog like Fiery, what will they do to us? The pups will be fine, look. Just for a moment or two. They will! See?"

Breeze shook her head. "No, Thorn! We have to get them before they go farther into the water."

"Breeze is right." Storm stared at Thorn. It surprised her that it was Thorn having doubts, and not her litter-brother. She usually had far more nerve than he did. . . . "We can't wait, Thorn."

"Look at the longpaws, Thorn," said Beetle, nudging her encouragingly. "They don't look scary at all. And we're faster than they are. Much faster!"

"Come on. Leave Thorn here." Storm was aware how ruthless she sounded, but the pups were more important right now. "We can't afford to delay when the pups are in danger!" Leaving Thorn shivering and shamefaced, she took a deep breath, broke out of the grass, and bolted toward the pups, Breeze and Beetle sprinting alongside her.

From the corner of her eye as she raced across the shore, Storm could see the longpaws, who had turned toward them and were pointing and giving sharp barks. *They don't sound like the bad long-paws,* she thought, *the ones who trapped and poisoned Fiery.* Their voices weren't muffled or angry, just clear and curious. One of them was staring straight at Beetle, and Beetle paused to eye him back, warningly, but neither the longpaw nor the dog looked afraid.

All Storm and Breeze could do was ignore the longpaws and run as fast as possible toward the pups.

"Come away from the water, pups!" Breeze's high, horrified bark rang out on the clear salty air. But the pups took no notice; perhaps they didn't even hear her, because they were having too much fun splashing and playing in the gentle waves. Tumble and Fluff were darting after the breakers as they receded, yelping at them in fierce delight and attempting to bite their foamy tips.

Most of the waves looked innocuous—but another breaker was building, high up behind the pups as they splashed back toward the sand. This one was far bigger than the other little ripples, and growing larger as it rolled toward the shore. It was curling up now, rising to a terrifying crest. Storm's gut twisted inside her, and as she ran, her lungs started to ache, and she gave a desperate, pleading howl.

Too late! Too—

The wave collapsed, gushing up the beach with incredible speed and power. A wall of foaming water hit the pups from behind. It shoved Tumble and Fluff forward, and as they surfaced, their claws scrabbled desperately at the sand. Nibble and Tiny were bowled over, flung head over heels into spume, and as the water receded, it dragged the smaller pups with it.

Breeze, Beetle, and Storm were in the lake by now, seizing the panicking pups by their scruffs and dragging them free. Storm hauled Tumble out of the water, astonished at its power as it sucked at the pups. *Is there a Lake-Dog?* she wondered, as Tumble squirmed and salty spray blinded her for a moment. *Let them go, Lake-Dog, please! If you're there—if you can hear me—don't take our pups!*

Gasping, she dropped Tumble onto the wet sand beyond the reach of the waves, then, coughing and trying to catch her breath, she bolted back to the water. Breeze was already on dry land, licking frantically at Nibble's sodden little form, and Beetle was struggling out of the lake with Fluff clutched in his jaws. He shook himself violently, giving Fluff an unintentional good shake at the same time, and silver spray from his coat blinded Storm as she plunged into the lake again, turning, paddling wildly with her paws.

Three pups safe, she thought. *Three! Where's Tiny?*

A blur of pale gold caught her eye, and she spun around, desperate. Tiny's head bobbed above the surface for a moment as she was tugged out by the force of the tide. Her little mouth was open in a silent howl, and as her dark eyes met Storm's, they were filled with helpless, primal terror.

Then the lake sucked her under, and she vanished.

CHAPTER TWENTY

"*No!*" *Breeze's hysterical howl echoed from* the cliff face, louder even than the crashing roar of the Lake. "*No!* The lake has taken Tiny!"

Storm, her paws finding purchase on the sandy lake bed, could barely catch her breath. Imprinted on her mind was Tiny's terrified silent scream as she was dragged beneath the waves.

Memories battered Storm, like even more brutal waves, as she struggled toward where the pup had vanished. *The Fierce Dogs attacking the Pack, on the narrow lake road to the Light House. Twitch's litter-sister Spring, washed out to sea and drowned. The half-wolf Alpha, too, falling into the water, and believed lost.* Storm had had a chance to help him, but he'd howled *Savage!*—the name he had chosen for her against her will—and she had left him to the lake.

But that was Alpha. He was a bad dog! And we only thought he was dead, but he survived, and threw in his lot with the Fierce Dogs. Tiny was an inno-cent pup!

Storm herself had almost drowned, fighting the Fierce Dog Blade beneath the ice of the river, and she shuddered as she remembered how cold that water had been, and the weight of Blade, dragging her down.

Another memory shot across her mind's eye: her litter-brother Grunt, swept away by the River-Dog, and Martha diving into the swirling waters to rescue him. . . . Storm took a deep breath. *Please. River-Dog, if you are here; Lake-Dog, if you exist. And Martha! Martha, be with me now! Help me!*

There was no more time. Storm launched herself into the deeper water, feeling her paws leave the safety of the sand, feel-ing the power of the Endless Lake as it enfolded her. Striking out with her paws, she swam desperately out into the open waters of the lake.

There was no sign of Tiny; her head did not reappear above the rough surface. Clenching her jaws, beating back every instinct that urged her to stay above the water, Storm dived beneath the surface.

Down here it wasn't blue and silver and sparkling, she real-ized with an inner shudder. It was green and dark, and her vision was obscured by drifting weeds and swirling sand. Blinking hard, Storm shot back up, gasping in breaths of cold air. *I don't want to go back down there!*

Tiny, she reminded herself. *Tiny . . .*

Gathering her courage, she ducked her head and swam down again. Pulling strongly with her paws, she plunged deeper, twisting and turning in the cold grip of the lake. *Move with the water.* Was that Martha's voice she heard, from long ago? *Don't fight it, Lick . . . let the River-Dog embrace you. . . .*

Once again Storm shot up into the dying daylight, her lungs burning. This time she waited only long enough to suck in more air, then dived immediately. *I have to try, one more time. . . .*

Fury and remorse constricted her lungs, threatening to drive her back to the surface again. *How could I lose Lucky's pup?* Her muzzle curled, and she snapped in useless anger, her jaws made slow and clumsy by the pressure of the water—

And her mouth closed on something soft.

Storm's eyes widened, and she tightened her jaws gently around the soft, limp bundle. Striking out for the surface, she burst into the air and paddled furiously for the shore. Was the pup still alive?

Breeze and Beetle bounded toward her. "Storm!" yelped Breeze. "We thought—"

Storm dropped the bundle of soaked golden fur to the sand. "I'm fine," she snapped, panting. "But Tiny . . ."

Breeze and Beetle both gasped in horror. The little pup lay there limp, like a discarded rabbit pelt, and she wasn't breathing. *Just like Grunt,* Storm thought, *all that long time ago . . .*

"Look after the others!" barked Storm. As Breeze and Beetle backed away to stand protectively over the other three exhausted, terrified pups, Storm lowered her head to lick hard at Tiny's face and belly. She could hear Tumble's pleading, feeble voice. "Is she all right? Breeze, is Tiny all right?"

"Hush," Breeze said. "Leave it to Storm. Only she can help your litter-sister now."

Storm couldn't even turn to look at the brown dog. *I'm not sure I can help Tiny.* Once again she licked fiercely at the little dog's muzzle, trying to clear away weed and sand and water, trying to force warmth and life into that cold, still body. *It's too late. I've lost her—*

No, Storm. Again she thought she heard that distant voice. *It's not too late. Remember everything I taught you. All of it.*

Martha . . . Oh, Martha, I can't remember. . . .

And then, suddenly, she did. She rolled Tiny's limp form onto her back, then drew back a paw and thumped her hard on the belly.

Behind her, Beetle gave a strangled whine, and Breeze gasped, "Storm!" But she ignored them both, thumping Tiny hard again, and again.

What if I crush her? What if I kill her?

It's all I can do! I have to try!

One more thump with her paw, and abruptly Tiny's body spasmed, and water exploded from her jaws. The little pup jerked and coughed and tried to wail, and Storm almost slumped onto the ground in relief.

But she couldn't afford to do that. Bending down to the crying, gasping pup, Storm began to lick her again, with firm, fast strokes, till Tiny had coughed up the last of the green water inside her. Instantly her body began to tremble violently, and Storm carried on licking warmth back into her.

It seemed a very long time before Tiny blinked, shuddered, and raised her head. Then she flopped back to the sand, her sides heaving.

"Oh, Tiny." Storm nuzzled her, the relief overwhelming. "We thought we'd lost you."

Tiny could only whimper with incoherent terror and misery,

but Storm glanced up at Beetle and Breeze to see the shock and delight in their eyes. Tumble, Fluff, and Nibble were whining their relief and gratitude.

"Oh, well done, Storm!" barked Breeze. "Well done!"

"Tiny," Storm growled softly. "You have to get up. Come on, now. We need to get away from this place." She glanced anxiously at the longpaws, who seemed to be paying them a lot more attention now. Just as she did, and just as Tiny managed to stagger to her little paws, Beetle gave a bark of alarm.

"The longpaws. They're coming this way!"

"Let's go," growled Storm urgently. Seizing Tiny by her scruff, she began to lope back toward the cover of the long grass. Beetle grabbed Tumble, and Breeze took both Nibble and Fluff in her jaws, and they followed her.

Storm was hugely relieved to reach the shelter of the grass; Thorn pushed through it to meet her, her face a picture of anxiety and guilt. "Oh, Storm, thank the Sky-Dogs—I'm sorry I couldn't—"

Storm laid Tiny down on the grass. "Never mind that," Storm bit out, shaking herself vigorously. As Breeze ran into the grass behind her, she added, "Thorn—take Fluff, now! We need to move fast."

"Why—" began Thorn, but just then she raised her head. Her eyes widened at the sight of the longpaws running toward the grass. "Oh! Yes!" Seizing Fluff in her jaws, Thorn turned and bolted. Breeze picked up Nibble again, and together with Beetle and Tumble she fled.

Storm skidded and turned, pausing for a moment at the edge of the lake grass that shivered stiffly in the breeze. With Tiny laid protectively between her paws, she lowered her head, hunched her shoulders, and glared at the approaching longpaws.

The first of them slowed its pace, and she looked directly into its eyes. As it came to a halt, she gave her fiercest Fierce Dog growl.

You won't take this pup, longpaw. You won't take any of them, no matter how weak they are. You won't do to them what you did to Fiery. I'll make sure of it. . . .

The longpaw raised its forepaws. It did not drop its gaze from Storm's, but after a long moment of standoff, it spoke in a low growl.

Storm cocked her head, unsure. The growl did not sound aggressive; it sounded almost conciliatory. Almost admiring, in fact . . . almost friendly.

Clenching her jaws, she snarled again. *You won't fool me, longpaw. You won't fool any of us, ever again.*

For a moment it continued to gaze at her. Then, slowly, the longpaw backed off, its paws still held up in a gesture that seemed to Storm like surrender.

Quickly, Storm once more picked up the trembling Tiny in her jaws and turned to race after the others. She came to a halt higher up the slope to glance back before hurrying on, and then turned again at the crest of the ridge before it sloped down into the forest.

The longpaw hadn't tried to follow. Storm hunched her shoulders and narrowed her eyes, alert for trickery, but it seemed the longpaw had really given up. It was striding back down the beach toward its companions and its floatcage.

Putting the longpaws out of her mind, Storm bounded to catch up with Beetle, Thorn, and Breeze. They had stopped higher up the path and were licking warmth into the shivering pups. Gently, Storm set Tiny on the ground, lay down at her side, and began to wash her, too. The little dog was looking much more herself now, and at last she stopped quivering. Her whimper was still hoarse with salt water, but the glint of terror had left her eyes.

Now that the danger and the horror were over, Storm could feel a sting of pain from the wound in her shoulder. *I didn't have time to feel it before; I was too worried about the pups, and getting them away from the longpaws. But I guess the salt water must have burned it, like it burned poor little Tiny's throat.*

As she licked at her shoulder to dull the pain, she felt something warm and soft snuggle against her. Surprised, she glanced down at Tiny, who was gazing up at her with adoration. A surge of unexpected affection warmed Storm's heart and gave her a twinge in her gut that was almost more painful than the one on her shoulder. *I'll protect these pups from any danger like we saw today,* she thought suddenly and fiercely. *Tiny and the rest—I'll do everything in my power to keep them safe.*

"Are you all right, Tiny?" she murmured.

"Cold," whimpered Tiny, nuzzling Storm's flank. "Cold, Storm. I'm wet. Brr."

Storm licked her again, very gently. "Is that better?"

"'Es," agreed the pup sleepily.

"But you're not hurt? Nothing sore?" asked Storm.

"No." The little pup shook herself awkwardly where she lay. "I'm okay, Storm."

"Well," said Storm, managing to put some sternness into her tone. "Don't go wandering off like that again, Tiny. Not even if your litter-siblings are with you."

"Tumble's brave," protested Tiny. "Fluff's brave too!"

"Yes, I know, but I don't care how brave they are," said Storm severely. "None of you are ready to go off on your own, not without telling a grown-up dog. The world is very exciting, Tiny, but it's dangerous, too."

Clambering to her paws, she nudged the pup. "Come on. It's time we got back to the camp." She glanced at the others. "Your parent-dogs are very worried about you, you know."

"Sorry, Storm," they chorused, sheepishly.

This time the pups managed to walk on their own paws, so Storm and the other adult dogs had a chance to talk among themselves about the terrifying moments on the beach. Breeze was full of admiration for Storm's rescue, yelping her approval, but Thorn was far quieter, and Beetle walked close beside her, nuzzling her in reassurance.

"It's all right, Thorn," barked Breeze at last. "You don't have to worry. We won't tell any dog you were afraid of the longpaws. We promise. Don't we, Storm, Beetle?"

"Of course we won't tell," agreed Beetle, but as Thorn glanced back at Breeze, Storm saw confusion and nervousness in her face.

"I really don't think," said Storm slowly, "that it would do any harm if we *did* tell the others. It's nothing to be ashamed of, Thorn."

"No," protested Thorn, licking her jaws. "That's good of you, Storm, but I *am* ashamed. I should have helped." She gave Breeze a grateful woof. "I'd appreciate that a lot, Breeze. And I'm still really, really sorry. . . ."

"Don't worry, Thorn. Truly." Breeze let her tongue loll. "We won't tell any dog. *Right, Storm?*"

"Well," growled Storm. "I suppose not. If it makes you feel better, Thorn, that's all right with me."

"It really does," sighed Thorn. "Thank you, Breeze."

"Don't mention it," said Breeze affectionately. "And we certainly won't."

I suppose Breeze is right, thought Storm, though she still felt vaguely uneasy. *But there was no point hurting Thorn's pride by bringing that up again. It all turned out fine in the end. No harm done.*

She had no more time to think it over, anyway. A slender shape was racing toward them through the trees, her tail high and her eyes shining. "My pups! You found them!"

"Mother!" The four pups yipped with joy and raced to meet Alpha, their traumatic experience apparently forgotten. Wagging their stumpy tails, falling over one another, they scrambled to lick her muzzle and be licked in return.

"Oh, my pups!" Alpha gazed at the four rescuers, gratitude

shining in her eyes. "Thank you. Thank you, all of you, for bringing them back!"

Storm began to mutter something formal, about it being no more than her duty as a Pack Dog, but she was drowned out by the pups' excited yelps.

"Mama, mama! We had an adventure!" squeaked Tumble.

"Storm's brave," butted in Tiny, falling over her Mother-Dog's paw.

"Really brave!" squealed Fluff. "Mamamamama—"

"And Breeze! And Beetle! And Thorn!" yelped Tumble, squashing Fluff's muzzle down with a paw. "All the dogs saved us! From the lake and—"

"Funny monsters—" yelped Nibble, desperate to get a word in.

"Longpaws!" Fluff corrected her bossily.

"And the *waves*," whined Nibble, with a glare at Fluff. "*Big* waves!"

"Storm *saved Tiny's whole life*," finished Tumble triumphantly.

"By the Sky-Dogs!" exclaimed Alpha, almost laughing with relief. "I must hear the whole story, pups. But let's get you back to the camp, my little runaways." Gently herding them with her nose, she urged them toward the clearing as Storm and Breeze shared a happy glance.

Alpha was positively bouncing with joy as she shepherded her pups through the trees. The Pack members who had returned to the camp leaped to their paws at the sight of the pups, barking their delight. Alpha quieted them with a friendly growl.

"Packmates, to me! The pups have been found!" she announced joyfully. "And we have four true heroes in this Pack." She turned, her tongue lolling happily at the rescuers; Storm felt almost embarrassed as the eyes of every Pack member turned to her and her friends.

"Pack, please thank our heroes. The good dogs who saved my pups' lives: Storm, Breeze, Beetle, and Thorn!"

CHAPTER TWENTY-ONE

Storm felt buffeted by affection as the Pack surrounded the returning dogs, yelping questions and exclamations and congratulations. It was dizzying to feel quite so much approval from the dogs who had so often looked on her with suspicion. Even Bruno nudged her flank, his tongue lolling as he barked with admiration.

The pups were bustled rapidly away by Alpha and Lucky, shepherded into their den, and even though the Pack members crowded into the entrance, growling and yelping their joy, the four of them curled up almost straightaway and fell into an exhausted sleep. Daisy crept forward to lick their slumbering bodies, her eyes still filled with guilt.

"It's all right, Daisy," murmured Alpha gently, licking her ear. "My pups are safe."

"We need to hear the whole story!" yipped Sunshine, her little black eyes shining.

"Yes, we do!" agreed Mickey.

Chase echoed him in a woof. "Please! Tell us everything!"

"It was mostly Storm," Breeze was telling the other dogs just as Storm backed out of the den after checking the pups just once more. "She was magnificent!"

"Yes," agreed Beetle. "She dived right into the lake—not a moment of hesitation."

Storm opened her mouth to say that wasn't *quite* true—she had certainly paused to think, or Martha's words would never have come back to her as they did—but there was no quieting the excited barks of the Pack.

"I heard she swam *under* the water to get Tiny!" exclaimed Snap. "Is it true?"

Thorn nodded. "She was amazingly brave," she whispered in awe, her eyes a little downcast.

"So were you," put in Storm, determined not to let Thorn down. Thorn had after all dashed to the beach with the rest of them, and it was hardly surprising she was afraid of longpaws. *Maybe she was the one with the most sense!*

"The pups never saw the wave coming," explained Breeze. "It rushed in behind them when they had their rumps to it, poor things."

"They'll know better next time," said Lucky, a little gruff with emotion. "Thank the Sky-Dogs you four got there when you did."

"There won't *be* a next time," said Alpha fervently, as she squeezed out of the den. "Not till they're old enough to be wandering off on their own! What in the name of the Earth-Dog came over them?"

Lucky nuzzled her neck. "A sense of adventure," he suggested, with a glimmer of his old relaxed humor.

"Even the longpaws didn't deter Storm," Breeze told Bruno and Snap, who were hanging on her every word. "She drove them away when one of them started to come after us."

"Storm's always been brave," said Bruno, glancing at her with respect.

"And loyal," added Mickey.

"An all-around Good Dog," agreed Snap.

Even though the stares and the praise and the admiration almost made Storm's fur crawl with discomfort, she couldn't help a shiver of pleasure. There wasn't a single member of the Pack who didn't appreciate her right now, she realized. *It feels good to be a hero in the eyes of the Pack. It feels good to be looked at with appreciation instead of suspicion!*

A small spark of hope kindled in her chest. Maybe after this, the Pack wouldn't be so mistrustful of Fierce Dogs. Maybe they'd accept now, once and for all, that it wasn't a dog's blood that mattered, but her heart.

But I won't point that out right now, Storm decided. *That would be pushing my luck, I think!*

Besides, Breeze, Thorn, and Beetle were getting their share of admiration and affection from the Pack, too—and that was as it should be. *We really did work as a team,* thought Storm proudly. *We worked together to save the pups. Just as a Pack should.*

"It's prey-sharing time," announced Alpha over the hubbub of excited dogs. Her dark eyes turned to rest affectionately on the four heroes. "And tonight, Storm, Breeze, Thorn, and Beetle will eat first. Before even I or Beta take our share!"

Storm pricked her ears in shock. Such an honor was unheard of, and a horrible trepidation skittered across her hide. What if the other Pack members resented it?

But glancing nervously around, she realized she needn't have worried. The dogs were nodding and scratching the ground in agreement, wagging their tails, sending up yips and howls of approval. Storm's eyes met Breeze's; the brown dog looked as surprised and gratified as she felt. Waving her own tail, Breeze walked forward to Alpha and crouched on her belly, panting.

"Thank you, Alpha!" she barked.

Storm joined her, lowering her forequarters before Alpha, and Beetle and Thorn joined her at each flank. "Yes, Alpha, thank you," Storm whined. "This is an honor."

"Especially for me," added Breeze humbly. "I'm not even a hunt-dog!"

"No less than the four of you deserve." Alpha's tongue lolled. "And the Pack agrees."

"Yes," barked Bruno. "Honor to Storm and Breeze and—"

"And Thorn and Beetle," yapped Moon, finishing for him. Her voice was bursting with pride, and Storm suddenly felt even happier for the brave Farm Dog than she did for herself.

Patiently the Pack settled to wait their turn while the four rescuers paced up one by one to select their prey from a plentiful pile. Finding a fat rabbit, Storm lifted it in her jaws and carried it to her place, where she sat contentedly tearing at it while the rest watched without rancor. It tasted better than any prey had, for a long time. When she had crunched the last bones and licked the blood from her paws, she settled happily to watch the other rewarded dogs eat, followed by Alpha and Beta and the rest of the Pack.

Storm was glad the prey pile had been so large tonight; there was no need for any dog to feel slighted, and certainly no reason for any of them to go hungry. The preference Alpha had shown the four rescuers was purely ceremonial—but no less thrilling for that. Full and quite sleepy, Storm laid her head on her paws and watched her Packmates. After finishing his share, Lucky had gone to wake the pups, and they had now joined the Pack circle and were happily chewing some soft and juicy voles.

The Sun-Dog had long gone to his rest by the time Omega was munching on some mice, and all that remained of his light was a faint gray blur beyond the trees. Deeper shadows gathered between the pine trunks, shadows that the new Moon-Dog didn't penetrate.

Storm blinked, staring into the forest, her heart suddenly tripping. Were the shadows *moving*?

No. There was no breeze tonight, and the branches were still. Yet she was sure she could see the darkness shifting, could see the pools of blackness stir and quiver.

It's my imagination, Storm thought, *after a tiring day. We're all exhausted—no wonder I'm seeing danger all around.*

Still, she couldn't help remembering her awful dreams: the shapeless black dogs made of shadow, the dark chasms that had opened to split the Pack apart and swallow them up.

She gave a deep, silent sigh of sadness. *Yes, there is still a darkness in the Pack. Today doesn't change that. I only wish it could—but I know better. Our troubles aren't over just because the pups were saved today.*

There was a bad dog stalking them—but who could the traitor be? Storm gazed at her Packmates one by one. Many of them, she knew, would still distrust her when the memories of today began to fade. *Bruno has always been suspicious of me; Snap too.*

But she couldn't imagine, however hard she tried, that Bruno was capable of sabotage and murder. He could be awkward and grumpy and snide, but malicious? *No.* And Snap—she was Mickey's mate! However blunt and aggressive the small hunt-dog could be, Storm trusted Mickey's instincts. Mickey could never love a bad dog, Storm knew it in her heart.

So who?

Her eyes roamed around the resting Pack. Twitch, the brave, determined, loyal Third Dog? *Never!* Quiet, stolid Chase? *I don't think it for a moment.*

Moon, Thorn, or Beetle? *No. They would never defile Fiery's memory that way.* Kind and sensible Breeze, whose love and care for Lucky's pups shone out of her dark eyes? *No, not Breeze.*

But that left only gutsy little Daisy, and the gentle Omega, Sunshine. *The very idea it could be either of them —it's ridiculous!*

So if none of the remaining Pack could be responsible, was it one of the dogs who had abandoned them? It seemed more likely. Woody, perhaps, or the resentful and ambitious former Omega, Ruff? Or Rake? Even Dart, who'd been one of their original Pack, had been bitter at the turn events had taken. . . .

No. Some of those dogs never liked me, but that doesn't mean they're bad. I knew them. I trusted them.

Storm gave another heavy sigh. She wished she could stop thinking about it and simply enjoy the peace of the evening. It was a relief when Alpha got to her paws, clearly preparing to address the Pack. Storm lifted her head and pricked her ears eagerly.

Little Sunshine, the last dog to eat, licked her jaws clean as Alpha began to speak.

"My Pack," declared the swift-dog in a clear, resonant voice. "There are some things I want to say to you all, and now is a good moment." Once more she met all their gazes. "I swear one thing to you tonight: we will find the dog who is trying to cause us harm. We will identify the bad dog and we will deal with him or her; but one thing we will not do is run from our trouble. We will not give this dog what they want! We will not abandon our Pack or our territory, and we will not flee with our tails between our legs, like Twitch's former Packmates did, or Bella and Arrow. We will face this—together!"

Lucky rose to his paws at her side. Storm saw sadness tighten the muscles of his face at the mention of Bella's name, but he too spoke levelly and clearly.

"Bella and Arrow have now left our territory," he said, "for good. The situation was not acceptable; we all knew that. But I want to say this: it should never have been necessary. They should never have had to leave us in the first place."

"I agree with you, my Beta." Alpha gazed at him with sorrow and sympathy. "It's for the best that they have left our territory now, but we must not allow the Pack to be further divided. We will root out this traitor, Packmates—and those of us who are true and loyal will do it *as* Packmates. Without turning on each other."

There were growls and murmurs of agreement from the dogs watching her.

"There's something else," Alpha went on, after a pause to let her solemn vow sink in. "I have been guilty too. I have been less than fair to some of you—especially our Third Dog." She turned to Twitch, dipping her head slightly, and he pricked an ear, intent. "I have doubted his loyalty without good reason—without *any* reason—and I have failed to listen to his good advice and counsel." She turned again, this time to face Moon's offspring.

"Beetle. Please come forward."

With a glance at his sister, Beetle did. "Alpha?" he said apprehensively.

"Not every dog is cut out to be a hunter," Alpha told him, swishing her tail thoughtfully. She sat back on her haunches. "Our Pack needs good Patrol Dogs, now more than ever. Therefore, Beetle: you will be returning to patrol duties, as of this moment."

"But, Alpha!" exclaimed Beetle, his dark eyes shocked.

"Alpha, he's learning—we both are!" protested Thorn.

"I know," said the swift-dog kindly. "And you have both tried your best. But Beetle will return to patrolling. This is my decision, and you must respect it."

"I agree," said Moon sternly, stepping forward a pace. "Respect the Alpha, my pups!"

The two of them subsided, muttering low growls.

"Tell me." Alpha gazed deeply into both the young dogs' eyes. "Did either of you ever truly think Beetle was meant to be a hunter?"

There was silence for a moment. Then Thorn gave a defeated growl, and Beetle muttered softly, "No, Alpha."

"I guess not." Thorn clawed sulkily at the ground.

"You are both good dogs," said Alpha, "but this is my decision, Beetle."

Lowering their heads, the two drew back into the circle. Storm wasn't surprised that Beetle had argued the point, but Alpha was right. He was no natural hunter. *Poor Beetle! His pride is hurt, that's all.* She watched him slink over to Breeze's side; the brown dog was close enough for Storm to hear Beetle's truculent growl to her.

"How's that fair, Breeze?" he complained in a low voice. "I was one of the dogs who saved the pups—and I did more than Thorn—but I'm the dog who gets demoted!"

"Hush, Beetle." Breeze consoled him with a lick of his ear. "There's no shame in being a Patrol Dog—and you're so good at it! The Pack needs you more than ever, Beetle, don't you see? It's so important, this work. And you know what I think? Patrol Dogs have to be a lot braver than hunters!"

Eyeing them from the corner of her lidded gaze, Storm saw Beetle's ears prick up and a proud light come into his eye. He suddenly looked far happier, and Storm let her tongue loll with relief and secret pleasure. *Well done, Breeze! She's a clever dog. And in a lot of ways, she's right.*

Glancing up, Storm saw the Moon-Dog peep out from behind a cloud. She was not showing herself fully; she'd only recently started to return to view as she did every round of her journey. Her silver glow was only a little more than a quarter visible, but her light was still strong and bright. Alpha gave a woof of cheerful summons.

"Pack! We will have a special Howl tonight," she announced. "It will make us strong, and reaffirm our links to one another. And it will celebrate the rescue of the pups!"

Storm blinked and shook herself as she stood up, preparing to join the circle. *Is that really . . . proper?* she wondered. *Should dogs howl when the Moon-Dog is partly hidden, when she isn't ready for us? Maybe it will be a bad omen. Maybe it will bring bad luck, not the good kind. . . .*

Once more she shook herself, more vigorously this time. *Don't be a silly pup, Storm!* It was superstition to think that the Moon-Dog would be offended by any honest tribute—and surely Alpha had the right to honor the great Spirit Dog in whatever way she saw fit?

As the dogs settled in their places, as heads were raised and voices began to sing out their first tentative howls, Storm found her anxieties shrinking and vanishing into nothing. Slowly the voices around her grew louder, drawing together in strength and harmony, and their sound filled the night sky.

The Howl held no tone of desperation or fear tonight, Storm realized; indeed there was a calm power to it that filled her with a sense of ease and belonging. She hadn't known it to feel so natural, so united, for many turns of the Moon-Dog. Her own howl came easily to her, blending with the sweet, high-pitched song of Sunshine at her shoulder. She could hear the eager, raw song of the four pups, somehow mingling perfectly with the deeper baying joy of the more experienced dogs. With a glance to her other side, Storm realized with a surge of delight that even Breeze had joined in this time.

Storm raised her voice, letting it grow louder and louder without dominating the others. Her hide and bones tingled with happiness as she watched the drifting clouds through her half-closed eyes. Shapes formed out of their shapelessness: a great, long-haired, shaggy dog, bounding through the sky on webbed paws. Happiness filled her.

Is that the River-Dog, showing us her pleasure at what we did today? Or is it . . . is it . . . Martha?

Perhaps they are one and the same now. A sense of peace and joy rippled through Storm's body. *Perhaps, after Martha's voice helped us save the pups . . .*

Storm let her blurred gaze drift to the four little shapes who were straining so eagerly to howl like grown dogs. Their moonlit bodies, tan and brown and gold, were distinct against the darkness of the trees behind them. . . .

The trees!

Shadows were among the trunks again, and they were moving. *They were moving.* There was no denying it now. Darkness shifted, weaving sinuously through the forest, and it coalesced into a recognizable shape: a vast dog, pacing back and forth, too big to be truly real. . . .

But it's there!

Cold horror drove out all the warmth that howling had brought to Storm's body. *It's the Fear-Dog! I know it is!*

She had seen a shadow-dog like it before. She had wondered if it was perhaps the watch-dog Arrow had spoken of, the spirit that looked over Fierce Dogs.

But this isn't it. She knew it in her chilled bones. *This is no watch-dog.* It was hard to see its shape, because of the shifting shadows. One moment it was there, clear and savage; the next it dissolved into darkness before re-forming again. It changed subtly, shimmering and undulating with shadow, but it was there, and real: terrifyingly, brutally beautiful.

A hideous notion choked Storm's howl in her throat: *Am I creating it? Am I singing that thing into existence?* She fell abruptly silent as the Pack howled on around her.

But the Fear-Dog didn't fade. It paced, and weaved, and stalked the Pack through the trees, always a little out of reach but never disappearing.

The Fear-Dog was here. It did not soar through the sky with the other Spirit Dogs, but walked on the earth *right beside the Pack.*

Terrifying chills rippled through Storm's bones, making her shudder uncontrollably. *The traitor that wants to harm us, the bad dog— it's no flesh-and-blood dog. It's with the Pack. The Fear-Dog walks with the Pack. . . .*

It's the Fear-Dog that hunts us!

It was little Sunshine's voice that broke the awful spell: the Omega's warm, real, flesh-and-blood body trembling beside her. The urge to turn tail, to flee from the glade and never look back, faded into the reality of the Pack. Storm glanced down at little Sunshine, shocked but grateful.

The little white dog's eyes were closed as she murmured

through the Howl, her voice intense and desperate and passionate.

"Please, Sky-Dogs," Sunshine cried softly, "please help our Pack."

Storm closed her eyes, too, and silently added her pleas to Sunshine's. *Please let things be better now.*

A NEW WARRIORS ADVENTURE HAS BEGUN

1

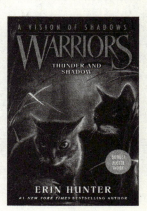

2

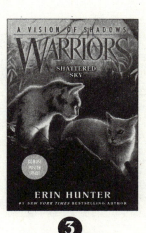

3

Alderpaw, son of Bramblestar and Squirrelflight,
must embark on a treacherous journey
to save the Clans from a mysterious threat.

FOLLOW THE ADVENTURES!

WARRIORS: THE PROPHECIES BEGIN

In the first series, sinister perils threaten the four warrior Clans. Into the midst of this turmoil comes Rusty, an ordinary housecat, who may just be the bravest of them all.

HARPER
An Imprint of HarperCollinsPublishers

www.warriorcats.com

WARRIORS: THE NEW PROPHECY

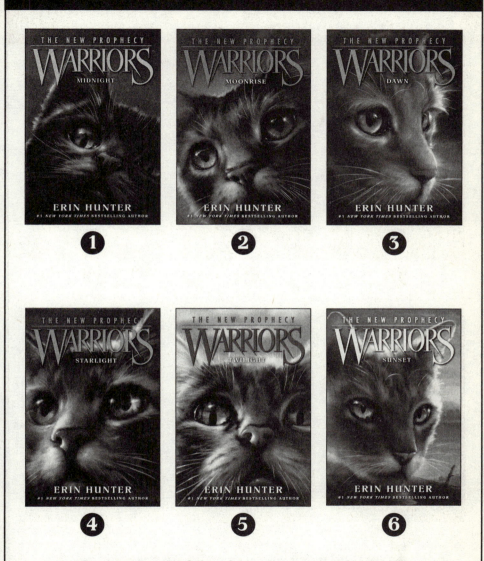

1 — THE NEW PROPHECY — WARRIORS — MIDNIGHT — ERIN HUNTER — #1 NEW YORK TIMES BESTSELLING AUTHOR

2 — THE NEW PROPHECY — WARRIORS — MOONRISE — ERIN HUNTER — #1 NEW YORK TIMES BESTSELLING AUTHOR

3 — THE NEW PROPHECY — WARRIORS — DAWN — ERIN HUNTER — #1 NEW YORK TIMES BESTSELLING AUTHOR

4 — THE NEW PROPHECY — WARRIORS — STARLIGHT — ERIN HUNTER — #1 NEW YORK TIMES BESTSELLING AUTHOR

5 — THE NEW PROPHECY — WARRIORS — TWILIGHT — ERIN HUNTER — #1 NEW YORK TIMES BESTSELLING AUTHOR

6 — THE NEW PROPHECY — WARRIORS — SUNSET — ERIN HUNTER — #1 NEW YORK TIMES BESTSELLING AUTHOR

In the second series, follow the next generation of heroic cats as they set off on a quest to save the Clans from destruction.

HARPER
An Imprint of HarperCollinsPublishers

www.warriorcats.com

WARRIORS: POWER OF THREE

In the third series, Firestar's grandchildren begin their
training as warrior cats. Prophecy foretells that they will
hold more power than any cats before them.

HARPER
An Imprint of HarperCollinsPublishers

www.warriorcats.com

WARRIORS: OMEN OF THE STARS

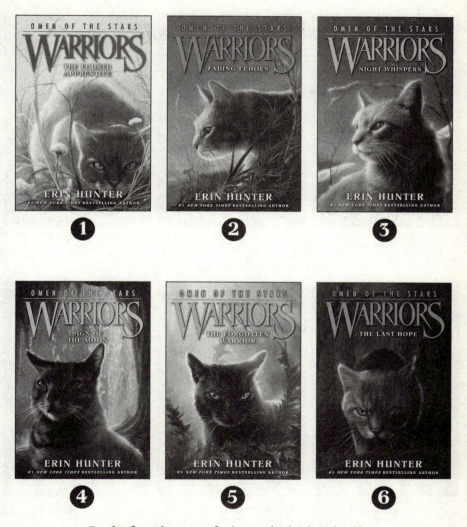

In the fourth series, find out which ThunderClan apprentice will complete the prophecy.

WARRIORS: DAWN OF THE CLANS

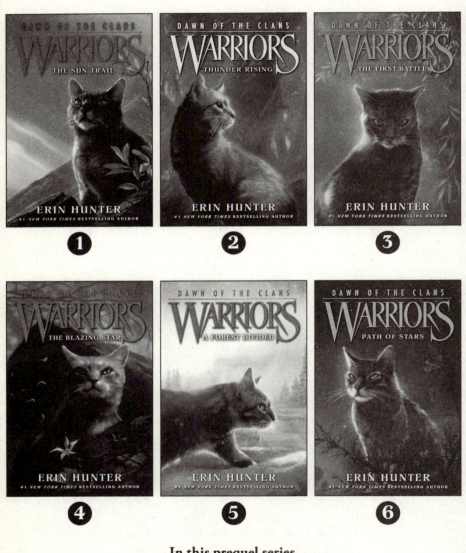

DAWN OF THE CLANS
WARRIORS
THE SUN TRAIL
ERIN HUNTER
#1 *NEW YORK TIMES* BESTSELLING AUTHOR

1

DAWN OF THE CLANS
WARRIORS
THUNDER RISING
ERIN HUNTER
#1 *NEW YORK TIMES* BESTSELLING AUTHOR

2

DAWN OF THE CLANS
WARRIORS
THE FIRST BATTLE
ERIN HUNTER
#1 *NEW YORK TIMES* BESTSELLING AUTHOR

3

DAWN OF THE CLANS
WARRIORS
THE BLAZING STAR
ERIN HUNTER
#1 *NEW YORK TIMES* BESTSELLING AUTHOR

4

DAWN OF THE CLANS
WARRIORS
A FOREST DIVIDED
ERIN HUNTER
#1 *NEW YORK TIMES* BESTSELLING AUTHOR

5

DAWN OF THE CLANS
WARRIORS
PATH OF STARS
ERIN HUNTER
#1 *NEW YORK TIMES* BESTSELLING AUTHOR

6

In this prequel series,
discover how the warrior Clans came to be.

HARPER
An Imprint of HarperCollinsPublishers

www.warriorcats.com

These extra-long, stand-alone adventures will take you deep inside each of the Clans with thrilling tales featuring the most legendary warrior cats.

WARRIORS: BONUS STORIES

Discover the untold stories of the warrior cats and Clans
when you download the separate ebook novellas—or read
them in four paperback bind-ups!

HARPER
An Imprint of HarperCollinsPublishers

www.warriorcats.com

WARRIORS: FIELD GUIDES

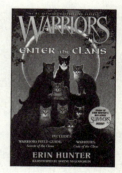

FOR THE ULTIMATE FAN!

Delve deeper into the Clans with these Warriors field guides.

HARPER
An Imprint of HarperCollins *Publishers*

www.warriorcats.com

ALSO BY ERIN HUNTER:
SURVIVORS

Survivors: The Original Series

The time has come for dogs to rule the wild.

HARPER
An Imprint of HarperCollinsPublishers

www.survivorsdogs.com

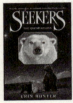 

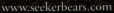